Venom
AND
STONE

ERIN O'KANE

Venom and Stone

Cursed Women Book One

By Erin O'Kane

Published by L. Guyatt as Erin O'Kane

Erin.okaneauthor@gmail.com

CONTENTS

Preface   vii

Chapter 1   1
Chapter 2   11
Chapter 3   29
Chapter 4   41
Chapter 5   55
Chapter 6   77
Chapter 7   91
Chapter 8   111
Chapter 9   121
Chapter 10   141
Chapter 11   153
Chapter 12   175
Chapter 13   193
Chapter 14   209
Chapter 15   231
Chapter 16   243
Chapter 17   259
Chapter 18   275

Acknowledgments   289
About the Author   291
Also by Erin O'Kane   293

DEDICATION

To everyone who fights their own battles and doesn't wait for
the prince to rescue them.
Heroes come in all shapes and sizes.

Once upon a time...

That's how all good stories start, right?

Legends of knights in shining armour on horseback, racing to save the damsel in distress, fighting the great sea monster or slaying the dragon who is terrorising the town. The story of the fair maiden who sacrifices herself to save her family. Myths of objects of power so great that they will grant your every wish and desire.

But not every story has a happy ending.

Who hears the tales of the cursed? Those who are tasked with guarding these objects of power your heroes are so determined to steal from us?

My name is Maya, and I am one of the cursed. Love is what cursed me, and love is what will free me, but I've learned the hard way that men only want me for what I guard, and I will kill every last one of them before I let them take it from me.

Chapter

1

The metallic thump of the guard's staff against the stone floor echoes around the large hall, waking me from where I was drifting off. Thankfully, no one noticed because of the veil concealing my face.

A flash of gold catches my eye, and I turn my head ever so slightly, taking in the king who is resting against his ornate throne to my left. He's glancing my way, and although he's wearing a benevolent expression, I can see the annoyance in his eyes. Correction, no one but the king noticed I was drifting off. He knows me better than anyone else in this room, so even though he couldn't have seen, he always seems to *know*. His hand taps against the arm of the throne, the golden ring on his finger flashing again, another tell that his patience is wearing thin.

It's a ghastly thing he sits upon, a large, jagged slab of white stone that's been carved into an ostentatious display of the king's might and power. Carvings of crouched men form the base, looking as though they are being crushed by the weight of the throne. He once explained to me that it's supposed to be a homage to the citizens of the city, showing that he wouldn't be here without the strength of his people, but to me, it just looks like they are being crushed beneath the weight of his wealth and power. Rich red velvet cushions pad the stone in an attempt to make it comfortable, and the back of the throne towers above him, splitting into three spiralling towers inlaid with magical, glowing gems to represent the past, present, and future. It looks uncomfortable as hell, but I can't deny its imposing presence seems to have the desired effect on people.

A wooden throne sits beside it to the left, also carved, but this is made to look like it's composed entirely of twisting tree roots and branches, all intertwined. If the queen's stiff-backed posture indicates anything, I'd say hers is just as uncomfortable as the king's.

One of the pages standing by the large, double wooden doors calls out a set of names, but I'm not really paying attention as Lord and Lady So-And-So make their way through the long hall towards the king. Absent-mindedly, I watch as they try to keep their eyes forward. There is a fake smile on the lord's face, but it's the lady's expression that catches my interest. She looks terrified— not of the fifty heavily armed guards positioned around the hall, but of little old me, standing to the king's right. I suppose in that case, my purpose has been fulfilled.

Weak, the hidden monster within hisses, scraping her nails against the inside of my mind, wanting to break free of the mortal body I currently possess. *Tear, maim, kill. All of the bright red blood would look lovely against her pale skin...* I can still see the frantic fluttering of her pulse beneath the skin on her neck, even from this distance with the dark half veil distorting my vision. I may be here to terrify everyone into submission, but I can't say the king would be particularly pleased if I tore into the couple. Besides, blood is so hard to get out of brushed velvet.

Glancing down at my luxurious outfit, I brush my hands over the dark skirts of the dress. It's black, the king's colour, and he has me wear it constantly. It drives the queen insane, but then she's always been jealous of me. Sure, I may be the one who warms her husband's bed, but I know for a fact that's not a job she wants. Her snivelling, judging, and plotting drives me mad, and it's an endless struggle to stop my gorgon from tearing into her—not that I can allow that to happen, since I have my orders, after all. Silently sighing, I reach up to adjust the veil covering my face, but a terrified whimper echoes around the hall. My eyes instantly snap up and lock onto the trembling form of the lady. Her husband, realising that something's happening, turns his attention to her, only for his eyes to widen in horror when he sees me. To my disgust, he takes a step back, leaving his petrified wife to face me alone. This only stokes my monster all the more.

Now he would make a fulfilling meal, even if his fear and cowardice would taint his blood, she muses, and I tilt my head to one side as I eye him up, much like a predator does before it pounces on their next victim.

"Maya." The king's cool voice cuts through my regard, and I slowly force myself to turn from the quaking couple.

"My liege?" I dip my head in a sign of respect, my deceptively delicate voice ringing around the room.

The corner of the king's lips tugs up into a semblance of an amused smile as he pins his blue eyes on me.

Despite being in his mid-forties, he's still just as hand-some as the day I met him. His blond hair is peppered with a few greys, and his smooth, lightly tanned skin is just starting to show signs of age. None of it takes away from the sense of power and self-confidence he exudes, however.

He makes a gesture with his hand that says *tone it down*, but that's not what he says aloud. "If you could refrain from eating any of the guests, I would be most grateful," he drawls, drawing a laugh from the watching guards and lords. Turning his attention from me, he looks around the hall and grins. "You can take the woman out of the monster, but you can never take the monster from the woman." The laughter is louder this time, and I dutifully nod and take a step back.

I've heard it all before, but the words sting none-theless. Despite the fact that I've done nothing except look at the blubbering couple, I'm still the one to be chided. The king likes it when people remember what hides beneath my skin, even occasionally ordering a little demonstration—not that he would ever admit it to his people—and this gives him the chance to chide me and remind everyone who holds my leash.

None of this is new to me. I've been at the king's side for over twenty years now, so I should be used to holding back, scraping, and bowing. It's not within my monster's nature to hold back, so I have to manage the constant strain as she pushes to escape. Honestly, it's getting harder and harder, because I'm beginning to agree with her opinion of humans. They are all weak, cruel, and self-absorbed, so why shouldn't I be the same?

The king speaks again, and I know he's telling the lord that he can continue with whatever he was going to say, but I've tuned it all out. My emotions twist and turn within me, souring, and I have to remind myself why I'm here.

One of the only times I'm ever grateful for this awful veil I'm forced to wear is during these monthly meetings, as it hides my true feelings and the fact that I'm usually falling asleep. I really hate these things. Once a month, all of the local lords make the trek up to the castle to pay homage to the king and queen.

Scribes stand in the corner of the room, making note of what each family brings. In this kingdom, if you don't pay your respects with material objects or gold, then you don't receive protection from the king. They all pay taxes, but this is just an additional gift to show how appreciative they are—a gift that is forced, and if one should fail to provide said gift, it would result in being ostracised from the very society that's supposed to protect them.

In an attempt to block out the monotony of the seemingly endless line of lords waiting to see the king, I focus on the building around me. Even though I've seen this room on many occasions during the last nineteen years of Marcus' reign, I still can't get over the grandeur of it. Much of it has changed since Marcus took over, such as the thrones and huge tapestries that decorate the walls, depicting his glorious ascension. However, there are things he can't change without knocking down the whole hall and rebuilding it, which I'm sure is something he's considered. It's a dark stone, gothic style building with tall pillars and alcoves, and huge, gravity defying archways that reach all the way up to the roof. Golden chandeliers hang from the ceiling, casting shadows over the stone, and matching golden lamps line the walls, lighting up the otherwise dark room.

When I'm bored, I like to imagine the previous generations of kings and what they would think of how King Marcus has changed their castle and city. They would probably view it with horror. His father, the old king, certainly hadn't been his biggest supporter, very much focused on the way things had been run for the last couple of centuries. He would be turning in his grave if he knew the changes Marcus has wrought. That thought brings a smile to my lips. I had never liked him. When the former king died of alcohol poisoning, no one had questioned it since he had, after all, been an alcoholic. However, I did hear some of the nobility making comments regarding how timely his death had been, and how convenient it was that his wayward son, who had been travelling the continent looking for magical objects, had suddenly returned just as his father died.

Those whispers soon stopped when they realised *what* I was under the dresses, veils, and jewellery Marcus bestows upon me. He's been using me to instil fear among his people and keep them in line ever since.

It's the sudden hush that brings my attention back to what's happening in the room. I've mastered the art of looking around without moving, and with the veil covering my face, no one will know that I was just staring up at the arched ceiling. As I scan the scene before me, I'm filled with mixed emotions—dread, because I know what's about to happen to the dishevelled man kneeling before the king, and excitement, but for the exact same reason. This truly shows how much of a monster I've become.

The atmosphere has changed in the room. All the pomp and circumstance from before is now heavy with the rich tang of fear, and now everyone seems tense—

everyone, that is, apart from the king, who is leaning back lazily against his throne.

My gaze instantly zooms in on the kneeling male. He must be in his late forties, and his clothing, which would have once fit him, seems to hang from his body. Seeing his hollow cheeks and the grief etched upon his face, the human part of me wants to reach out and comfort him, but I know better than that. Several days' worth of scruff coats his chin, and from the way he keeps glancing back at a group of children by the door, I would guess he's their father.

"Please, Your Highness," the man begins, his voice rough with grief. "My wife recently passed, and I spent our savings on healer's fees. I have no money left to give you. My taxes took every penny I had left."

The healers. I barely manage to hold back a disgusted shake of my head at the very term. Whilst some possess magical abilities, most are just well-educated humans who do their best to heal the sick and injured. With an ever-growing population and the conditions in the city being as poor as they are, there are always more people who need services than there are healers. As such, their prices are extortionate. Rather than helping those who need it most, as they originally started out doing, they now only cater to the rich or those who are willing to bankrupt themselves looking for a cure.

When the king doesn't respond to the lord's plight other than to raise a brow, the kneeling man's face falls. "Please, I have four children to feed. Without me, they'll starve."

I glance at the children standing at the back of the room. The eldest, a daughter in her teenage years, is holding a young boy in her arms, while a small girl hides in her skirts. By her side is a boy of about ten. He's standing tall, his body stiff as he tries to appear strong for his family. They look frightened, but none of them cry or call out, not even the youngest. They are going to need to be strong, because this life isn't kind to orphans. Doesn't the lord know that pleading to the king will only make things worse? That his cry for help will only fall on deaf ears? Either he doesn't truly know what his king is like, or he's desperate enough to try.

"Do I look like a charity to you? Maya, am I known for my charity?" Turning slightly in his throne, he looks at me with an expectant expression.

"No, Your Highness," I reply obediently, knowing the part I am to play.

True terror enters the lord's eyes as he turns to look at me, then back to the king. That's when I realise that it was absolute desperation that's brought the man to this point. He has nothing left other than his family, yet he still came here today to face the king, despite knowing it wouldn't do anything to change the outcome.

Gripping his hands together before him, he pleads, "Please, give me another month and I'll find the money. I'll give double next month."

The king gestures for the scribe to approach. He does so, scuttling forward and presenting a roll of parchment to the king. Marcus hums low in his throat as he looks at the list and slowly shakes his head as if he's disappointed by what he sees. I know better though. That gleam in his eye tells me everything I need to know—he's enjoying this.

"Your contributions have been getting smaller and smaller, Oliver. Last month, it was less than satisfactory, but we let it slide." Handing the scroll back to the scribe, he slowly climbs to his feet. "And this time, you come to me without anything whatsoever." Gesturing wide in a way that says *what can you do*, he solemnly shakes his head and clasps his hands in front of him.

"This is your family?" Marcus asks suddenly, striding towards the four children, their faces pale. Behind my veil, I squeeze my eyes tightly shut to stop the emotion and dread rising within me. Of course no one sees.

At a frightened, tentative nod from the lord, Marcus tilts his head to one side as if contemplating something. "You could offer one of your children. It will pay off your debts and keep Maya satisfied for a while," the king suggests lightly, gesturing towards me, his eyes gleaming with sick delight. I know that when he turns back to look at the lord, that expression will be gone and he'll play the role of a patient, benevolent ruler.

The lord pales as if all the blood has drained from him before an angry red flush appears on his cheeks, his face contorting with anger. Staggering to his feet, he hurries towards his children and puts himself between them and the king, throwing his arms out wide. "No, I won't let you touch them!" His voice is stronger than it's been, his conviction making him stand tall. "I would rather offer myself than let you harm them."

This time, I can't hold back my quiet sigh. What the lord doesn't know is that he's just been baited into offering himself. This is exactly what the king wanted.

Smiling, the king claps his hands together. "Offer accepted. Although you don't look quite as tasty." He turns his smug expression on me. "Maya, it's dinner time."

CHAPTER

Once again, the atmosphere of the hall shifts, this time to one of eager anticipation. The guards and nobles don't get to see me in action all that often. It's disgusting, but exactly what I've come to expect of humans after my many years of walking this land. Blood sports always seem to incite an excitement within them, even when the victim is one of their own.

The lord instantly realises his mistake in offering himself up, and the sour scent of fear fills the air, increasing all the more as I slowly step forward. Standing tall, he turns from me and faces the king. I'm sure we're about to hear him beg, because that's how these things usually go.

"What about my children?" His voice doesn't even waver, his expression firm. This is a man who's accepted his fate but is still fighting for his family.

Marcus raises a single eyebrow once more. "The orphanage will take them, I'm sure, although perhaps not the older girl." His eyes rove over the teenager who must only be sixteen at the oldest, and I feel my stomach churn. "I'm sure she can find work in one of the brothels. She's pretty enough."

To say I'm surprised is an understatement—not with the king's response, but the lord's. When faced with the prospect of becoming my next meal, most men beg for their lives and offer up everything they own, but not this one. Instead, he's fighting for his children, knowing their lives will be all the worse without him. The brothels are not somewhere anyone wants their child to work, where they are essentially sold to the house madam and forced to pay back the ridiculously high training fees. Most of the whores never manage to pay off their debts, and their lifespans aren't long. The orphanages aren't much better. No man should have to go to their death knowing their children will be left to suffer without them.

Again, I feel torn. The human part of me hates this. The lord hasn't paid his dues because he's become a widower and has to feed his children, it's not as though he's committed a crime and needs to be taught a lesson. Sure, over the years my human heart has begun to harden, tainted by the monster within, but I still possess *some* empathy. My other half, the beastly part of me, relishes her time in the spotlight.

You're too soft, she whispers in my mind. *Release me from this mortal body and I will take away your concerns.* She's not wrong. Sometimes, I think about just letting her loose so I can be numb to the horrific things I have to see and do, but I know that once I returned to this form, I would be horrified. So I keep that leash on her and continue my slow walk across the hall.

I pause just behind the king. He smiles at me and

gestures for me to continue before stepping back and returning to his throne. He wants the best view of the show, after all.

The lord whispers to his crying children, telling them he loves them and saying his last goodbyes. He knows it would be futile to try to escape, instead choosing to spend these last moments with them. I wait for him to turn around and face me, while the children are pulled away so they don't get caught up in what's about to happen.

I don't actually eat human flesh, but it's something someone once accused me of, and the king never denied it. Now, everyone believes that I'm a flesh-eating demon. They either don't know or don't care that I was once one of them, that I was human before I became cursed with this form. They'll never accept me as one of them, even when I wear my human body.

Now that the children are clear, I stretch out my arms and allow the change to take over, throwing my head back as the otherworldly power consumes my body. It's agony, but I don't allow a single sound to escape my lips as my body twists and transforms. A heavy weight settles around my head, and the pain in my legs starts to abate as a gasp of horror fills the hall. Opening my eyes, I smile as the snakes, which now form my hair, brush against me, eager to touch me after being confined for so long.

I should shift more often and let my alter out more, then I wouldn't feel such a huge struggle when I change. It's not like I have another being within me, but my other self is a second presence in my mind. I'm a gorgon, and as such, I have two forms. *I* control both, but I've pushed my monstrous self down so much that she's developed a personality of her own, and her actions are often more rash due to being confined.

Other than having snakes for hair, my upper body is almost identical to my human form—although if you look at me under the light, you might see very faint iridescent scales along my skin. The scales change colour at my waist and become thicker, forming a V below my belly button and covering a full, snake-like tail. I usually keep it wrapped beneath me, but if I were to stretch to my full height, I would be as tall as two men. It's my eyes, however, that are the most dangerous thing about me. As with all gorgons, I have the ability to turn humans to stone with a mere glance. My gaze is intoxicating, which is why I'm bound to wear this veil at all times, covering my eyes and protecting the king and his subjects.

Typically when I do change, I give myself over to my gorgon, allowing her to revel in dealing out the king's justice, as it helps with any guilt that I may feel, but today, I hold back. Something about the way he offered himself to protect his family stirred something within me.

The lord is looking at me now, but I'm again surprised by the fact that there's no disgust in his expression, just fear and sadness. With deliberate movements, I raise my hands to my head and release the tie that holds my veil in place, watching as the hated fabric flutters to the floor. My snakes hiss with anticipation, and I tilt my head to one side as I assess my latest victim. He's staring straight ahead now, his body stiff.

End this. The words hiss through my mind, and the urge to lunge forward, to strike and put on a show for the king, pulses through my body. It's an urge that is so much harder to resist in this form. There's nothing I can do for this man. He is destined for death whether I deal the blow or not. A thought comes to mind, and I realise that although I might not be able to help him, I could help his family.

This is stupid, really stupid, and I'm bound to get caught, but I can't help myself. I close the distance between us, feeling all eyes on us, my gorgon loving the attention. I grip the lord's shoulder, piercing my sharp nails into his skin and eliciting a grunt of pain. Embracing him like a lover, I lean in and trace a line across his neck with my tongue, tasting the faint saltiness of his skin. His breaths come in quick, sharp bursts, and it takes everything within me not to let my gorgon take over and sink my fangs into his neck.

"I can't help you, but I'm going to help your family. They will be safe," I promise in a whisper.

Before the lord can react, I pull back in a whirl of speed not possible for humans, grip his chin, and force him to look at me. His eyes widen in surprise, but he doesn't try to pull away from me, accepting his fate. The process of turning to stone doesn't take long, and within seconds, he's solid and has breathed his last breath.

I know I'll get chided for this later once we're out of public view. The king wanted a drawn out, grisly execution, where I bit him and let him bleed out on the floor with my snakes crawling over his body. Instead, I gifted him with a quick, painless death.

The tug in my chest is so strong that I'm almost physically moved by it, the magical noose around my neck reminding me just whom I belong to. Leaning down, I retrieve my veil, put it back in place, and sigh with relief as the feeling disappears. There's no point in resisting, because the spell that binds me to Marcus will only increase its grip on me, slowly tightening around my neck until it chokes me into obedience. There's an audible sigh of relief once my eyes are covered. I know this form makes the nobility uncomfortable, but I don't rush to shift back, allowing my tail to stretch out as I turn and make my way back to the king.

"Have him moved to the gallery," Marcus orders the guards, waving a hand dismissively, his tone suggesting that this is all a mighty inconvenience for him. What a shame. A man just lost his life, making his children orphans, but I've put out the king by making a human statue. The gallery is a quiet part of the castle that most people avoid, but the king enjoys frequenting it and often goes there when he needs to think. He relishes seeing the forms of the many men and women I've turned to stone over the years. This will be the home of the newest addition.

"Maya, you are dismissed for the rest of the evening. I think this demonstration has reminded everyone what happens when they choose to disobey or cross me," he says loudly, and I know this is more than a warning to everyone. Still, I dip my head in agreement and make my way over to the door at the back of the hall.

"See me in my rooms later," he orders as I slither past him, his eyes trailing over me. Marcus has been one of the only people to look at me in this form and not shy away. Once, I believed it was because he loved me, and I know deep down he does love me, but he loves power more, and that's what I offer him as a gorgon—power.

Again, I nod my head and make my exit. As soon as I'm free from the room and the door shuts behind me, I let out a sigh. My snakes fuss, knowing I'm about to shift back into my other form, but I'm going to need my human legs for what I have planned this evening. Raising a hand, I let them twist around my fingers as I pet their heads in comfort, hushing them in a low voice as I move through the dark passages. Marcus doesn't like me moving around the castle in this form unless it's on his orders, so once I've shifted, I have to use these passages where no one will see me.

Changing forms is exhausting and leaves me weak afterwards, so I can't change back immediately without suffering the consequences. Usually, I would go back to my room, stretch my tail and bathe, then change back before I attend to the king or head to bed. Tonight, though, is different.

Your human heart is going to get us killed. I push that thought away. I know how dangerous this is and that I'm risking everything. It doesn't take long for me to cross the castle in this body. My tail is strong and muscular, making me far faster than I am with my usual two legs. Reaching the door that leads out to the main corridor, I push it open to find my personal guard, Noah, waiting for me. Most would think that he's here to protect them from me, or that he's my constant shadow to stop me from escaping, not realising that I'm bound by magic and *can't* leave whether I want to or not. Of the four men who guard me, Noah is the one I like the most. We've struck up an unlikely friendship.

He's way too grumpy and world-weary, considering he's only thirty-six, but I know something traumatic happened whilst he was serving the king and that he's been part of my guard ever since. The others treat me with respect but are all wary of me, only speaking when they absolutely have to. Noah, while not the most talk-ative, will have the occasional conversation with me, and he is the only one I would trust with what I'm about to do.

Wearing a black uniform with golden stars embroidered over his heart, he looks menacing. His sword gleams at his hip as he eyes me, taking in my current form. His tanned skin is starting to show signs of his age, a few fine lines appearing on his face—not that I would ever tell him that. His short, cropped hair is darker than most of the citizens here, which makes me think he's originally from a different kingdom. It's his eyes that really make him stand out though, the dazzling blue so bright it reminds me of the magical lake I used to visit before I met the king.

He leads me back to my rooms in silence. It's not far from here, and thankfully, it's all on the same level—navigating stairs when you have a tail isn't the easiest. We don't come across anyone on our short journey, as all of the lords are still in the hall and the servants know to avoid me after these events. When we reach my rooms, Noah steps in front of me and holds up his hand to stop me. Opening the door, he walks in and looks around, checking for anyone or anything that might be there. We've had assassins sent after me before, so the king ordered this as a precaution. What I don't understand, though, is why they send the vulnerable human in first. I can protect myself, but whenever I ask Marcus, he always just mutters something about keeping up appearances.

Noah gives me the all clear and I enter the rooms, shutting the door behind me. They are luxurious, far more so than I care for. I used to live in a cave, and while I did hoard my possessions like a dragon, all I needed was space to stretch out and a place to make my nest. Moving past the plush loungers and coffee tables ladened with sweets and pastries, I slide over the marble floor and into the bedroom. It's even worse in here. Hanging fabrics cover the walls, mimicking curtains, and there's a huge, ostentatious bed that fills most of the space. It's ridiculous. The only person I'm permitted to share my body with is the king, and he never comes to my rooms anyway, so why he believed I needed such a thing is beyond me. Ignoring the bed, I move into my favourite room. Carved deeply into the floor is the bath, which is more like a small pool, where the hot water is already waiting for me.

Undoing my dress and removing my veil, I slide into the water and groan with pleasure. I could spend hours in here, soaking up the warmth like the cold-blooded reptile most of the world seems to think I am. Closing my eyes, I let the change take over me, the angry hiss of my snakes dissolving into the white-hot agony of my tail splitting into two as my legs form. The heat of the bath helps, but I'm still left gasping from the effort, and sweat drips down the side of my face as I attempt to catch my breath. Changing twice within the space of an hour is challenging, so I'll just have to rely on my wit and fighting skills should everything go tits up tonight.

My heart slowly returns to its usual rhythm and my breathing settles, so I quickly wash myself before stepping from the tub, my legs shaky. Without bothering to cover myself, I walk naked into the bedroom. My skin is pale and smooth, unchanged from the day I was cursed to carry the gorgon within me. While I may look like I am in my early twenties, I'm actually over sixty now. My dark hair falls in waves down my back, and my unusual green eyes mark me as someone from a different nation. Unlike the more buxom, broad people of Vaella, with their tanned skin and pale hair, I stand out like a sore thumb. Well, it's not hard to recognise who I am when the king dresses me from head to foot in his colours and decreed that no one can cover their face but the king's blade. That's what he calls me, his blade. I sit at his right hand and cut down his enemies with a single look.

Reaching my dresser, I move the gowns aside and pull out the dark shirt, jacket, and trousers I've hidden at the back. They fit tightly, binding my chest, and when I pull on the black cloak I also had stashed, I inspect myself in the mirror as I fix my veil in place via sturdy clips in my hair. With the hood up like this, you can't even tell that my face is covered beneath. Black, knee-high boots finish the outfit, and I stride back into the living area to find Noah leaning against the door.

Seeing me back in my human form and taking in my outfit, he simply sighs and shakes his head. "Again?" Despite his words, he doesn't sound all that surprised.

I don't bother to respond, instead heading over to the large bookshelf that fills one of the walls. Pulling aside two heavy tomes, I retrieve the dagger I hid there and slide it into the sheath at my waist.

"You're going to get us both killed," he mutters with a weary voice.

"You don't have to come," I point out, replacing the books and turning to face him with a shrug. "Stay here and guard the room." I already know what his response will be, but I always give him the option. He's the closest thing I have to a friend, and if anything were to happen to him, I'd feel awful.

He snorts and rolls his eyes, his body language confirming what I already knew. "That's not going to happen."

Despite knowing he can't see it, I smile at him. It's not the nicest smile, full of teeth and the promise of violence, but he seems to know anyway. Pinning me with a look, he strides over to the door and gestures for me to hurry up.

"Let's get this over with."

Opening the door, Noah steps out and checks that the coast is clear before gesturing for me to follow. I dart from the room, and we make our way through the castle corridors. Thankfully, everyone is still busy in the hall with the party that follows the giving of gifts, and all the servants will be serving them or cooking in the kitchens. Silently, we make our way to the back of the castle and into the servants' quarters. The short staircase that takes us down is deserted, which Noah confirms with a nod. It's not as nice down here as the rest of the castle—undecorated, plain, and cold from the winter chill seeping through the stone walls—but it's a hell of a lot nicer than the conditions down in the streets, and they also have what we need here, which is an unguarded exit.

Arriving at the wooden door, we sneak out into the castle grounds. The bitter winter wind whips around us, nearly taking my hood with it. Grasping onto it tightly, I stalk towards the stables, attempting to ignore the sting of the cold. As we round the back of the castle, I see the stables and a ramshackle cart, with the four children of the now deceased lord huddled together under an alcove to hide from the wind. This must be the wagon that's going to take them away. We arrived just in time by the look of it. Disgust makes me feel sick. They couldn't even wait and let the children eat before tossing them out? Then again, how could the lords possibly enjoy themselves at the party with the orphans of their peer who was just murdered?

"You speak to the children, I'll find my contact," I instruct, keeping my voice low and not even bothering to check if he'll obey. We've done this before, and the less Noah knows the better.

Despite my hard exterior and general hatred for humans, I have a soft spot for children. On several occasions over the last nineteen years, I've helped children escape and make it to foster homes where I know they'll be cared for. Before Noah was my guard, it was more difficult, as I had to find a way to sneak around them, but with him helping me, it's been easier. I know we risk being caught each time we do this and that it could ruin everything, but these children deserve a better life and I owe their father this. I am the reason they are now orphans, after all.

Sneaking past the stable master and into the building, I scan the area, ignoring the smell of horse manure and hay as I hurry from stall to stall until I find him. The stable hand can't be much younger than Noah, his straw-like hair already starting to thin, but he was just a boy the first time I came to him.

Slipping into the stall in near silence, I clear my throat. "I have four more for you."

He drops his rake in surprise, a high-pitched squeak escaping him that has me ducking and glancing around in case he attracted attention.

"Heavens above!" he curses quietly when he spots me, pressing his hand against his chest. I can hear it pounding from here. He needs to pull himself together, otherwise he's going to draw attention to us. "Fuck me. You scared the crap out of me! You've got to stop sneaking around like this," he whispers furiously, his face twisting up in anger as his embarrassment makes itself known.

The blush across his cheeks is easy to see in the moonlight shining into the stall. Bending down, he picks up his rake and starts his duties once again, shaking his head. "I can't keep doing this. We're going to get caught."

The shift in his voice has me standing and tilting my head to one side as I observe him. I know this stance disturbs many people, that it makes them suddenly remember just who and *what* I am. I'm dangerous, and they need to remember that.

"Are you going to help me or not?" My tone conveys my displeasure at having to ask this question, and he quickly blanches, but he doesn't instantly reply like I thought he would.

Slowly, as if considering the risks, he looks up and just over my shoulder, which is as close to looking at my veiled face as he will bring himself to. My estimation of him goes up a few notches. Not many would risk looking at my face, even with the veil covering my eyes. "We will help you." Walking to the stall door, he peers over to check that we're still alone, and then he glances over his shoulder once he's sure. "You should work for us. You could save many more lives than the occasional child."

Ah, this again. The mysterious *us*. I'm aware of a rebellion within the city. Hell, the king often uses me to help find some of these so-called rebels, yet they are still trying to recruit me. Their methods are just as brutal as the king's, and I want nothing to do with it. However, they are useful when I need them to help children escape. I know there are far more of them in the castle than just the stable hand, but I couldn't tell you who they are and that's fine by me.

"I don't think so." There's a hint of a smile in my voice, but I don't elaborate on my answer. "They are outside. Make sure they can stay together. They just lost their father, but I don't think you have to worry about them staying quiet. They seem sensible," I explain quietly, giving him the facts so I can get the hell out of here and back to my rooms before anyone notices Noah and I are missing.

Sighing, he just nods and slips from the stall, not bothering to try and convince me otherwise. I appreciate the fact that he didn't try to argue back. I know how difficult it will be to try to house four children together.

I wait a few moments for him to get far enough away, my ears pricked and listening to the sound of quiet children's voices. If I go out there now, I might scare them, and I need them to leave with the stable hand as quickly as possible. I'm listening so hard that I don't immediately notice the person sneaking in behind me until the crunch of straw gives them away.

Instinct takes over as I grab the dagger on my thigh, spin in a whirl of black fabric, and lash out, catching them on the arm. As they bite out a curse in a low, gruff voice, I realise my assailant is a male. He clutches his arm to his chest and steps back to assess me. I expand my senses to make sure he's alone, and once I'm reassured I'm not going to be jumped by anyone else, I take a moment to assess him right back. He's wearing clothing similar to mine, all dark and close fitting, with a cloak that covers most of his face.

"Relax," he mutters, raising his hands as if to calm a startled horse. "I just want to talk to you." I can just make out a sharp chin and dark stubble before he's moving again. Darting forward, he tries to grab me. I instantly shift away from his arm, but I don't notice what the rest of his body's doing. I blame the fact that I've just shifted and it's left me weak, but as his leg swings around, he takes my feet out from under me and the whole world shifts as I crash to the ground. Before I know it, he's pinning me in place with a knee on my chest.

"This is very forward of you if all you want to do is chat," I spit. My gorgon is screaming to be released, to tear this mystery assailant to pieces with my fangs and claws, ordering my snakes to bite and let him taste my venom. If I could just shift my head enough for my veil to slip, then I could easily turn him to stone—although then I'd just be trapping myself under a heavy statue. It's not ideal, but if it's the only way to survive this, then I'll let my pride take the blow.

The man above me pulls back in shock, his surprise palpable. "You're a woman."

Shit, I need to get out of here before he figures out who I am. I still don't have a clue who he is, but his words are slightly accented, making me think he's from another kingdom.

"Very astute of you," I retort, bucking to try and throw him off me.

Gritting his teeth, he makes a noise in the back of his throat as he puts more of his body weight into holding me down. With a grunt of pain, I stop fighting for a moment, considering my options.

Where the fuck is Noah when I need him? *No, Maya, you're going to have to get out of this mess by yourself.*

"I just need to talk to you," he insists. "We need to know who's been helping the rebels."

I'm about to demand to know who this *we* is, as he makes it sound like he's separate from the rebels, only he reaches out and pushes my hood back. My veil slips a little, but it doesn't move from my face, and I can't decide if that's a good thing or not. He rears back when he sees the black and gold material covering my face. Even in other kingdoms, they know of the woman who wears the veil, the king's blade.

"It's you."

He's distracted by his shock, so I reach within me to borrow the last of my gorgon's strength, bucking and writhing. Managing to displace him, I roll from under him and grab my dagger, which fell to the floor when I was knocked down. Jumping to my feet, I adopt a defensive stance and raise the blade.

"Don't come any closer," I order, allowing some of my monster to enter my voice, the words sounding more like a hiss. Now that he knows who I am, there's no point in trying to hide it.

The order doesn't seem necessary, however, as he just gapes at me. I can't see his expression, thanks to the large hood hiding his face, but I know he's surprised. Although he's holding himself defensively, ready to fight if I were to strike, he seems to have lost all of his desire to attack.

"Maya," a hissed voice calls. Noah is coming to find me, probably growing concerned when he didn't find me waiting for him.

The mystery attacker turns his head slightly before returning his attention to me, and then he slowly raises a finger to where I imagine his lips to be. On deft feet, he backs into the darkness of the stables and disappears.

What in the hell was that all about? Should I follow him and demand answers? Light footsteps approach as Noah nears, where I just stare into the darkness. Taking a deep breath, I ground myself and slowly release it, sliding my dagger back into its sheath and pulling my hood back up. Stepping out of the dark stall, I meet Noah's concerned expression.

He raises an eyebrow in question, but I just shake my head. We're not in any danger now, so there's no point telling him about the mystery man. I know he'd only just shout at me for letting my hood slip and revealing my identity.

"The children are safe?" I ask as I start making my way from the stables. My nose wrinkles. I'll be glad to get into the fresh air, although I'll have to have another bath before I see to the king. It would only raise questions if I were to see him smelling of straw and horses.

Falling into step beside me, Noah nods. "They are on their way to a safe house where they will stay before a new family will take care of them."

I dip my head once in acknowledgement. Something settles inside me now that I know they are safe. We hurry into the castle in silence and make it back to my rooms unnoticed. My mind replays my interaction with the mystery attacker, and I come to a conclusion—my soft, human heart is going to get me killed one day, but thankfully, that's not today.

Chapter

Pushing down all thoughts and feelings from my earlier encounter, I knock firmly on the wooden door three times. There's a brief pause, and then I hear Marcus' voice call out.

"Come in, Maya."

Some might be surprised that he instantly knew it was me, but this is a regular routine of ours. There's only one person who would visit the king this late in the evening, and everyone else knows not to disturb the king, as it's practically a death sentence.

Pushing open the door, I enter without fanfare, letting it shut softly behind me.

The room looks the same as always. There is a huge bed in the corner of the room, very similar to mine, and the four posters are carved with images of sirens reaching up into the sky. To my left is a large wooden table covered in trinkets, maps, and open books, all strewn about as if he had just been pouring through them for information. A large fireplace takes up most of the far wall, the fire currently blazing, and before it are three large armchairs. Draped in one of these is the king, who is lazily swirling a drink in his glass. He doesn't look up as I come in, just continues to stare into the fire.

This isn't good. Whenever he's in a mood like this, I'm the one who tends to suffer for it. Something has upset him and is weighing heavy on his mind. Was it the lord I turned to stone, or something else that I missed?

"Good evening, my king," I greet from my spot by the door, dropping into a slight curtsy.

Although I knew him long before he became who he is today, in this setting, he loves it when I call him by his title, and I can see I made the right decision. Raising the drink to his lips, he throws it back before turning his attention to me, his eyes gleaming at the honorific. His gaze roams over my body, and I can almost feel it against my skin as he takes in the dip of the dress lingering on my cleavage.

He stands and prowls towards me. "Maya, you look stunning, as usual."

After my second bath of the evening, this one much more luxurious than the first, I dressed in the practically see-through gown he likes me to wear for these meetings. It's black, like all the outfits he provides for me, and the neckline is a deep, plunging V that exposes half of my cleavage with black and gold lace edging the bodice. This allows for the amulet I always wear to be clearly visible. The bodice beneath the lace is black and fastens in the back, showing off my slim waist. The black fabric just covers my nipples, giving me at least some dignity. Loose, gossamer sleeves go to my wrists, the fabric light and see-through. The skirt is made from the same light fabric, long at the back and gradually getting shorter as it reaches the front.

My skin has been anointed with oils to make it soft and supple, and a light dusting of shimmering powder was applied across my collarbone and down my cleavage. This is the only time I allow anyone to help me dress, and that's only because the king ordered it.

Usually, I make myself at home in his rooms, taking a seat and helping myself to the sweets laid out on the coffee table before the fire, but when he's in a mood like this, I know better. Something has made him feel out of control, and because of that, he wants to take it back. Instead of finding the source of the issue, he does it with me. He knows he always walks a fine line with me, that one slip of my veil could kill him, but he enjoys the danger and the fact he can order me around and I'll do as I'm told. No one else in the world would have the power over me to do this, but Marcus does, and on nights like this, he likes to remind me of it.

"Would you like a drink?" I ask, trying to walk past him to get to the drink trolley in the corner of the room, but he reaches out to stop me.

"No, I just want you." He eyes me once more. "Take off your dress."

My mind becomes distant as I follow his orders, reaching behind me for the laces. With one tug, the dress slowly slips off my body and falls to the floor. Wearing only my black heels and veil, I watch as his lips tug up into a smile. Slowly, he closes the distance between us and crushes his mouth to mine, pushing me back until I'm pressed against the door.

I open my mouth to allow him entry, returning his kisses with vigour. His hands skim over my body, knowing all of the places that turn me on. I reach for him, trying to undo the buttons of his shirt.

"No," he says against my lips, gripping my wrists and pulling them down. "I want to have you like this."

Fiddling with the fastenings of his trousers, he removes his cock and gives it a few hard pumps.

"Should we move to the bed?" I murmur, my breaths coming in pants as desire courses through me. We may have a complicated relationship, but he still knows how to bring me pleasure.

However, when he shakes his head and grips my arms, I realise that my pleasure is going to have to wait.

"No. Turn around, I want to take you here."

Gritting my teeth, I turn and shift into position as he thrusts into me.

Collapsing on the mattress in a sweaty mass of limbs, I allow a smile to play on my lips.

After he fucked me against the door, he took me to the bed and covered my body in kisses, ravishing me once his need to dominate passed. Then together, we explored each other's bodies and made love, slowly and passionately, until we both climaxed.

A soft piece of fabric is pressed into my hand, and I know it's my veil. Stretching on the bed like a cat, I sit up slowly and untie the blindfold that's been covering my eyes. We learned long ago that my veil can slip, so a blindfold is a necessity when we come together like this. Keeping my eyes closed, I raise the veil and fix it in place. Blinking my eyes open, I glance around to see where my dress is and spot it by the door. I go to stand, but a hand on my wrist stops me.

Looking back, I see Marcus gazing up at me. He lies on his side, the sheets covering his nakedness, and watches me with a warm expression. "Don't leave just yet."

"What about the queen?"

I don't know why I ask. Perhaps some jealousy is creeping in? Not that I should feel that way. The queen has separate chambers, and they rarely share a bed, something I know she's bitter about. She's always hated me, not understanding why the king holds me in such high regard and loves me like he does. They both respect each other, but there is no love between them. Perhaps when the queen first married him she hoped that something would blossom between them, but over time, she put in less and less effort to engage with Marcus, and the only time they are ever seen together is at events like the one held this evening.

Really, though, she knows nothing about my relationship with the king. I know he loves me, but it's a love that's become twisted and possessive over time. I wish I could tell the queen this and that she wouldn't want to be in my place. Maybe that would ease her hatred of me. Of course my gorgon is possessive over the king, even if she wants to eat him at times, so my sympathy for the queen only goes so deep.

There are many rumours about their relationship, and the fact that she hasn't produced an heir yet is something that's caused controversy and speculation across the kingdom.

Marcus raises an eyebrow at my question. "She's with one of her lovers, I'm sure." He says it so casually, like a throwaway comment, and it shows just how much he doesn't care. Waving it away, he holds out a hand. "But please, just stay for a little while longer."

The use of the word please makes me pause. Usually when he asks for something, he expects it to be done immediately and without question. I'm sure he's trying to make up for his rough fuck against the door earlier. I've come to know that Marcus occasionally needs to release some of his frustrations, and that often comes out during sex. Afterward, though, he's usually kind and gentle.

My gorgon wants to be alone, since we're tired and it's been a long day, but the human part of me wants to bask in this moment. I don't get to see him like this often, so I make the most of it when I can. Lying back down, I roll onto my side, making sure my veil is still secure. Marcus smiles and traces lazy patterns against my skin.

"I wish we could always be like this," he murmurs, his soft touch helping me to relax against him. "It reminds me of the old times, when we used to travel and didn't have to worry about the responsibilities of the kingdom. Everything is so different now."

He's right. I never would have known how much my life would change when I first met him over two decades ago. I'd been cursed for over twenty years by that point and living alone in my cave. It took time for me to trust him, because everyone else who sought me out was trying to kill me for the amulet I guarded, so I'd assumed the same about him. However, he was patient and kept coming back. It was just the two of us, but now I have to share him with the kingdom.

"I know." My reply is quiet and full of longing, wishing we could go back. Not physically, because the castle is much more comfortable than the caves we would sleep in, but our bond was so strong. It's different now. *He's* different now.

There's a heavy pause as his hand trails up the valley of my breasts and comes to a stop where my amulet rests.

"Things could be different if you gave me the amulet." His fingers hover over the emerald set in the middle of the diamond encrusted amulet.

I stiffen, and my good mood immediately disappears. Why does it always come back to this? Sitting up, I pull my legs to my chest, trapping the amulet against my body and out of sight. "You know I can't do that."

I'm not looking at him, but I feel his mood change in an instant. "You don't trust me." It's a statement, not a question, and one I'm not going to deny. This is a conversation we've had many times before.

My amulet is the cause of my curse, and if I hand it over to him, then he will have absolute control over me. What I say, what I do... I would be his puppet, locked within my own body. Currently, I'm bound to him by magic, something I agreed to out of love, but there are loopholes with that, and I still have my own free will. Handing over the amulet would take that away completely.

Yet it always seems to come down to this. It's always the same fight, the same argument, that gets us nowhere. He promises me he wouldn't use it unless he absolutely had to, that he'd let me live my life. He claims that he doesn't even really *want* the amulet, that he wants me to give it to him in the ultimate show of trust. The fact that I won't really gets to him.

We used to travel the land together, not long after we first met, and I fell for him. Marcus had been searching for magical objects when he found me, his research leading him to the amulet I guard. No one can take it from me unless I choose to give it to them or they slay me. However, if I'm dead, the amulet's curse will just pass to the next person, turning them into a gorgon. And so it goes on. He knows he can't take it without becoming like me, something he would never allow.

Deep down, I know I can't trust him with something so powerful. There's a mania that surrounds him when it comes to magical objects, one he just can't seem to shake. So no, I don't trust him, not when it could cost me my life.

Resting my cheek on my knees, I watch him through the veil.

"I love you," I answer instead, and it's the truth. I do love him, and a broken part of me will always love him even though sometimes I barely recognise him. Power has changed him over the years—not physically, but mentally and emotionally.

He snorts. "That's not the same," he replies, but he reaches out, brushing his fingers against my leg so I know I'm forgiven. We're silent for some time, and my eyes are just starting to drift shut, the weight from the day taking its toll, when he hums low in his throat. It's a light, musing sound, but something about it has me on edge.

"You didn't bite the lord today like I told you to," he comments, and again, his tone is light and deceptively calm, but I can feel his frustration in the background like a looming thunderstorm.

I have to bite back my sigh. Can't we just enjoy this moment together? We get less and less of them nowadays. Frustration flares within me, and it's not just from my monster's unending anger, but my own this time. He might be my king, and I might be bound to serve him, but we're more than that, and I've never been one to hold back my thoughts, not when it's just the two of us.

"You wanted me to torture a man, to painfully kill him in front of his children, because he couldn't afford to give you a *gift*."

Despite wearing my human form, the words come out in a hiss. Ever since he started this practice, I've voiced my dislike of it. Killing or threatening people who hurt others is one thing, but this is something different altogether.

Pulling away from his touch, I sit on the edge of the bed, gripping the mattress tightly. "I'm not a performing monkey to accommodate your nobles' bloodlust. The result was still the same, I still killed him. You just wanted to send a message to the lords." The accusation hangs in the air between us. He doesn't deny it, we both know what I said is true.

The bed shifts behind me, and I feel the heat of his skin against my back as he moves closer. "You don't usually have trouble causing men pain," he whispers, his warm breath brushing against my ear.

He's right. When I let my gorgon out, she revels in it and wants to bathe in their blood, gorging on it until we're sick, but this doesn't apply to helpless men who offer themselves up to protect their children.

"I might be a monster, but even I have limits." Climbing from the bed, I walk over to where my dress lays on the floor in a pool of fabric. Shimmying it back on, I turn and see he's not moved. He is watching me with the covers draped over his lower body, but I can see his erection pressing against the sheet.

He holds out his hand, and I know he wants me to return to bed, but frankly, I don't want him to touch me right now. Anyone who gets turned on at the thought of someone else being murdered is someone to be wary of. Shaking my head, I place a hand on my hip to show him exactly what I think of his offer.

He rolls his eyes and falls back onto the bed. "Saint Maya," he mutters, raising a hand and placing it over his eyes. "You can leave now. You need to rest. We've got an important day tomorrow, and I need you to be on your best behaviour."

The dismissal is clear, and I don't wait for him to change his mind.

"Yes, my king." I bow, despite the fact that he's not even looking at me anymore, and leave the room, ignoring Noah who's been waiting outside for me the whole time. We walk back in silence, and for the first time, I feel ashamed of my relationship with the king.

CHAPTER

The castle is abuzz with activity this morning. Usually, the day after the monthly giftings, everything is quiet as the nobility nurse their sore heads from the night before. Not today, however.

Dressed in my usual conservative black and gold dress, I frown as the servants hurry around. Most of the time they cower away when they see me, but today seems different. Marcus' parting words from last night stand out in my mind. Perhaps all of this is related to that?

Owen is my escort today. The young soldier seems excited to have the position of guarding the king's blade, but he's also terrified of me at the same time. He's wearing his armour this morning, which is unusual when we're just walking around the castle. I catch up with him so we're walking abreast and clear my throat.

"Owen, do you know what's going on? Why are the servants so worked up this morning?"

He glances over with obvious discomfort at our close proximity, but he stays professional and keeps walking.

"Dignitaries from another kingdom are visiting today, my lady. I'm sure the king will explain everything to you when we get to his rooms."

So that's what Marcus was alluding to. We've had dignitaries visit before, however, and it's not caused this much of a fuss, so what's different this time?

Hearing the shutdown in Owen's comment, I don't bother to speak again and just follow him through the corridor. I hadn't slept well last night, visions of the lord I killed replaying over and over in my mind. When I was eating breakfast in my room this morning, Owen informed me that the king wanted to meet with me in his assembly room. I don't get called there often, only when he's planning something and needs my input.

Reaching the room, I hear raised voices before we even enter. *This is a good sign*, I think sarcastically. Owen knocks on the door and steps aside as it opens so I can enter, no matter how much I would rather stay outside. Marcus and his three advisors are sitting around a huge wooden table, all in conversation as they stare down at a map spread out before them.

They stop talking when I walk in, the scent of fear reaching me instantly. Two of the advisors, Paelo and Rogers, instantly look away for fear of catching my eye. My face is covered, as always, and even if I wanted to kill them with my stare, Marcus would stop me. The two advisors have been at the king's side for over a decade, yet they are still terrified of me. The third advisor, Jarred, hates my guts. He stares at me as if his own eyes could turn me to stone. I'm not sure what I've done to make him hate me so much, but I find it amusing and take every opportunity I have to piss him off.

"You requested my presence, Your Highness," I purr,

watching as Jarred bristles. He thinks I'm nothing more than the king's whore. Let him. I don't care what little men like them think of me.

Marcus looks amused, knowing full well what I'm doing.

"Today, we've got dignitaries coming from Saren."

My eyebrows shoot up in surprise. Saren is a neighbouring kingdom to ours, and almost as large. The smaller kingdoms of the land have pledged allegiance to us, knowing we could crush them if they went against us, but Saren has always stood its ground. They have an abundance of minerals, rock, and iron ore that they mine, making them wealthy. They also have some of the best blacksmiths in the land.

There's a large mountain range that separates our two countries, and it's one of the only things that has stopped an all-out invasion. Marcus wants to be in charge of it all, creating a united group of countries where he sits at the head, but Saren has other ideas. A tentative truce was called between them several years ago, but all attempts at diplomacy and setting up trade have failed—until now, apparently. No wonder everyone is on high alert.

"They finally agreed?" I don't bother to hide the surprise in my voice or the fact that I know more about our situation than most would. Perhaps I should have pretended not to know anything, because Jarred's expression goes dark.

Marcus, however, ignores him, finally looking up from the map and running his eyes over me. There's a slight glimmer in his gaze, and I know he's remembering our encounter last night. "Yes, and we have to get them to agree to unite with us, or at least agree to a trade deal."

"We need access to their mines. We're gaining less and less resources from ours," Paelo chimes in, a concerned frown taking over his wizened face.

Jarred slams his hand down on the table, startling the other two advisors. Marcus turns his head slowly to look at him, but Jarred is too busy gesturing towards me in anger, so he either doesn't see the look of reproach from his king or doesn't care. "Not that you need to know any of this," the advisor sneers. "You just need to stand there and look threatening."

Allowing my gorgon to come forward a bit, I hiss from behind my veil, watching in satisfaction as all three advisors flinch away. I know it's childish, but I don't care.

"Maya," Marcus warns, raising an eyebrow. I'm usually better controlled than this, and on a day like today, he needs to be sure I'm not going to do anything to screw this up. I feel the magic that binds us tighten around me for a moment, making it hard to breathe, but it releases after a couple of seconds, just a reminder of what he could do. "I need you to keep an eye on everything. Watch the dignitaries closely. I don't trust their king, and I certainly don't trust them. Report anything you see to me." There's no room for questions. This is an order, plain and simple.

There's a light, cursory knock at the only other door in the room, and I know from experience that it leads to the king's private rooms. Without waiting for an answer or order to enter, the queen bustles through. Clutching my hands in front of me, I will myself to be as still as one of my stone statues, pushing down my dislike for her. My monster hisses inside my head, wanting to tear her apart and revel in her blood... Taking a deep breath, I focus on nonviolent thoughts, like the startling green day dress she's wearing and how it reminds me of the wild grasses on the mountains where I used to live. The black accents and detailing are the only links to the king. Her hair is brushed and pinned to within an inch of its life, and her crown is carefully perched on top.

Smiling airily at the advisors, she glides into the room before seeing me. Scowling, she places her hands on her hips. "Oh, it's you."

I want to roll my eyes at her behaviour, but I know it's not just her. From the short time I've spent around the ladies of nobility, I've noticed they all seem to have this pampered, childish attitude. I doubt any of them have suffered or wanted for anything a day in their lives, so it makes it difficult for them to appreciate what they have.

When I don't respond, she narrows her eyes and waves her hand dismissively. "We don't need you to kill anyone right now, so perhaps you should go. That's all you're good for," she spits out.

Paelo and Rogers gasp quietly as if fearing my retribution.

"Phoebe, that's enough," Marcus says sharply. He's never had much patience for her theatrics, and he knows the thin line I walk with her. It would be *so* very easy for me to kill her, and I wouldn't even need to shift into my gorgon form.

I stalk towards her, swaying my hips seductively as I walk. The closer I get, the more anxious she looks, her arms dropping to her sides as she shoots a desperate look at Marcus, realising her mistake. The king just shrugs. She got herself into this mess, so she can deal with the consequences.

Stopping just a handspan away, I lean forward ever so

slightly, dropping my voice into a low purr. "That's not what your husband said last night as I warmed his bed."

"Maya," Marcus calls, but I hear the amusement in his voice, which is opposite of how he spoke to his wife just moments ago.

Queen Phoebe's face contorts in anger, and her cheeks flush red with her embarrassment. Should I feel bad for flaunting our relationship in her face? Perhaps. Do I? Hell no. Marcus and I were together as lovers *way* before he ever met her. However, he needed to marry and have a queen. No one was ever going to accept a gorgon as a queen, so he found Phoebe. In public, they may appear to be the perfect couple, but that's all for show. I'm pretty sure she hates him—maybe not as much as she hates me, but close.

I don't step back, I refuse to, but I look at Marcus, holding my hands loosely behind my back. "Yes, my king?" My voice is light and sweet, and I know it bugs the crap out of the queen.

The corner of his lips tugs up into a smile, but as Queen Phoebe steps back in a huff, his expression drops. "Try not to wind up the queen. I need you on form today. You'll do as instructed?"

"Don't I always?" I think I manage to hide the slight edge of bitterness that tries to worm its way into my voice.

"You're dismissed. Make yourself useful before they arrive."

I'm glad he can't see my face at his casual dismissal and the implication that I'm not always useful, that my sole purpose is to *be of use*. Without another word, I spin on my heel and ignore the stares as I stalk from the room, closing the door behind me far harder than necessary.

Owen is waiting for me with a wary expression, sensing my sour mood, but he wisely doesn't say anything. Gathering my skirts in one hand, I turn to the right and march through the corridors.

"I'm going to the gardens. Either hurry up or stay here," I bite out. I know none of this is his fault, but he's a constant reminder of how my life has changed, and I don't have the energy to hide those feelings right now. Thankfully, he doesn't argue, simply nodding and taking up a position a few steps ahead of me as he leads me out to the garden, where I can try to find some peace.

IT'S COLD OUT. It is still winter, after all, so I'm the only one in the garden. Even Owen has retreated to one of the overhangs on the back of the castle, watching from a distance. I want to be alone, so this suits me. It's midmorning now, and I can hear the sounds of the castle preparing for our visitors. This time of year, the gardens are bare and the evergreens are overgrown, so I sometimes feel like I can get lost out here. It's the closest thing to freedom I have.

A weak beam of sunlight manages to break through the clouds and bathes me in pale yellow glow. Smiling, I tilt my head back and enjoy the gentle warmth of the winter sun. It's not much, but I'm going to take it as a sign that things are about to change. Today isn't going to be easy, I know the role I must play, but being universally hated is tiring.

I've been sitting on this rock for at least an hour, enjoying being away from the expectations of the castle, but it's also not far from the stables. Thanks to my monster, I have superior hearing. It's not as good as when I'm in my gorgon form, but enough that I can make out the conversations of the stable hands and guests who arrive. From what I've gathered, I believe half of the dignitaries' party has already arrived to ensure everything is up to standard.

Snorting, I shake my head. That's not going to go down well with the king.

"Is something amusing?"

The male voice startles me so much that my gorgon almost rips through my carefully constructed barriers. Whirling with a speed no human could possess, I crouch defensively with a menacing hiss as I search for the source of the voice. It's not hard to find him. Leaning against a tree is one of the biggest guys I've ever seen. Not only is he tall, but he's broad too. He must be about double my size, and with his arms crossed over his chest, his biceps look like they are about to burst from his tunic. A dark cape is tied around his neck, but it does nothing to hide his size. With the hood down, I can make out his dark cropped hair. His hazel eyes shine with an intelligence that I'm sure many overlook when they see his build. Peeking out from the top of his tunic is a tattoo that looks to continue down, and I see more ink on the backs of his hands.

Even I can admit that he's intimidating.

How the fuck didn't I hear him approach? Taking in his dark green uniform, I assume he must be part of the dignitaries' party. Shit, this is not a good way to meet one of them. From his build, I'd say he's probably a guard, yet he looks at me with knowing eyes that see far too much. I need to pull myself together and decide if he's a threat or not. Usually, I'd dismiss most humans, but there's something about this one that has me on edge.

He continues to lean against the tree, his stance easy and casual, not at all intimidated by who I am. My gorgon pushes against my barriers again, irritated at the lack of fear shown by the stranger. She wants to put on a show and make him realise exactly who I am. Of course he knows who I am, everyone does. Assassins from Saren have been sent to kill me before, and my clothing and veil clearly mark me for what I am. Pushing away my irritation and frustration that he was somehow able to sneak up on me, I straighten and loosely clasp my hands in front of me. Tilting my head to one side, I observe him for a moment longer.

"Just an inside joke," I finally reply, my voice quiet and steady.

Something flares in his eyes as I speak, and his lips quirk. "You're all alone out here."

I'm not sure what the purpose of this conversation is. Could he be trying to point out that I'm vulnerable alone? That he could be a threat? Or is he taking note that I wander alone in the gardens, ready to report the information to his master? Either way, he's wrong.

"Not quite." I nod my head towards Owen sheltering in the overhang, gazing off in the wrong direction. Stifling a sigh, I return my attention to the stranger, noting the amusement in his expression.

Pushing away from the tree, he slowly makes his way towards me. Even with the distance between us, I realise I underestimated how tall he was as I crane my neck upward to take him in, a walking behemoth. Thankfully, he stops just as I'm considering stepping back, something my gorgon would never let me do.

"You shouldn't be alone out here. I hear the king has a monster on the loose, one he keeps chained to him."

Again, that trace of amusement laces his tone. So he *does* know about me. I'm taking his comment as confirmation. The question is, do I allow him to bait me?

Humming in the back of my throat, I decide that two can play this game, and a thrill of excitement courses through me. I don't get verbal sparring partners often, as most are too afraid of me to even try it. Crossing my arms over my chest, I tilt my head once more. "How can she be on the loose if she's chained?" I challenge, my lips twitching beneath my veil.

"You know there are more ways to keep someone prisoner than physically chaining them," he replies, his voice softer.

I feel as though someone's dropped a bucket of water over me, and my amusement instantly flees. This conversation has suddenly taken a huge turn that I am not prepared to dive into, and it hits a little too close to the mark. What is this guy trying to get at? I don't know, and I don't care. Sympathy is the last thing I need from a Saren grunt.

Clearing my throat and standing tall, I take in his dark green uniform beneath his cloak. He's not wearing armour, and I notice golden symbols stitched into the collar of his tunic. Perhaps he's more important than I first suspected. Captain of the guard maybe?

"You're from Saren." I'm stating the obvious, and it's clear I'm trying to change the topic, but he doesn't call me out on it.

"I am." He inclines his head. "From your accent, I would guess that while you live here, you grew up far from this land."

He's right, of course, not that I'll tell him that. Something about what he said and his earlier comment are making me nervous. I don't think I've shared this many words with anyone other than the king and Noah in years. In part, it's thrilling, but it also feels like he knows too much. I should leave. I should turn around and walk back into the castle, where I don't need to worry about him tracking me down and asking more uncomfortable questions. Only, I don't.

He seems to realise that I'm not going to reply to his comment, and really, he doesn't need me to confirm it, because it's obvious he already knows about me. "What's your name?" he asks instead.

Do I tell him? Part of me wants to, but this whole interaction has shaken me. I better return before the king finds out. "A lady never tells," is all I say as I begin to turn away, making as if to leave.

"Lady Maya!" Owen shouts, panicking as he realises I'm not alone. He's in such a hurry to reach me that he trips over his own feet. Shaking my head, I glance back at the stranger and see all amusement has left his face.

"Your prison guard is here." He lowers his voice as if he doesn't want the guard to overhear, but I don't miss his quiet amusement.

"He's here to protect me, not the other way around." Even as I say it, I know deep down it's not true. I hate the constant presence of the guards, of my protectors. In all honesty, what could they ever do to protect me that I couldn't? During all of the assassination attempts, I was the first to react and save myself. We all know I don't need anyone to protect me, yet we still go through this game of pretend.

"Of course," the stranger replies, his sarcasm loud

and clear as he shakes his head. "Lady Maya," he says by way of farewell, bowing slightly at the waist. Owen arrives at my side just as the stranger turns and walks away, but not before scowling at my protector.

Owen bristles, watching as the stranger stalks off towards the stables. "You shouldn't speak to them. They are all rapists and murderers in Saren."

I raise my brow at his ridiculous statement. "The whole kingdom?"

He starts at the edge in my words, having the decency to look ashamed of his sweeping generalisation. Is this how they feel about us too? King Marcus isn't seen in the best of lights, even in the kingdoms we're allied with. His tactics aren't always clean and honest, but he tries to offer everyone a better life with a solid infrastructure. Of course, many see this as a dictatorship. He doesn't share much about politics with me these days, but I know there are many who are unhappy with the way he leads. I imagine that Saren believes us to be the biggest threat and probably views us in much the same way.

Cheeks heating with embarrassment, Owen dips his head slightly, but he doesn't back down. "Maybe not all of them, but I've heard about the type of people their king hires. They are not good men."

Rumour or truth? I imagine we'll find out at the ceremony later.

"I suppose we better head inside," I say on a sigh. Despite the cold weather, I'd stay out here all day if I could. It's far better than being near the constant scheming and plotting of the nobility.

"Yes," Owen begins, sounding relieved that I'd come to this conclusion myself. None of the guards feel comfortable with me outside. "The king has supplied you with something to wear."

I want to groan, knowing it will be something flashy and ostentatious or ridiculously revealing. He likes to ensure everyone knows whom I belong to, especially when dealing with nobility from other lands.

"Then I guess I better get changed."

Chapter

I was right about the outfit. I'm seething with anger as I stare at myself in the mirror. There are many things I would do without question for my king, but this is not one of them. When I see him, I'm going to make it very clear that I am *not* happy.

The top is little more than a tightly fitted black bra with beading around the cups to show off my cleavage, and boy does it show. The bottom half of the outfit is made up of loose black trousers, which gather together in golden cuffs at my ankles, and a gauzy over skirt that's open at the front and gets longer towards the back. Small golden bells have been sewn to the bottom of the skirt, which chime quietly every time I move. I look like the belly dancers I saw when Marcus and I travelled to the desert cities far away when he was searching for a magical lamp. We never found it, but the style of clothing they wore obviously stuck in his mind.

Flicking one of the bells on the skirt, I scowl at the bright tinkling noise. The king is going to know exactly where I am tonight, even if he can't see me. Does he not trust me after all this time?

The clothes leave nothing to the imagination. I don't mind wearing clothes like this in private, and they are beautifully made, but to insist I wear this to a formal meeting this important is something different altogether. The king might as well have written *mine* all over me, his possessiveness stepping up a notch in the presence of his enemy. Funnily enough, my gorgon isn't too upset by it. She likes being dressed up and is looking forward to terrifying the dignitaries while looking fabulous.

A knock at the door pulls me from my musings, and I quickly adjust my veil to make sure it's secure before I take one last look at myself. Making a disgruntled noise, I turn from the mirror and pull open the door. Noah is waiting for me, having swapped shifts with Owen, and he simply raises his brows as he takes me in.

"I know. Don't say anything," I bark, the order coming out far harsher than I meant it to.

Raising his hands in a gesture of surrender, he steps back. "I wouldn't dare."

Grumbling, I stalk past him, noticing the corners of his lips turning up as he tries to suppress a smile. Stalking through the hallway, I take a left when I reach the main corridor, heading towards the grand staircase.

"Where are you going?" he calls, his voice getting quieter the farther I get.

"To see the king." It should be obvious, and I let my frustration bleed into my voice.

"He's already in the hall, Maya. The guests are about to arrive."

Cursing, I stop in my tracks and spin to see him waiting for me at the junction in the corridor. Stalking back to him, I gesture for him to carry on and follow behind him. I guess my conversation with Marcus will have to wait.

Come on, Maya. Focus, I tell myself as we walk in silence. Today is important, and I should be thinking about how I can best serve my king. Everything else can wait until later when we're not hosting our enemy. I can't help but wonder what the dignitaries will be like, and an image of the stranger I met earlier today flashes in my mind. He didn't seem to be afraid of me at all, yet he seemed to know who I was, or at least had an idea, judging by his comments.

Ahead, Noah begins to slow as we reach the main hall, nodding to the guards who stand by the tunnels. The king must already be in position if he doesn't want me walking in on his arm. My frustration makes itself known once more, causing my monster to push against my boundaries. I hate making my entrance like this. They already fear me, and making me enter this way only affirms their association with dark tunnels and the serpentine body of my other form.

Noah gestures for me to enter, and I know he'll join me shortly, taking the side door into the hall like the rest of the guards and castle staff. After all, this passageway is just for me. Releasing a sigh that ends on a hiss, I push past him and make my way through the dark alone. You'd think that I'd struggle to see, given that there are no lights in here and my face is covered, but thanks to my other form, I can see perfectly. In fact, I prefer to be in the dark.

I can make out the voices of many people gathered in one place. The king must have invited all of the nobility in the kingdom for it to be this full. Then again, he's achieved something his father was never able to—having peaceful negotiations with dignitaries from Saren—so he's going to want to show off this achievement.

Light starts to filter through the tunnel, and as I round a corner, I see that the doorway is open, showing me the back of the two thrones. Hovering at the entrance, I briefly debate if I should just stay back here in the dark. Marcus wouldn't drag me out, not in front of the dignitaries, but I'd pay for the insubordination later. Closing my eyes, I force myself to remember why I'm here and who I pledged my life to.

Marcus. The young man who found me in a cave when I had nothing. The man who gave me a reason to want to live again. The only person who ever looked at me without fear. He's the one I gave up my solitary life for and travelled across the land with. Sure, I never thought my life would pan out like this and power has changed him, but deep down, he's still the same Marcus I met all those years ago. Feeling stronger, I open my eyes and step out into the light.

With my back straight and head high, I take slow, measured steps as I walk around the thrones, ignoring the hushed whispers and gasps as I seemingly appear from nowhere. Turning my back on the gathered nobility, I face the king and queen and drop into a low curtsy, the bells on my clothing jingling quietly. I stand without waiting to be dismissed, and my eyes immediately land on the queen. She's staring daggers at me, her hate and jealousy obvious as she takes in my outfit. The dusky pink of her conservative gown makes her look soft and delicate, whereas mine makes me look alluring and dangerous.

"Maya," the king calls with a note of reproach.

Satisfied, I look away from the queen and step towards Marcus, who is holding his hand out for me to take. His eyes gleam with gratification as he runs his gaze over my body. I'm still not happy over the clothing, but seeing him look at me this way takes away some of the sting from my frustration.

As I take his hand, he draws me closer. "I knew I made the right outfit choice," he says in a low, hungry voice. He tries to pull me into his lap, but I place a hand on his chest to stop him.

"You could have warned me," I point out, my tone icy. This isn't the place for me to disagree with him, but he needs to know I'm not happy.

He watches me, his gaze skimming over my veil as if he can look straight into my eyes. The slight incline of his head is the only acknowledgement I get, and I know it will have to do for now.

"I want you to stay close to me today. We need to show a united front."

Sitting on the arm of his throne, I lean down so my lips almost brush his ear and lower my voice to whisper, "Of course, my king." A grin spreads across his face, and he wraps an arm around my waist, anchoring me in place. It's uncomfortable as hell, but it sends a powerful message. Leaning back, I rest my arm on his shoulder. I know how to play this part. I also know how it will look when the dignitaries arrive. The blade of the king is practically draped over him, dressed to entice and snare.

Ignoring the snort of disgust from the queen, and now in position at the king's side, I take a moment to look around the room. It's been dressed up for the occasion. Hundreds of candles fill the chandeliers, bathing the room with light. The king's banner hangs from the wall, the golden thread gleaming against the black backdrop, and long wooden tables laden with food are positioned against the walls. The waiting nobility and other guests mill around, leaving a long pathway clear in the middle of the room. Beside me, I notice the king incline his head slightly, and before I can ask what's about to happen, the two huge wooden doors are pulled open. It takes three men on each side to open them, but my gaze is locked on the group of people waiting beyond them.

Without waiting to be introduced, they start to move. Three guards dressed in light armour bearing their king's sigil march into the hall, followed by a page. Beyond is a group of three men who have to be the dignitaries, based on their clothing and stature. The rest of their guards bring up the rear. No one says a word as they make their way towards us.

There's something different about the dignitaries, and it takes me a moment to realise what it is. They all walk together with an easy confidence, but one of them takes the lead and is obviously the one in charge. He just has that look about him. Broad-shouldered, he's muscled from many years of training, not something I'm used to seeing in representatives sent from other kingdoms. Usually, pompous advisors are sent, and I can tell they have never lifted a sword a day in their lives, but not these men. The male in charge wears his brown hair tied back in a bun, his face is all sharp angles, and several days' worth of stubble coats his chin. His blue eyes scan the room briefly before landing on us.

I shift my attention to the man on his right. He's different from the other people in his party. His skin is paler, and his hair is so blond it's almost white. It looks so soft I want to run my fingers through it. His eyes are also blue, but not the deep blue like that of his companion. These are a light sky blue, and they are so unusual that I just want to keep staring and commit him to memory. His lips are twisted up into a smirk, and although he's smaller than the other two, his swagger more than makes up for his stature.

Looking at the large man beside him, I only just manage to hold back my shock when I realise I've already met him—the stranger in the garden. He changed, although he looks uncomfortable in the smart clothing of the dignitaries. His eyes are locked on me, and a single brow arches as he takes in my new outfit and position on the king's throne.

The king hisses in a sharp breath beside me, and his face is twisted in anger. His entire body seems to tremble with rage, and I can't help but notice as several of the watching lords who are closest to us start to back away. They have all witnessed the king lose his temper before, and no one wants to be in the line of fire.

Following Marcus' furious glare, I see he's looking at the three dignitaries. What the hell is going on? I place a hand on his shoulder, but he brushes me off like I'm nothing but a pesky fly buzzing around his head. He surges to his feet, and I have to move quickly so I don't end up sprawled across the floor. My hiss of anger would usually cause a gasp from the watching nobility, but all eyes are locked on the king right now.

"What is the meaning of this?"

The whole room seems to freeze from the wrath of the king, and then the spell is broken and everyone reaches for their weapons. Both sides stare at each other, their swords drawn as they wait for someone to make the first move. The Saren guards have gathered around the dignitaries, but I see they are the only ones who haven't pulled out weapons. That's not to say they are not being cautious. They appraise the situation with their hands hovering close to their swords. Our guards seem hesitant, glancing back at the king for an order. The room is silent save for the shuffle of feet, and the atmosphere is tense.

"Your Highness," the page from Saren calls out, stepping forward and attempting to continue with diplomacy. "May I introduce—"

A low growl emits from the king, cutting off the page. Frowning beneath my veil, I look between him and the dignitaries. I've seen him angry over many things during our time together, but I've never seen him like this. It's obvious that I've missed something.

He steps forward and descends the dais, his face twisting into a sneer. "I know who they are." Stopping just before the line of palace guards that separate us from everyone else, he glances at me over his shoulder before turning back to the dignitaries. "King Kai's team of monster hunters."

I go cold. I stay away from court gossip, but even I've heard of the monster hunters. They are famous across the land for their tracking and fighting skills, and they haven't yet come across a monster they couldn't beat. What I hadn't realised was that they were from Saren. I suddenly understand the king's anger, and judging by the whispered voices filling the hall, the watching nobles have too. It's a huge insult for King Kai to send his personal monster hunters when they knew Marcus had a monster of his own. Was the Saren king deliberately trying to spark a war between our two kingdoms, or are the hunters here to kill me?

My gorgon relishes the challenge, and before I realise

it, I'm stepping forward, my hands loose at my sides but ready to react in a moment. I pause at the lip of the dais, my gaze flicking over to the huge male I met earlier today. Unlike the others, who are watching the king, the stranger from the garden is watching me. If the rumours of the hunters' skills are to be believed, then he could have easily killed me when he had me alone, or at least tried to, yet he seemed more intent on discussing my invisible shackles.

"I invited you here for discussions of peace and trade," Marcus continues, his voice shaking with barely suppressed rage, "and your king insults me by sending his monster killers. If you think I'm going to allow you to take her, then you're mistaken." Stepping back, he turns to me, his face distorted with hatred. "Maya, change. Kill them."

I look at him in shock. He can't be serious. If I change, I'll kill them, I won't be able to stop myself, but I don't think that's what the dignitaries want. If they wanted to kill me, they would have had the opportunity to do so several times already. It doesn't make sense for them to go about it this way, and jumping straight to offence will only make *us* the instigators of war.

Reaching out to lay a hand on his arm, I attempt to beseech him. "My king, maybe we should—"

My words are cut off as a tight band of magic clamps around me. Marcus watches me with anger and disapproval written all over his face. He expects me to obey him without question, especially in front of his kingdom, but in this case, I can't blindly kill, not when the consequences are so high. I may think most humans are evil and only care for themselves, but I know what this will cost Marcus if war breaks out between the kingdoms. I wish I could portray all of this with my face, that he could see my reasons in my expression, but no, he just stares at my veil as if I'm betraying him.

The magic that binds me to him gets tighter with each second I disobey. I grasp my throat as panic begins to set in, my airway constricting. I'd expect my gorgon to be pushing against my barriers, since killing is something she loves, but for some reason, she's retreated deep down inside me. Is it out of fear for these supposed monster hunters, or is it another reason entirely?

"Your Highness, we're not here to kill your pet." The male voice sounds familiar, and I see the male in charge of the dignitaries frowning up at the king.

The pale male at his side stays silent, watching me with a frown. He has a dagger clasped in his hand, yet I feel no threat from him. Taking a wheezing breath, I glance at the third male of the group, the man from the garden. He shifts his weight from foot to foot, looking like he's about to spring into action at any moment.

"We're here to trade," he insists, his deep voice strained like he's trying to hold back his feelings. "And we have a service that might be of interest to you. Don't throw this opportunity away out of fear and greed."

Marcus rears back like he's been struck. He might have agreed had it not been for that last comment. No one insults the king and lives to tell the tale.

"Lies," the king hisses, his temper flipping as he enters a sort of mania. "I won't let you have her. She's mine." Possessiveness rings in every word, and I realise in that moment that I will never be free of the king. The idea of belonging to him before was never something that bothered me, I *liked* being the king's favourite, but that was when I thought he considered us equals. He just made it clear that I'm little more than a possession to him, which tears at my human heart. I reach within myself for the strength of my gorgon, both for the physical and emotional pain.

Striding up to me, he grabs my shoulders and shakes me. "Maya, do it."

My head falls back as a bolt of pain surges through me like lightning, and when he lets go of me, I fall to the ground, shaking with agony as I try to fight against his order. That invisible band tightens around my neck even further, restricting my throat until I can't breathe. My gorgon awakens, sensing my dire need, and rushes to the surface, pushing against the restraints holding us as she tries to force the change. I feel the magic stretching as she tries to break the spell on us, but it's no good. Even if we could break free, I wouldn't let her. If I change, I won't be able to stop myself from obeying the king and killing the dignitaries. In doing so, we'd lose all hope of trade deals and peace between our two kingdoms. Besides, there's something inside me that's whispering that these three are important, and if they die, then all hope is lost.

My vision wavers, and I fight against the panic. Beseechingly, I look up at Marcus, but he just watches me with disappointment. He wants me to give in and follow his orders, and this is my punishment for going against him.

A presence appears at my side, and then a gentle hand rests on my back. From the corner of my eye, I see it is Noah. He looks worried, which is an expression I've not seen on his face before. I expect him to tell me just to follow the order, but he doesn't, instead staring up at the king.

"You're killing her yourself," the dignitary states

plainly, crossing his arms over his chest. "Why would I try to stop you if I wanted her dead?"

His words make sense, but the king just snarls at him. This is it. After all these years, I'm about to die, all because the king can't see past his hurt pride. I should shift and save myself. I've killed for the king before for lesser insults, but even the thought of harming the dignitaries makes something in my soul cry out. I can't explain it and I certainly don't understand it, but until I figure out why these three are so different, I can't allow that to happen.

The stranger from the garden has a hissed conversation with the other two before pushing past them and making his way over. The male in charge is shaking his head at his colleague's back, but he makes no move to stop him. When the large man reaches the line of guards, he stops and glares at them. I know he could snap them in two without a thought and push through, but instead, he takes a deep breath and pulls his tight gaze from me to look up at the king.

"I could snap her neck right here. It would take me less than a second to get past your sorry excuse for guards. You've handicapped her and made it so easy for us to hurt her." He's making an obvious attempt at restraining his temper, but I can hear the anger he's trying so desperately to hold back. Without giving the king a chance to reply, he turns his attention back to me. "We're not here to hurt you, Maya." There's a promise in his voice, and for some unknown reason, I believe him.

I'm not sure exactly what makes me look towards the king, but because of this, I catch the look of pure, undiluted fury in his eyes. I don't know it now, but I'll realise later that it's because the stranger knows my name and he spoke it with familiarity. It seems to take a moment, but the king suddenly takes in the shocked silence around us and realises that the whole room just witnessed his freak-out. Backed into a corner, he knows he has no other choice, so with a dismissive wave of his hand, the magic over me is suddenly released.

Choking, I fall forward as I gasp for air, my lungs burning with each sweet breath. Closing my eyes for a moment, I focus on taking steady breaths and slowing my racing heart. My head is pounding from the lack of oxygen, and the world is spinning around me so much that I know I won't be standing for a while for fear of falling. It wouldn't do for the king's blade to be stumbling around the room, not after so obviously disobeying him.

As if able to read my thoughts, the king walks over and slides his hand through my hair in a way that's supposed to look loving, but as his fingers tighten and pull my head back, I gasp at the pain in my scalp. Stooping, he presses his lips to my ear.

"We'll discuss your disobedience later," the king hisses.

I know he meant his words for my ears only, but the stranger stiffens. Most would have missed this little detail, only seeing the king touching his favoured, yet from the male's narrowed eyes, I know he sees through it all.

Marcus either doesn't notice or doesn't care as he stalks back to his throne. The atmosphere in the room is still tense, but isn't as electric as it had been before, and many of the guards' swords lower as they wait for orders.

I'm still staring at the stranger as he runs his eyes over me like he's checking that I'm okay. Convinced, he inclines his head towards me and returns to his party, speaking in a low voice to his two companions. They saved me, and I don't know why. Was it because I disobeyed my order to kill them so they are returning the favour?

"Are you okay?" Noah asks in a voice so quiet I nearly miss it.

Am I okay? No, not really. Not wanting to attract the king's attention, I merely nod my head. If I were to tell him how I really felt... I don't want to say the words out loud. Noah doesn't look convinced, but he takes my silent answer and stands, returning to his position. The king starts to speak, and I drag my gaze up to watch him. He doesn't even look my way, his voice bright as he explains the situation, weaving his own narrative of the events that just took place. Like the good lords they are, many nod their heads and accept his explanation, despite having just witnessed what happened.

Staying in my position on the floor, I just watch the king in numb disbelief. My body is still in agony, and my gorgon seems to have disappeared within me again, but all I can ponder is that Marcus nearly killed me. He shook me. The king actually laid his hands on me then watched as I suffocated from his order. I almost died because he wouldn't listen to what the males from Saren had to say. His pride got in the way, and he almost lost me because of it.

I've watched him change over the years and made excuses for him, but not anymore. I need to guard my heart so I'm not hurt like this again. This stirs my gorgon, and her agreement helps me build a barrier around my heart. I'm strong, stronger than any man in this room. Those words repeat over and over in my mind. I was tricked into this curse, and if the legend is true, the only thing that will save me is love. I thought Marcus loved me, but I'm not so sure now.

The king continues to speak, and I know introductions are made, but I'm too busy recovering and building internal shields. Eventually, the king gives the word and the party begins. Music fills the hall as everyone mingles and discusses what they just witnessed.

Marcus ignores me as I stay on the floor and gather my strength, and once I feel strong enough, I climb to my feet. He glances over at the movement, and after a heavy stare, he gestures for me to come to his side. I'm glad I'm wearing the veil, which hides my expression, as I slowly walk over, each step painful.

Staring out at the party, he clears his throat. "You're to mingle with the dignitaries from Saren. Remind them that they should be afraid of you." He finally looks at me, his expression one of mild annoyance, but I see the fury in his eyes. "Do you think you can obey *that* order?" he spits. Without waiting for a response, he shakes his head and looks away again. "Come to my room tonight."

I'm in trouble, and he's going to make me pay for it. I had hoped that I could just return to my room and recover, but no, he's going to make me stay here, despite knowing how much pain I'm in. Thankfully, most of my *mingling* is simply meandering through the crowd and finding a pillar to lean against. I hate this, and Marcus knows it. In fact, it's probably why he told me to do it. It just reinforces people's fear and hatred of me, although it's the people from my own land who react more to my presence than that of the Saren visitors. Shying away, the nobility blanch as they realise who just brushed against them. Inevitably, I end up with a clear radius surrounding me as I lean against one of the pillars at the back of the hall.

The nobles seem to be enjoying themselves, eating and drinking far too much and speaking in too loud voices about our visitors. Unsurprisingly, the visitors from Saren stick together by one of the tables, their gazes alert as they observe their hosts.

It's been at least an hour now since the dignitaries' disastrous entrance, so I'm sure I can slip away quietly without too much fuss. Pushing away from the pillar, I make my way across the hall. I don't have to weave through the gathered guests as they all jump from my path. I'm about halfway across the hall when a shadow falls over me. I instantly know who it is before they even say a word.

"Maya."

Hearing him say my name sends a thrill through me, but I'm not sure if it's from excitement or anticipation. Turning, I see the male from the garden, and beside him are his companions.

The male with his hair tied back who seems to be in charge of the group steps forward and presses a hand against his chest. "Let me formally introduce myself. I'm Lord Elias of Saren, this is Theo." He gestures to the pale man to his right.

Theo grins at me in a way that should be disconcerting, but I find it oddly charming. He doesn't say a word, and before I can speak, Elias talks again, pointing over his shoulder to the tallest of the three of them.

"And you already met Mason." The hint of exasperation in his tone suggests that he doesn't approve of our earlier encounter, but his half smile takes the sting from his words.

Something about what he just said is bugging me, however, and I can't figure out why. I commit his face to memory, and that's when I realise it's not what he said that seems familiar, but *how* he said it.

"I know you." Images of a hooded man pressed against me in the dark flash through my mind. "You were the man in the stables." The certainty in my voice shocks me as I stare at him.

I don't need him to confirm it, I know I'm right, but when Mason and Theo stiffen, their actions confirm it. Elias, on the other hand, doesn't seem fazed in the slightest. Tilting his head to one side, he seems to consider something. When conviction flashes in his eyes, I'm suddenly nervous about what he's going to say next. "And you, Maya, are so much more than the monster the king paints you as."

Cursing internally, I realise that I've just given myself away. What the hell had these men been doing in our city that required a disguise? Several days early at that. I'm sure that if Elias was here, then the other two were as well. Are they a threat to my kingdom? I hadn't thought they were, but now I'm not so sure. My back stiffens as I look over the three of them. I just disobeyed my king to save these men, trusting my gut feeling. Was I wrong? If they do turn out to be threats, then I will kill them, despite the little part of my mind that shrinks away from the idea.

Part of me also acknowledges that the sudden anger I'm feeling isn't purely because of what they might be doing here, but because of his last comment. I'm not ready to think about why that would upset me so, however.

"How long have you actually been in Vaella?" I

demand, glancing between the three of them. I attempt to sound intimidating, but a sudden onset of fear makes my voice tight. "If you tell the king I helped those children he won't believe you," I hiss, backing away. I need to put some distance between us. I'm not worried what the king will do to me if he discovers what I've been doing, but I am concerned about how it would affect our already fracturing relationship.

"We arrived a few days early to scope out the city and see what it was really like without the pomp and circumstance. We heard of someone within the castle who was helping people escape the king," Elias explains, watching me closely.

There's a slight wariness to him now, as if he's remembering who I am and what I'm capable of. Good.

"I was trying to meet you that night," he continues. "I wanted to talk, but I had no idea the king's blade was the one behind it all." He raises a single brow as if to challenge me to deny it.

I'm too caught up in my own mind, however, to retort. What was only ever going to be a one-time thing started to become more regular, and I always knew that I'd eventually be caught. But for these men from a different kingdom to have heard about me... I've not been careful enough. They were able to track me down. Excuses pour through my mind, like I had just shifted, but that wasn't good enough. I was weak when I should have been able to fight him off.

Striding forward in a move too fast for human eyes, I jab my finger against his chest. "Keep your voice down," I order, my gorgon entering my voice.

He looks down at my hand in surprise, and I notice

his two companions stiffening behind him, but neither move to stop me.

"Maya, I meant what I said earlier." Mason frowns, shaking his head. "We're not here to hurt you."

"Then why are you here?" I demand, my confusion evident in my tone.

They share a look before glancing around at the nobility who are pretending not to watch us. None of the guests are close enough to hear us, none would risk coming that close, not with me here, but these three are obviously here for another reason other than visiting my king. I'm pretty sure they are not going to tell me, so when Theo speaks, it takes me back.

"We want you to help us." His voice is quiet but sure. There's something seductive and melodic about it that makes me want to listen to him speak all night. He's been the quietest of the three, and I get the impression that he doesn't speak often.

I have no idea how to reply to that, and it only brings up more questions. Help them how? Why do they need me, the king's blade, to help? This is certainly not the place for a conversation like this, and I can feel the king's gaze on me. I've been here long enough, and I need to make my excuses before I irritate the king any further.

"Is everything okay here, Lady Maya?" Noah asks, rescuing me and giving me an excuse to get out of this conversation.

Only just managing to hide my relief, I turn towards my protector. The slight glint of humour in his eyes tells me I've not fooled him. Ignoring that, I dip my head in acknowledgement to his question. "I think I'm ready to return to my rooms."

He nods and takes a step back, gesturing for me to follow him.

"Maya, wait," Mason calls, and for a moment I pause, but I don't turn around, instead continuing to walk across the hall, very aware of the gazes on me. Had we been alone, would I have done anything differently? Asked them questions or at least said farewell before running away with my tail between my legs?

Stopping in front of the thrones at the foot of the dais, I bow deeply and look up at the king through my veil. He stares at me for a long time before nodding and dismissing me with a casual wave of his hand, as if he's shooing a pesky fly that's been bothering him all evening. Usually that might hurt, but tonight, I'm just grateful I don't have to hang around. Pulling myself up to my full height, I move behind the thrones to my tunnel and make my escape.

CHAPTER

Nodding my farewell to Noah, I shut the door behind me after I enter my room. I should bathe and get out of this ridiculous outfit, but I'm just so tired that I can't even face that just yet. My mind feels numb, and it's so full of everything that happened today that I can't even begin to process it. Spotting my bed, I drag myself over and ungracefully flop down onto it, not bothering to pull back the blankets. I groan in pleasure and close my eyes. I'll rest just for a moment.

A loud banging sound startles me awake. Jerking upright, I turn towards the noise, my hands raised and talons extended as a partial shift occurs before I can even try to stop it. Marcus stalks into the room, his eyes blazing as he slams the door shut behind him, not seeming bothered by my rumpled state or raised hands, the sharp points of my claws glistening in the torchlight. I can smell the wine on him from here, and when I glance at the timepiece on the wall, I realise that I must have fallen asleep, because several hours have passed. He must have come straight from the hall.

He never comes to my room, so I know I'm in trouble. Standing tall, I lower my hands and take a step forward to meet him.

"Do you know what you did tonight?" He stops just before me, his words dripping with acid and contempt. My greeting dies on my lips. There will be no pleasantries tonight then. I've never seen him like this before, and it takes me aback. If anyone else dared to speak to me like this, they would be dead before they could even take their next breath. I'm weak when it comes to him though.

I try to hold back my anger. If I shout, it will only escalate things, and that's not going to help either of us. What I did in the hall made him look bad, and I'll apologise for that, but when he's drunk like this, I know nothing good will come of it.

"Marcus—"

A slap across my cheek stops me in my tracks, and my head turns with the force of the blow. I could have held strong, only I wasn't expecting him to react this way. My face stings, but the real pain isn't physical. No, I can't believe that he just did that.

"I am your king, and you will address me as such," he growls through gritted teeth, making me wince as he grabs my shoulder tightly. For the first time, I see contempt for me in his expression, and that hurts me more than his words.

No, this is enough. I refuse to be treated like this. I am not some pathetic weakling he can push around. My pride has been injured too, something that my inner beast finds most insulting of all. We are not human, we are not subservient, and we will not be treated as such.

"Get off me!" I shout, ripping myself out of his hold. Rounding on him, I feel my body grow as my gorgon presses against my control. It would be so easy for me to give in to her right now and teach him a lesson, but my human heart pleads for me to remember my compassion. I want to laugh at myself. Compassion is something I lost many years ago.

"How dare you?" There's a challenge in my voice as I tilt my head to one side, the rest of my body unmoving like the predator I am. "Do you not remember who I am? I gave up everything for you, and this is how you treat me?"

My gorgon rises to the surface once more, and I'm so tempted to let her out. That's what shocks me the most and makes me blink, my bravado faltering. When did our relationship become so toxic that I would consider using my monster against him?

He must sense this, however, as a cruel smile pulls at his lips. "Go on then! Shift! Show your true colours!"

This time, I can't hold it back, and the change takes over me. A cry escapes my lips as the transformation rips through me. Pain like no other blinds me as I fall to the ground, my legs becoming one long, thick tail. The sound of hissing around my ears and the heavy, warm weight of my snakes tells me the transformation is complete as the pain starts to fade.

My body is weak, my chest heaving with laboured breaths as I look up at him. I don't recognise the man standing before me. Striding over to the fire, he grabs the poker perched against the wall. Disgust ripples over his face as he looks at my shifted form and shakes his head with a sneer.

"You want to be a monster, then you'll be treated as

one." He lifts the poker and swings, the metal connecting with my back. A cry rips from my lips at the pain that lashes through me, my back arching with agony. He hits me over and over, spitting hateful words that I try to block out. Had he given me time to recover after my shift, I could have defended myself, but I'm too weak. My snakes lash out and try to bite him as I shuffle away, willing my tail to work. My anger and conceit builds. What had been an ember within me begins to burn hotter and hotter, fuelled by the fact my gorgon is currently in control, her anger fed by the betrayal of our lover.

I could remove my veil and end this once and for all, but when it comes down to it, I can't kill him. Even my gorgon shrinks away from the idea.

The door smashes open, but Marcus doesn't stop, and I'm too busy protecting myself to see who just forced their way in.

"Stop!" The deep voice resonates through the room. Several footsteps sound, and the blows stop, the poker suddenly dropping to the ground with a loud clang. Flinching away with a hiss, I manage to get my tail working and use it to push myself across the floor, away from the sounds of a scuffle that currently echo around the room. My back bumps against the wall as I reach the back of the room, and I can't stop my groan of pain.

I sense someone approaching before I see the booted feet in front of me and jerk my head up, my snakes hissing a warning. Elias stops in his tracks and raises his hands in a universal gesture to show he's unarmed. When I make no move to attack him, he slowly lowers himself to a crouch. With my breaths still sawing out of me, I take a moment to scan him. His expression is solemn, but there's a simmering anger in his eyes that I don't think is aimed at me.

"How dare you?" Marcus snarls, his words slurred by the alcohol he clearly drowned himself in this evening. "I am king. I'll have you all hanged for this." He's not jesting, I can see how serious he is, but the three dignitaries don't seem to be bothered in the slightest. What's happening here? Are they going to try and kill him? If they did, would I try to stop them? Before this, I would have said yes without pause, but now I'm not so sure.

He's currently being restrained by Mason whilst Theo pats him down. I don't know what they are looking for, and the smaller man gives nothing away. Mason's expression, however, makes him look fierce, and murder dances in his eyes.

"Stop talking." Theo's voice is light, but the order is obvious, and the musical quality to his voice makes me pause.

To my eternal surprise, Marcus does exactly that. He even stops struggling against Mason, and a sense of calm settles over him. In my painfilled state, I can't figure out what's happening. None of this makes sense.

"Maya," Elias calls, snapping my attention back to him. He looks me over and shakes his head. I'm sure I look a right state. The gauzy outfit I'd been wearing is hanging from my body, torn from the blows of the poker, not to mention the fact I'm huddled in a corner with my snakes slithering around my shoulders as if trying to find a way to comfort me. "I'm sorry we didn't get here sooner. We should have realised he'd take what happened out on you."

I knew there would be consequences to my actions, I just had no idea he'd hurt me the way he did. However, that's not what I'm worried about right now. "How did you find me?"

Elias sits back on his heels and seems to ponder the question for a moment. Decision made, he nods towards the still open door. "Your guard came and found us when he heard you shouting."

Surprised, I turn my head to see Noah standing in the doorway, his expression dark. He looks away as if unable to hold my gaze and instead looks at the king, and I'm shocked to see contempt there. He's the king's guard, and his solemn duty is to protect Marcus, yet tonight he went against that, and he might have just saved my life.

"Are you okay?"

I'm just turning back to Elias when he reaches for me. I instinctively flinch back, my snakes hissing, and he pauses, except there's no fear or disgust in his expression, just concern, like he actually cares about the answer. Shaking away that thought, I pull myself together. I don't answer his question, instead asking one of my own. "Why are you trying to help me? I'm a monster."

Elias arches an eyebrow. "I'm a monster hunter, remember? I've seen plenty of monsters in my time, and not one of them would risk their life by saving orphaned children, or the lives of dignitaries from other kingdoms." His last comment is said with a wry smile. "He, however" —he looks back at the king with a scowl, his voice hardening— "is another matter entirely."

Ignoring the feelings that try to rise up at his comments, I focus on the immediate danger. "He'll kill you for this. All of us." The king might be strangely calm at the moment, but that will soon fade. Marcus is a proud man, perhaps even more so than my gorgon. He won't let a slight like this pass, especially not when he's been physically manhandled. He'll order the dignitaries to be put to death for "attacking" him, and I'll be the one who has to carry out the sentence. After everything tonight, I'm sure he'll decide that I'm too much of a hassle and order my execution. What good is having your own personal monster who won't do as ordered?

Elias doesn't seem concerned by this though. "That's not a problem." Glancing over his shoulder, he meets the gaze of his pale companion. "Theo."

More questions rise in my mind, but before I can ask, Theo nods and reaches up to cup the king's cheek. He does it gently, like a lover, and I'm stunned into silence.

"You haven't seen us." The statement is almost conversational, and I find myself wanting to nod, but I stop myself when I see the king doing the same.

"What—" I cut myself off as I listen to his words and the soothing, almost lullaby effect they seem to be having on the king.

"You will now return to your rooms and fall asleep," he continues. "You won't remember any of this in the morning, only that you came to this room and disciplined Maya. No further action is needed, you are satisfied."

The king isn't struggling at all now, and Mason lets him go, stepping back as if just being close is disgusting.

"Theo's a siren," I murmur in shock. I've never met one in person, but there used to be one in the great lake near where I lived after I'd been cursed. She never showed herself to me, but I sometimes heard her singing, calling me to the water. Sirens don't have the best reputation, known for luring men to their watery deaths. I've heard rumours that they can shift into human form, but I wrote that off as hearsay. It makes so much more sense now—his unusually pale skin and hair, his almost painful good looks, and how he doesn't talk often.

"Half siren," the male in question replies, throwing me a toothy smile that would intimidate most, and I realise now that his canines are sharp and pointed.

Half siren. One of the famous monster hunting team members is part monster himself. I can't decide how I feel about that. Does he track down and kill his own kind, or is there something else going on here?

"As you can see," Elias begins, staring at my veil as if he can see right through it to judge my reaction, "there's a lot we need to talk about."

He's not kidding. The last thing I want to be doing right now, though, is having this conversation. Gritting my teeth and making sure my veil is still firmly in place, I curl my tail beneath me and push myself upright, managing to keep my pained noises to a minimum. I'm glad he's not able to see my face. I don't want them thinking I'm weak, they could use it to their advantage.

They promised that they wouldn't hurt you, and so far, they have kept that promise. They pulled the king off you, risking their own lives in the process, my mind reasons. Releasing a long breath, I push those thoughts aside.

I roll my shoulders back, noting I'm as tall as Elias like this, but he doesn't back down. If anything, his brows pull down in concern. "You've been badly injured. Let us help you."

Ignoring his comment, I glance over just in time to see the king being bundled from the room. Trying to keep an eye on Elias in front of me and listen to the hushed conversation by the door, I can just make out Mason's order for Noah to take the king back to his room. From the corner of my eye, I see my guard pause, but after a second, he nods and takes the silent king's arm, leading him away.

Shaking myself out of my stupor, I try to regain control. "You need to leave." My words are seething, the order punctured by the resounding hiss of agreement by my snakes.

I have no idea how long the king will be under Theo's spell or if someone will come to check on me. Is a half-siren's spell as potent as their full-blooded relatives? If they come across Noah whilst the king is still mute... I don't even want to think about the potential consequences.

"Maya..." Mason steps towards me with reproach in his voice and a scowl to match.

My gorgon reacts to the tone of his voice, hissing in distaste. However, it soon becomes apparent that Mason isn't about to step down either. Sensing that things are about to get out of hand, Elias raises a hand and motions for the other man to stop as he returns his attention to me. "At least let us see the wound."

Taking him in, I deliberate if I should show them or not. They already know about it, so there's no point trying to deny it, and I get the feeling they won't leave me alone until they have seen it. Hissing out a sigh, I slowly turn and allow them to see my back through the shreds of fabric that cling to my body. Their sharp inhales make me snarl, and embarrassment has me lashing out. "I'm fine, I've had worse." My intention was to get them to back off, but it only seems to upset Mason more, if the low growl he's emitting is anything to go by.

"I heal faster in this form. I just need to rest, and I'll be fine by morning." My protest seems to fall on deaf ears, however, as the atmosphere in the room is still tense.

"She needs a nest," Theo says, and I throw him a glare despite him not being able to see it.

Who the hell do these males think they are? They just came into my space and witnessed one of my most embarrassing and degrading moments, and now instead of giving me the peace I so desperately crave, they are spouting nonsense about nests.

I throw my hands up in exasperation. "I can take care of myself."

Mason turns to his companion with a frown. "A nest?"

Crossing his arms over his chest, Theo nods. "Gorgons sleep in nests. I'm surprised you don't have one already." He aims the last comment at me, and as his voice ripples over me, I allow myself to be momentarily calmed by the sound.

Snorting, Elias shakes his head. "From what we've seen of this king, I'm not surprised."

All is still for a moment until Mason jerks his head once and storms through the room and into the bathroom. He makes a grumbling noise, and I realise he's talking under his breath. When he storms back out again, he ignores me completely and grabs the pillows and blankets from the bed. In a state of shock, I just watch him. Even in my gorgon form, I'm completely baffled by these three. I blame the post-shift weakness for not demanding to know what the hell he thinks he's doing.

It's quiet for a moment, save the occasional rustle of fabric in the other room. Slowly, I turn my head to look at Elias and Theo, hoping they can shed some light on what's happening, but before I can, Mason pokes his head around the door, his gaze going straight to me. "Is this okay?"

Theo walks straight past me without even a hint of fear and steps into the room. "Not bad. This should be enough to help her feel settled."

His voice travels out to me, and my gorgon hisses at being talked about like I'm not here. Elias just shrugs and gestures for me to go into the bathroom. Sighing, I slowly slither through, biting my lip as the movement pulls on my wounded back. I stumble to a stop when I see Theo and Mason looking down at their handiwork with satisfied expressions.

The bath, which is a large, sunken space taking up most of the room, has been transformed. Bedding lines the bottom, with blankets and cushions scattered around. It looks cosy and makes my gorgon's little black heart happy, and something within me feels complete. I hadn't realised how much I missed my nest. I always used to make them, and even when Marcus and I travelled, I would find the time, but when he became king and we moved into the castle, he told me that I had to act like a lady and he wouldn't be sleeping in a nest. It's been years since I had one.

Slowly, without even realising that I'm moving, I slide into it, arranging the pillows until they are just right. Instinct takes over as I brush invisible lint from the blankets. I curl my tail beneath me, and a low, happy humming noise emits from my chest. I don't think I've ever made a sound like that, and I quickly stop, feeling embarrassed. Looking up, I see that Elias has now entered the room too.

With the three of them looking down at me like this, I should feel cornered, vulnerable, but for some reason, I don't. *It's because I know I could easily take them in a fight*, my inner voice counters, but I'm sure it's more than that.

These three are from a neighbouring kingdom, one we've been at war with for years, yet they are helping me. In the short time they have been here, they have shown me more kindness than I've received in years.

"Why are you doing this?" I hate how vulnerable I sound, but I need to know the answer.

Any hope that I might find out is soon dashed as Elias shakes his head. "We can talk about that tomorrow when you're feeling better. But for now, you need to rest. One of us will stay here to make sure you're okay."

"I will," Mason volunteers before I can protest. I don't want them here, and I sure as hell don't *need* them here.

"That won't be necessary," Noah answers, appearing in the doorway, his face set in a heavy frown. "I won't let anything happen to her."

I hadn't even heard him return, because my gorgon is too busy planning how we're going to bury ourselves in our nest and make it pretty. Why the hell isn't she crawling out and demanding that they all leave us the hell alone? She's always so protective, and we don't trust easily, yet she's only irritated at their behaviour, not biting them like she would anyone else. Some secret part of me whispers that it's because she knows they won't hurt us. That's the most disturbing part of all this, not the infestation of men in my room or the beating that Marcus gave me, but that she seems to instinctively trust them and what that could mean.

"You allowed the king to hurt her," Mason grumbles with disapproval, pulling me from my terrifying thoughts and back to the present.

"That won't happen again," Noah promises, watching me with a strange expression as I absent-mindedly stroke the blankets beneath me.

The atmosphere is heavy when Elias finally sighs and nods. "Fine. You can stay, but you'll come and find us if anything happens."

It's a command, one I expect Noah to bristle at, but he just dips his head in acknowledgement. When did they earn his loyalty?

Mason makes that low grumbling sound again and steps towards his companion. "Elias, I don't like this—"

"Mason." The word is an order, followed with a shake of Elias' head, and to my surprise, the larger man stops in his tracks. Elias stares at Noah, sharing a long look, before gazing at me once more. "We'll see you tomorrow, Maya. Rest up."

All four men leave the room, and I can hear them speaking in low voices. I should go out there, or at least try to hear what they are saying, but I'm so tired and my eyelids heavy. I can already feel the skin pulling together and beginning to heal, and exhaustion pulls at me. I wasn't lying when I said I'd heal quickly in this form, but it always takes a lot out of me. They need to know that they can't just order me around like that, and that I don't need them to protect me, especially not from my king, but as my eyes start to drift close, I decide that I can set things straight tomorrow.

I'm not sure how much longer the men from Saren stay in the other room, as I'm asleep within minutes.

CHAPTER

A gentle knock on the door startles me awake, and with a jolt, I jerk upright. Disoriented, I look around in confusion. Why am I in my bathroom? Glancing down, I see I'm sitting in the middle of my bathtub with pillows and blankets strewn around me. The tatters of my ridiculous outfit fall off me, leaving me mostly exposed, and my back throbs, reminding me of the events of last night. Shit. Groaning, I let my head fall into my hands. What a fucking mess.

"Lady Maya?"

Noah's concerned voice has me lifting my head and straightening my veil. Grabbing the nearest blanket, I pull it around my now human form and clear my throat. "Yes?"

Noah walks in, his gaze lifted to give me privacy, and I can't help the small smile that pulls at my lips at the show of respect. "The king has requested your presence in the banquet hall," he informs me without a hint of emotion in his voice, which indicates that he's annoyed.

He always uses that voice when he's trying to hide his true feelings.

My fragile smile instantly drops. The king has *requested* my presence, and in the banquet hall of all places. Of course he has. Whatever reason he has for wanting to see me, he wants it to be public. That's the only reason he would call me there and not his rooms.

Just managing to hold back my huff of annoyance, I nod my head in acknowledgement. "Okay. Thank you. I'll get dressed and be out in a moment."

Noah makes to leave the room but pauses and places a hand on the doorframe, not glancing back at me. "Are you okay? Tell me honestly." There's anger in his tone now, and I realise that he must be furious if he's letting this slip. He's usually so good at keeping his feelings under wraps.

My back throbs as if in answer. The wound must have been far worse than I first thought if it's still hurting today. I know telling him this won't do either of us any good, so I lie. "I'm fine. I won't be long," I say again, gentler this time.

Noah leaves without another word, and I stand, letting the remaining scraps of fabric fall from my body as I climb from my makeshift nest. Walking over to the large, gilded mirror, I turn and glance over my shoulder, frowning at the brown and green bruises that mottle my skin. Sure, I'm almost healed physically and have certainly suffered worse wounds, but emotionally, I'm hurting, and honestly, I'm not okay. Marcus did this to me. Just the thought makes me feel sick, and now I have to face him like nothing's happened.

If Theo's siren spell worked on him, then the king won't remember how badly he hurt me and how he mocked me for being a monster. I can't let him remember what actually happened, as it would put a death sentence over our heads, but I sure can't forget what he did.

Striding out of my bathroom, I see that I'm alone, which means that Noah is waiting for me outside. I probably should have checked before I walked out here naked, although it wouldn't be the first time that I've shocked one of my protectors by wearing nothing but my skin. Making my way over to the wardrobe, I pull open the doors and look at the row of black clothing that awaits me. Without thinking about it for too long, I grab one of the long-sleeved riding style jackets and a pair of tight trousers. Marcus prefers it when I wear dresses, but today, I feel like wearing more clothing, as if covering my skin will protect me. Pulling on underwear, I don the clothes like armour, each piece making me feel stronger. I pull on a cloak and glance at the mirror once more. Something about having the fabric around my shoulders makes me feel better, like a shield is covering me, protecting the mottled skin of my back. Of course, no one but Noah and the dignitaries will know about my injury, however it helps to ground me all the same. I look fierce. Strong. Taking a deep breath, I vow to be just that.

Striding over to the door, I pull it open and nod to Noah. I'm ready to face the king. The walk is short, and before I know it, I'm standing in front of the two large wooden doors.

I enter the banquet hall and stride along its length, passing rows and rows of tables until I reach the large oak table along the back wall. The hall, whilst smaller than the grand hall where the party took place last night, is still just as grand. The king sits alone at the head of the table on a large wooden throne-like chair, but the matching one to his left, where the queen would sit, is empty. Behind him, three large arched windows allow beams of sunlight to stream in, bathing him in golden light. At the table closest to his on the right are the three dignitaries, as are several other men who I've not yet been introduced to, although they have the look of advisors. The king's top advisors sit at the table directly opposite them on the other side of the room. The rest of the huge room is empty. Marcus must be trying to impress or intimidate the dignitaries if he's eating breakfast here by having such an intimate meeting in such a large room.

Conversation comes to a halt as I enter, the sound of my sandals softly padding against the stone floor echoing around us. All eyes are on me, and their expressions vary from disgust to fear, all of which I'm used to. When I glance at the three males from Saren, however, I'm surprised to see concern and intrigue. Why don't I affect these three the same way I do everyone else? The rest of their party seems to fear me, some going so far as to lean away as I pass them, as if that could stop me from killing them in a second.

"Maya, come here."

The king's voice echoes around the room, and I have to swallow down the rush of mixed emotions that swell at the sound of his voice. I immediately head to his side, knowing that any refusal will just make things more difficult for me. Stopping just beside him, I drop into a small curtsy and watch his lips lift into a twisted smile, like he's got a secret he's not going to share and he wants everyone else to know it. Reaching out, he takes my hand and pulls me onto his lap with one sure movement. It's something he's done repeatedly over the years, and it's never bothered me, yet today, I have to fight my disgust at his touch.

The sound of clattering cutlery has my head jerking up, and I see Mason has just slammed his fork onto the table, the metal handle noticeably twisted. His face is thunderous, and I watch as Theo leans towards his companion before speaking to him in a low voice too quiet for me to hear.

"You seem to have gotten the dignitaries all riled up. They appear to trust you," Marcus whispers into my ear, his hand moving over my leg possessively as he watches the three foreign men. "I have no idea why when their whole job is to destroy creatures like you. Perhaps your little indiscretion last night was useful after all." His voice is a purr, and I can hear the scheming in his tone. His words sting, and it takes everything inside me to remain still on his lap. Creatures like me? Is that how Marcus views me? As a creature, a beast, a monster? How long has he felt this way? Things have changed between us over the years, but after last night, I feel like I'm finally seeing his true colours.

"I want you to get me information and find out what they are doing here," he continues. His voice is almost seductive as he speaks, and he keeps it low enough that no one but me can hear him. "I don't believe that the King of Saren would send his best team of monster hunters on a diplomatic mission. It doesn't add up. Do what you need to." I feel the tightness of the magic that binds us settling over me as he gives the order. His hand stills on my leg, and he squeezes tightly as I sense his shift of mood. "And, Maya, don't disappoint me again." All seduction and playfulness are gone, leaving me with the cold, cruel Marcus from last night.

With no room for discussion or negotiation, I simply nod, my chest tight with emotion. I hate this distance that's developed between us. Knowing that he's disappointed in me makes me feel uncomfortable, but at the same time, I know I did the right thing and I am not ashamed of my actions.

"Lord Elias," the king calls, his voice cutting through the low murmur of conversations that has since started up again after I reached the king. Everyone shifts their attention to us, attempting to avoid looking at me, yet I see the flicker of their gazes on me, the whites of their eyes showing their fear. I feel a little thrill of satisfaction. They should be afraid of me, this is the deference that I should be shown...except when I look at the three males from Saren, their gazes shift easily between the king and me, and there is no discomfort at all in their eyes.

The king either doesn't notice or doesn't care as his hand begins tracing patterns on my leg once more. "You were asking for a tour of the castle. My blade is at your disposal." Marcus' voice is light, gracious even. I've learned to be wary when he sounds like this, as his honeyed words often come back to bite me.

Mason raises an eyebrow but says nothing, while Theo tilts his head to one side, a move I'm fond of myself, his smile sending a shiver down my spine. My reaction, however, isn't out of fear, but a thrill that I can't quite explain. As I'm beginning to learn is usual for them, Elias is the one to reply, inclining his head at the offer. "That is very kind of you, Your Highness," he begins with a tightness in his voice that I can't quite put my finger on. "Perhaps afterward, we can meet to discuss those trade deals we mentioned."

Ah. The king is avoiding them. That doesn't make

things easy for a dignitary when the very person they have travelled all this way to meet won't do that very thing. Marcus waves a hand dismissively, the corner of his mouth twitching up into a smile. "That's what the advisors are here for. They can hash out a plan and negotiate. They will call us when the final decisions are needed."

Elias frowns and pauses, but he must realise that it's futile to try and change the king's mind, so he simply nods instead. "Of course."

The advisors from Saren are frowning, and I can practically feel Mason's anger from here. What an insult, especially given the taut history between our two kingdoms. They have travelled all this way, and the king can't even be bothered to meet with them. This is an important trade deal, and if it's handled wrong, war could break out. I'm not quite sure what Marcus is playing at, because he's been trying to get Saren on side since he became king. Is it because the Saren king sent his monster hunters? Is Marcus paranoid that they are here for another, more sinister reason?

Marcus goes back to eating his breakfast with me on his knee, not once offering me anything, and I know better than to ask. Eating in front of others will make them think I'm human and that I have needs, thereby forgetting my true purpose here. By not eating and watching their every move, it reminds them just what I am—the king's disciplinarian, his blade...his monster.

Everyone else slowly follows the king's lead and continues to eat their breakfast, albeit tentatively. Their eyes flick to me constantly, as if expecting me to pounce. This time, I don't feel the thrill of knowing they are afraid of me, my mood soured. I allow my mind to wander to inane thoughts of the weather and how long the harsh spring will last this year, focusing on anything but the expression of anger on Mason's face when the king touched me.

———

BREAKFAST SEEMED to go on for an eternity. Eventually, Marcus finished his food and left, giving me one final heavy look. The others finished not long after, and I was able to give them the grand tour, not that any of them seemed particularly interested. Well, perhaps all except for Theo, whose eyes glistened as he scanned each room. Now, finally in the garden, I'm well and truly done with being their tour guide. They make me nervous, which is something I've not felt in a long time. They want to discuss last night. I can feel their eyes on me, trying to decipher if I'm still in pain, but I don't give anything away. My wounds are pretty much all gone now, and the twinges from the bruises I felt this morning are barely noticeable.

Noah had finally clocked off duty and was replaced by Jason, one of the older guards who acts as my protector. He always gives me more room than the others, too hesitant to come close, which works in my favour. Now, as we walk through the gardens, he steps back even farther, just keeping me in his line of sight. Usually this pleases me, since it allows me to have more privacy than I'm afforded in the castle, but today, that just seems to encourage the dignitaries.

"Maya, are you okay? You're walking a little stiffly," Elias comments lightly, and I know he's not saying this out of concern. My eyebrows rise. Just how closely has he been watching me to have noticed that? And that, I realise, is the purpose of his question, to make me aware that he's been watching my every move. I spin to face him, my lips peeling back into a snarl, but I'm brought up short by his expression. His brows are furrowed ever so slightly and concern marks his face, although he quickly smooths it away. Not quickly enough, however. Perhaps his question was genuine after all.

Unsure how to react, I let out a long breath which sounds more like a hiss. "I'm fine," I bark out, then as the three of them raise their eyebrows, I sigh, realising how ungrateful I sound. "Thank you for last night. Not that I needed your help, but it was...kind of you." The words taste like ash in my mouth, and I'm sure they can hear my confusion. I just don't understand their angle.

"We didn't do it to be *kind*, Maya," Mason spits, stalking closer until his huge frame dwarfs me and I have to crane my neck up to look at him. "He was hurting you. No one should be able to get away with that, king or peasant."

This male is such a contradiction. He's huge, his biceps are larger than my head, and he has a scowl that would intimidate even the fiercest of warriors, yet he then comes out with comments like this. Saren is supposed to be a brutal kingdom, and when I first saw Mason, he was exactly what I expected. Now that I know him though, I'm beginning to wonder if he's an abnormality or if what I've been taught about their homeland is wrong. When I shift my gaze to Elias and Theo, who stand just behind the larger man, their expressions sober.

Giving up the pretence, I shake my head and gesture wide. "Look, you need to tell me why you're here. Why you're really here."

There's a beat of silence, and then Mason glances to Elias, waiting for his decision. Elias watches me closely, his eyes narrowed as if he's trying to decide how much to tell me. They are not going to tell me, and I don't blame them. After how Marcus has treated me and what they witnessed last night, I don't expect them to trust anyone here.

Elias surprises me when he begins to walk once more, gesturing for me to follow him. Frowning, I watch him stride away and then glance at Theo and Mason, who are already starting to follow their companion. Theo glances over his shoulder at me and grins, flashing me those sharp teeth. A laugh bubbles up inside me, but I quickly cover it up by clearing my throat and following them. I'm not supposed to let them out of my sight, after all.

Elias isn't walking fast, and when I reach his side, he looks at me with a measured expression. "Do you know the real reason our kingdoms have been at war?"

This isn't what I was expecting him to say, and it takes me a moment to recall the stories Marcus told me. I didn't grow up here, and I certainly don't make it my mission to listen to the politicians in court. Glancing over my shoulder to make sure my protector is still out of hearing range, I incline my head slightly.

"I was told it was because your king didn't want to conform to our way of life."

A strange sound has me jumping. I've never quite heard anything like it. It takes me a moment to realise that it was Theo snorting at my side. He rolls his eyes with a shake of his head. "Sounds like the kind of bullshit your king would come up with."

"Our king doesn't deal with slavers," Mason bites out,

disgust making his voice deeper and more menacing than usual.

Elias doesn't say anything, but he watches me intently as I slowly put together what they are implying. "Slavers..." I trail off, wrinkling my nose. Even the thought of that kind of filth in our kingdom makes my gorgon shift with rage. They don't comment and seem to be waiting for me to come to a conclusion. "Wait, are you trying to say that Marcus trades slaves?" Astonishment makes me laugh, but when none of them say anything, it pulls me up short. Reaching out in a move too fast for human eyes, I grab Elias' jacket and pull him to a stop. "Slavery was abolished here centuries ago. Just look in the streets, there are no slave markets," I insist, not quite sure why I'm so angry and adamant about it. Is it because they are implying Marcus allows this to happen and I'm defending my king, or is it because deep down, I fear something sinister might be going on that I didn't know about?

"Not the markets in the streets, no," Elias agrees, his expression saying everything his words don't.

The black markets. I've never been to them, at least not since Marcus became king. There was a time before when... No, this isn't about then and the atrocities of the previous king, this is about now and the illegal selling and trading of slaves.

"Marcus can't control what happens in the black markets. I'm sure he doesn't even know this is happening."

This feels like a lie, and even as I say it, I partially know it's not true. Those markets should have been shut down decades ago, but Marcus has always said that he keeps an eye on what happens there. He explained that if it did close down, it would just open up elsewhere, some-where he wouldn't have any control over the dodgy deal-ings of the underworld. So...he must know or at least suspect. My heart twinges in my chest, another piece of my heart fracturing. How did I not see the kind of person he's turned into? If I paid more attention, then I would have seen it. I should have done something. I might be a hideous gorgon, but like it or not, I still have a human heart, and when it comes to children and slaves, I just can't seem to harden myself as much as I should be able to.

"It's his job as king to know what's happening in his city," Mason states, stepping forward. For a moment, I think it's to pull me away from his companion, but he actually grabs my shoulder. Later, when I think over this, I'll realise that he was only trying to turn me around to face him, but being touched is the last thing I want right now, especially after last night. Instinctively, I jump back, releasing a long, low hiss, a noise that no human should be able to make.

Mason seems to realise his mistake and holds up his hands to show me he means no harm, frowning with anger and realisation. That doesn't stop him from contin-uing to shatter my illusions about Marcus though. "He *does* know, Maya. He's the one who's been shipping people off and selling them as slaves to other lands." His words make me feel sick, and as something shifts in his expression, I prepare myself for another blow.

"You must have known about it," he counters, step-ping closer and invading my personal space once more. Theo reaches out and places a hand on his arm, causing him to pause in his tracks, but it doesn't stop the poisoned words that flow from his mouth. "You were there at the docks only a handful of days ago."

If only I could turn myself to stone, all of this wouldn't be quite so painful. The worst thing about it is that he's right—I *was* at the docks with the king, I remember the occasion. I'm not taken from the castle often, but for this, he wanted me with him. Those weren't slaves we sent off though, at least I hadn't believed them to be. He told me we were shipping prisoners away, sending them to prisons outside of the city. He said that too many criminals within our walls made us look weak. They were all people who committed crimes, weren't they?

"He told me they were criminals being sent to other prisons..." Betrayal, pain, and rising nausea cause me to trail off, and I have to swallow against a lump in the back of my throat. Thinking over his words again, something in particular sticks out that I didn't notice at first. "You saw me at the docks. You've been watching me for that long?" They said they'd been here for a couple of days, but I hadn't realised that they meant they had been watching me the whole time.

"We had to know what we were dealing with," Elias explains in his steady, no-nonsense tone. "Until that night I bumped into you in the stables, we had no idea that you were anything other than the king's mindless killer."

It's hard to argue with him when he says it like that. If I'm to look at it from a purely strategic standpoint, I suppose it was a sensible move to check out the greatest threat to them when they first arrived. I certainly would have been considered a threat, but what am I to them now? They are not treating me like the beast they claimed to think I was.

"Maya," Elias continues, his gaze flicking over my veil as if searching for my eyes, his expression solemn. I don't want to hear what he's about to say, dread lining my gut. "Most of the people on that boat were citizens who couldn't pay their taxes or the vulnerable that no one would notice were missing."

No. I don't want to believe them. Marcus wouldn't lie to me about something like this, he just wouldn't. However, before yesterday, I never thought he would try to hurt me like he did. Do I really know him at all?

Crack. Another piece of my worthless human heart breaks. My eyes sting, but no, I can't—I *won't* fall apart in front of these men. I refuse. I should know better than this. Men only ever want me for what I offer them—power. I was cursed because I fell in love and ignored all the signs. When Marcus found me, I thought I was beyond love, but he was so genuine I believed he truly loved me, and so I fell again. Have I been locked in a relationship where he's been using me this whole time? No, Marcus does love me, at least he did. Can you truly love someone you harm?

We don't need him. We don't need any of them. We are stronger alone, my gorgon hisses in the back of my mind, and I'm inclined to agree. Pulling on the strength of my gorgon, I take a deep breath and stand tall. Whether Marcus loves me or not, something has to change. I won't go on like this any longer, especially now that I know he's been keeping the selling of slaves from me.

A strong wind blows through the garden, causing me to clutch my cloak, and I realise that I've been standing in silence for some time with the three males all waiting patiently for my response. Whether they are aware of my internal turmoil or not, I appreciate the fact that none of them have pushed me for an answer.

"So, what, you're here to stop him?" I finally reply, not sounding nearly as composed as I hoped I would, but none of them comment on the strain in my voice. I do notice Mason watching me closely though, the slight furrowing of his brow giving away his concern.

Theo glances at Elias, and when the other male nods, he clears his throat. "We're here to find proof of what he's been doing and bring him to justice."

I hadn't expected them to actually answer the question honestly, so that just goes to show that they either trust me or think I'm going to help them.

Stunned, I look between the three of them, waiting for the punchline or for them to tell me they are joking, but no. They are deadly serious. They are taking a huge risk in telling me, especially considering who I am. I should whip my veil off right now and turn them all to stone for threatening my king, or at the very least call out to my protector, but that's not what I do.

"What then? Will your king take the throne?" I ask incredulously. Their king is trying to take over our kingdom, but is he any better than Marcus, who's been expanding his empire since he took the throne? One thing will make it easy for the Saren king though—Marcus has no heir. Kill the king, and the throne will be open for the taking, no need to get his hands dirty by killing off relatives and children.

"No, he doesn't want that."

Elias is trying to reassure me, but I've been bitten by kings who speak this way. They say they want a peaceful kingdom, and then they expand into the smaller cities and kingdoms until they have no choice but to agree to merge with us. I'm sure my scepticism is obvious despite the fact they can't see it in my expression.

He raises a brow but continues anyway. "He would help the people take back their city and form a government of people they vote into power."

A foreign king would give the throne back to its people? Everything he says sounds so crazy that I can't even wrap my head around it. What I don't understand, however, is why they are telling me this.

"This is treason." I don't know why I'm whispering or slowly backing away from them, putting some space between us. "I should kill you right now."

Why does it sound like I'm trying to convince myself of this fact? The very fact that I'm not acting is treasonous. Marcus wanted to know why they were here, and I've found that out. Either I need to kill them, or return to my king and tell him what I've learned, yet I continue to stand here, staring at them in horror.

"But you won't," Elias counters, "because you've known there is something wrong with your king for a long time."

They can see right through me. Is this how the famous monster hunters slay their foes? By cutting them with the strongest weapon of all? Truth?

Hands balled into fists, I fight against the conflicting emotions within me. "I am loyal to my king."

Mason grumbles low in his chest, the sound more like a growl than anything a human would make. "He makes you kill, Maya! Surely you see that's wrong?" He's obviously trying to keep his temper, but I see him mirroring my actions, his fists clenched tightly at his sides.

Something snaps within me. In the blink of an eye, I

cross the distance between us and pounce. Grabbing the front of his shirt, I wrap my legs around his waist and clutch his chest, hanging on as I bring my face to his, a low rattling hiss coming from my throat. He jerks in surprise, and I feel his muscles tighten as if to react and shake me off, but to my shock, he drops his hands loosely to his sides. I see the other two step closer from the corner of my eye, but neither of them attempts to stop me.

I'm so close to him that our foreheads are almost touching, and my veil is the only thing stopping him from turning to stone in an instant, yet he still doesn't react.

"I am a monster! It's what I do!" I hiss, my voice menacing as my gorgon pushes at my boundaries. "Don't ever forget what I am."

His hazel eyes shift, but not from fear or anger. For a moment, I get caught up in his eyes. From here, I can see the green and brown flecks. His eyes are so pretty for a guy whose whole image is meant to intimidate. Right now, he's not looking at me as though I'm a threat, despite the fact that I'm clinging to him like a demon, but instead, he watches me with compassion that I don't want nor deserve.

"You're a monster because you let him turn you into one." His voice is soft, almost a whisper, but he might as well have shouted.

Releasing him like he's contagious, I jump back and continue to retreat from the three of them. I struggle to control my breathing, which is suddenly coming in great sawing breaths like I've just run five laps around the city. "You know nothing about me or what I am," I reply, shaking my head as I back away.

Elias steps forward as if to stop me, raising a hand,

but he quickly drops it when I instinctively flinch away. He frowns, his handsome face contorting. "We know that you go against your king to help others. Monsters don't do that."

Hating how I react to them and how weak they make me feel, I know I need to get away. Spinning on my heel, I stalk away, knowing that if I stay here, I'll do something stupid, something I'll regret. "This tour has concluded," I shout over my shoulder as I march towards my protector, who wears a pensive expression. I snarl at him, but I don't even feel a little bit of pleasure as he flinches away from me.

Without looking back at the dignitaries, I storm into the castle, their words haunting me as I try to figure out what the hell I should do.

Chapter

I run my hand along the spine of the old book and pull it from its shelf, wrinkling my nose at the dust the action kicks up. This library is wasted here. Hardly anyone uses it but the handful of scholars the king allows to live in the castle. It would be better suited in the city where its knowledge can be used, rather than just gathering dust.

I can feel the librarian's eyes on me as I begin to leaf through the pages of the book, but he doesn't dare say anything or try to stop me. I usually come here to get away, but I've been hiding out in here much more frequently over the last couple of days.

It's been a couple of days since the disastrous tour of the castle with Elias and his men, and I've been avoiding everyone. Thankfully, their duties keep the dignitaries busy and Marcus has been absent, attending to some issue in the city. It must be serious, as it's been taking all of his time and he's not yet called for me to learn what

I've discovered. He's also not called me to his rooms, but this suits me just fine.

Leaning back against one of the shelves, I finally find the section in the book I'm looking for. Shifting position, I attempt to settle myself and pay attention to what I'm reading, but I keep getting distracted. I've not let my gorgon out for several days now, and I can feel her impatience as she pushes against my boundaries.

I become aware of another presence nearby, and my gorgon perks up, but I keep my head down, flipping over the page as I continue to read. Whoever it is will soon pass by when they realise who's lurking behind this bookshelf.

"Most of that is all wrong, you know."

Slamming the book shut at the sound of the musical voice, I jerk upright and spin, only to come face-to-face with Theo. If I weren't so irritated, I'd be blushing at being caught.

Attempting to brush my actions off, I hold the book closely to cover up what I'd been reading and shrug my shoulders. "What do you mean?"

"Sirens." He gestures towards the book I clutch against my chest, the gilded title down its spine clear to see. *Monsters of the Land*. Shit. He must have seen the chapter I'd been reading, either that or it was a very good guess, one I just confirmed with my snappish behaviour.

Smiling in a way that tells me he sees right through me, he leans against the opposite bookshelf, crossing his arms over his chest. His posture is relaxed, and he's obviously not at all concerned that he's alone in a remote location with me.

"It's written by men who fear the sirens, who know

them only as the creatures who drown the innocent. It's mostly lies." He shrugs like he's not really bothered, but I see a tightness around his eyes that tells me otherwise. Most wouldn't pick up on it, but I've lived for a long time and am only alive today because I'm able to read the subtle signs of men's bodies. "Did you know that a siren can only capture the minds of those who are immoral or who have a stain on their soul? They cannot call to the innocent. The stories of children being stolen and eaten by the sirens are all wrong."

This is news to me, and he's right—the book certainly didn't say anything about that. It only claimed that sirens were beautiful and lulled people to a watery grave, no matter their age, race, or gender. It said they have an endless hunger that is never sated, and they are always looking for their next meal. Looking at Theo now, composed and calm as he watches me with a mischievous glint in his eyes, I can't say that he fits that description. Is that because he's only half siren, or is he right and the book is wrong? It wouldn't surprise me. I know from experience that what's written about gorgons is mostly incorrect. Pursing my lips, I think over what he said and what it must say about the king. If his mind was captured by Theo, and what he says is true, then Marcus' soul is tainted. Given what I've learned about him recently, I'm not all that shocked.

"You've been avoiding us."

Snorting, I bring my attention back to him, noticing some of that playfulness he seems to carry around with him has dimmed. For some reason, that disturbs me. I shake my head as if to rid myself of those thoughts. "Don't flatter yourself. I've been avoiding everyone," I comment lightly as I slide the book back onto the shelf and walk down the line of bookshelves, needing to put some space between us.

His light footsteps sound behind me. "You didn't tell the king."

He doesn't have to elaborate, because I know what he's talking about. I didn't run to Marcus and tell him everything the dignitaries told me.

Facing forward, I keep my back to him. "You don't know that."

In a flash, he's suddenly in front of me with a speed I wouldn't expect for a human, and he walks backwards so he can keep pace while looking at me. "Well, we're not dead or in chains, so I'm pretty sure you didn't tell him." His lips quirk up into a smile, but it doesn't reach his eyes. He knows full well I've not said anything, and now he wants to know why.

Anger, guilt, and regret churn in my gut. "Yes, and now I'm committing treason too," I hiss, my voice too low for anyone else to overhear.

Theo comes to a sudden halt, and I almost crash into him. He holds up his hands to steady me, and I quickly step back to avoid his touch. His brows pull into a frown. "I know how hard this must be for you—"

"Do you?" I step forward, crowding him now. Only seconds ago, I was trying to get some space, but now my anger is fuelling my actions. "You've been through the pain of discovering the person you love is potentially committing deeds so awful, it makes even *me* horrified? You discovered the person you love might not have loved you after all, but just wanted to use you for the power it gives them?" I refuse to allow him to hear the pain I feel at hearing it aloud, so I channel my gorgon's unending anger and frustration, watching his face closely. If I see even a hint of sympathy... I don't know what I'd do, but I'm sure I'd regret it later. Taking a deep breath, I step back, my hands shaking with how much effort it's requiring for me to stay in control. "No, I don't think you have even the slightest inkling as to how hard this is." Turning, I go to walk away.

"Maya—"

Whirling, I throw my hands up in the air. "What?" I demand, exasperated, no longer speaking in a hushed whisper. "What do you want from me?"

Hearing my voice break, he pauses. He appears taken aback, and a sadness settles over him that shifts something inside me. Gone is the grinning, teasing man, and left behind is a male who has experienced great sorrow.

"I may not know how that feels, but take it from someone who's been hated for who he is and been called a monster since birth. I know how hard it is to break past that word and see the person beneath the curse. You are good, Maya, and you are strong." From the emotion ringing in his voice, it's clear he's telling the truth. He's experienced these things too, and most of all, he truly believes what he's saying.

I just stare, my mind and heart in turmoil. What he's saying... It feels like I've been drowning all this time and finally got my head above the water. His words are my lifebuoy, keeping me afloat while I gasp for breath. Each agonised lungful of air is painful, but it brings with it a blissful sense of peace, of restoration. I feel like he can see past the veil, past the monster, and see *me*.

You are good, Maya, and you are strong. The words ring through my mind. He believes them, that much is obvious, but he doesn't know my past and the awful things I've done in the name of the king and to protect myself.

"I've killed, and sometimes, I enjoy it," I whisper, almost afraid to admit it aloud.

A sad smile crosses his face. "So have I," he replies, not bothering to justify his actions. He's close now, his pale hair falling forward as he tilts his head to look at me. Slowly, so I could stop him if I wanted to, he raises his hand until he reaches my jaw—the only part of my face he can see. Cupping my cheek, he regards me questioningly to see how I'm going to react. When I don't push him off, he does the same with his other hand, his fingers brushing softly over my skin. Slowly, he glides his hands up past the veil. My breath hitches in my chest, and I stiffen for a moment, fearing that he's about to remove my veil, and squeeze my eyes shut.

"Shh," he coos. "Trust me."

I don't know why, and later, I'll blame it on his siren voice, but I still and allow his fingers to continue up. He explores the contours of my face, gently brushing my cheekbones and the bridge of my nose. Skimming down, he pauses as he reaches my lips. Using his forefinger, he traces my Cupid's bow, and my mouth opens in a quiet, breathy gasp. I've not been touched like this in...well, I can't remember. Marcus has never been one for gentle caresses, and right now, Theo isn't treating me like a monster or the blade of his enemy, but like a real human.

I should stop this. It's just confusing me, and he's going to think that I'm something I'm not. However, all thoughts of stopping this, of walking away, disappear when he steps closer, his body almost pressing against mine. My back is pushed against the bookcase behind me, trapping me in as he lowers his lips, lifting the veil enough to press them to mine.

I'm so surprised that I freeze for a moment. The heat

of his lips on mine makes my heart soar, but reality soon crashes back in. Pushing against his chest, I force him to step back.

"What do you think you're doing?"

I don't bother to explain that I belong to the king, he already knows. A cheeky glint enters his eyes, and anger floods me. Is this all to get back at the king? Am I just a plaything to him? Were all of those sweet, honeyed words just to get him laid? My chest squeezes painfully at the thought, but I channel it into my frustration.

His expression sobers as he seems to sense my anger, and then he arches a single brow as if in challenge. "Don't tell me you don't feel this pull between us. Your monster calls to mine." When I don't immediately respond, he lets out a huff of annoyance. "You are so much more than he lets you believe, Maya. You deserve more."

Placing a hand on his chest, I tilt my head to one side as I look up at him. "I suppose you're going to say I deserve someone like you?"

He shrugs, and I want to shake him. I can't believe that he just kissed me. Sure, his touch had been pretty intimate, but I hadn't expected anything more than that. I should have stopped it, but I was just so caught up in being touched in a way that was revered. He's right—I *do* feel a pull towards him, but I have with all three of the dignitaries since they arrived. These men are trying to overthrow my king, and now I'm kissing one of them in the library. What a fucking hypocrite.

Realising that I'm still practically pressed against his chest, I step to the side, breathing a sigh of relief. After checking that my veil is still firmly in place, I brush down my outfit. If the king ever suspected that one of his enemies just kissed me...

Leaning against the bookcase opposite where I now stand, Theo manages to look calm and casual, despite what just happened. Perhaps it didn't mean all that much to him.

"I meant what I said, Maya. I'm not trying to seduce you into helping us," he says, somehow guessing where my thoughts have gone. "The kiss was just a bonus." He grins, his eyes sparkling.

Frustrated at how easy all of this is to him, I scowl beneath my veil. "It doesn't matter anyway. Even if I wanted to, I'm magically bound to the king." I don't specify if I'm talking about helping them or the kiss. Let him work it out for himself.

He frowns and hums low in his throat. "That's going to be a problem."

Something about the way he says it catches my attention. "What do you mean?"

"We need your help."

I get the impression he was going to say more, but he bites his tongue. He's already mentioned that they want my help, but this seems like more than that. Is there a specific reason he's come to me today?

"Help with what? I won't help you hurt Marcus."

Why am I even entertaining this idea? Everything that I thought I knew has been thrown up in the air and I'm reeling, unsure who I can trust. *No one*, my monster hisses, urging me to be cautious. They have answers for me, answers about what's been going on with Marcus, which is the only reason I'm listening—not because of this mysterious pull towards them.

Glancing around to make sure we're alone, he closes the distance between us once more. "There's a shipment of slaves due to be shipped out tonight, ordered by the king." His voice is low and serious. I don't react, hiding my disgust and rising dread as he continues. "They are all children from the orphanages. We were just here to get proof of what was happening, but we can't allow this to happen, not if we can do something to stop it." His eyes scan my veil-covered face as if he can see it, and I wonder if he's remembering what he felt only minutes before. "Will you help us?"

Children. They are selling children. There's no way I can just stay in the castle now that I know what's happening. Damn them. They knew that if they told me I'd have to help. Perhaps I can do some digging whilst I'm there and get proof once and for all if Marcus is behind this. A weight lifts from my chest. If I go, not only am I helping the children, but I might be able to prove that Marcus is innocent and the dignitaries will leave us alone. *Stop being so naïve*, my gorgon hisses in my mind. *Marcus is up to something. We've known that for a while now. We need to see it for ourselves.*

I wait for the familiar ring of restricting magic around my throat as I make my decision, but it never comes. I may be bound to follow Marcus, but there are loopholes. By going tonight, I'll be learning more about the dignitaries' true reason for being here, thereby following his order. I take a deep breath as resolution settles within me.

My gorgon and I are completely in agreement as I nod my head. "I'll help."

CHAPTER

I suspected this part of the plan would be the most difficult, and I was right. Getting out of the castle unseen? No problem. Meeting with the three of them? Yup, easy. Convincing my protective, grumpy guard to let me go? Now that's where we have a problem.

Pausing in the passageway, I spin to look at my protector, my cloak swirling around me in a wave of dark fabric. It's almost pitch black in here, save for the small torch he carries, the gentle crackling of the fire sounding loud in the confined space. With my hood up and veil firmly in place, I know he's struggling to see me in the dark, but I can easily make out his disgruntled expression.

"Noah, we've discussed this." Although we're alone and far below the castle in these forgotten passages, sound travels strangely down here, so I keep my voice low. "You either come with me, or you stay here and guard the room."

I know there's no way he'd let me go alone, especially

when he knows I'm meeting the males from Saren—he's made his opinion on them perfectly clear. However, his constant grumbling is starting to drive me mad. I need to be clear-headed and calm tonight so I can see the truth for myself, but his muttering is certainly not helping with that.

"I don't trust them."

That's something else he's told me over and over. He's trying to protect me, I understand that, but he needs to trust that I know what I'm doing. My gut is telling me that I need to be there tonight, and for better or worse, I'm going to find out the truth.

Holding my arms out wide in a *what do you want me to do about it* way, I huff out a breath. "It's not too late to go back."

His face shifts into an expression of disgust. "Who do you take me for?"

"Then stop complaining!" I hiss. Spinning on my heel, I stalk into the shadows, my gorgon's eyesight letting me see perfectly in the near darkness.

After I agreed to help, Theo explained the plan. I was to meet them down by the docks, and from there, they would take me to the area they suspected the children were being held. We decided that it would be best for us to leave the castle separately in case we were discovered. It would be much harder to explain why I was sneaking around with the dignitaries than if I were alone with my protector.

The passages beneath the castle are vast, a labyrinth of twisting routes that seem to have no logical pattern, but I memorised them years ago. They extend beyond the castle, with a single route that leads directly into the city. While I use the passages on a semi-regular basis, I've not used the one that leaves the castle boundaries in over a decade. Even if I'd wanted to, the magic that connects me to the king would have stopped me, and as we reach that tunnel now, I raise my hand to my throat, half expecting the magical noose to tighten.

A cold breeze tugs at my cloak, and I slow to a stop as the passageway changes from the castle's stone to rough-hewn rock, showing the entrance of the outer tunnel. Guilt twists in my gut. I shouldn't be doing this. I should turn around and tell Marcus what I've learned. That's what a good subject would do.

A subject. Is that what I've become? What happened to me being his lover, his equal in all things?

"You don't have to do this." Noah's tone is uncharacteristically gentle, and I feel the warmth of his body as he steps closer. I'm not sure what I've done to deserve his loyalty or friendship, and I appreciate it more than he'll ever know. However, I have to know the truth, I can't continue to live a lie.

"Yes I do," I whisper, but it's more to myself than to him.

Pulling myself together, I step into the rocky tunnel, crossing not just the physical boundary line of the castle, but a metaphysical one between myself and Marcus.

Noah says nothing, but I hear his quiet sigh as he follows me, our footsteps the only sound in the tunnel. It's cold in here, and the scent of damp earth reaches my nose. I know that when we get closer to the docks, the salty smell of the ocean will reach us on the breeze. As we walk, I take in the well-worn pathway, and I notice the lack of dirt and dust. This tunnel has been used recently, but by who?

I mull over these thoughts as we walk, and after

around fifteen minutes or so, the distinctive scents of fish and sea hit us. Wrinkling my nose, I slow as we round the final bend. Glancing over my shoulder, I see Noah treading carefully, making sure not to stir the loose stones.

"The torch needs to go now. We'll travel in darkness from here," I tell him, my voice quiet but firm.

Noah scowls but does as I say, cursing under his breath as we're plummeted into darkness. Grabbing his hand, I place it on my shoulder and start to walk forward, guiding him.

This tunnel leads to the back of a large, dilapidated warehouse on the outskirts of the docks. I just have to hope that nothing has changed since I last used it and find myself blocked in, but from the damp footsteps I now see on the rocky floor, I'd guess otherwise. Faint grey light filters in, and I can see the outline of the exit. Pushing aside the heavy wooden planks that hide it, I slip out into the warehouse, my eyes flicking around the room. It looks much the same as I remember, with empty shipping boxes strewn around and planks of rotten wood leaning up against the walls. The roof above us has broken in places, allowing the moonlight to illuminate the state of the room. It's designed to be uninviting, even to squatters, and it seems to have done the trick.

Reaching back into the tunnel, I pull Noah out, watching with mild amusement as he squeezes through the small gap and curses at the smell, cupping a hand to his nose.

"Stay here. Guard the tunnel. I'll be back soon." I secure my cloak around myself and turn to leave, but a tight hand grips my arm, stopping me. He knows better than to grab me. Hissing in warning, I slowly turn to face

Noah, staring first at his hand and then up at his face. I see his pulse jump in his neck, inviting me to bite him, but to my surprise, he doesn't back down.

Clearing his throat, he releases my arm but holds his ground. "I'm not letting you go alone."

Pushing away all emotional thoughts and feelings, I take the logical stance. I shake my head sharply and cross my arms over my chest. "I'll be quicker without you. You'll only get in my way." It's harsh, but it's true. Without him, I can slip through the darkness and use my supernatural speed and strength to help me hide. If he's with me, I'm only going to be using my energy to ensure he stays safe and out of sight. Not to mention if I get caught, he would be implicated in the fallout, and I'm not having that on my conscience.

Grumbling, he steps forward, not prepared to drop the subject. "Maya—"

Allowing my gorgon to enter my voice, I snarl, "No. Don't make me force you." We both know this isn't an empty threat. I could overpower him and tie him up here until I get back.

"You think I'm going to let you risk yourself without me being there?"

Again, I don't know what I've done to deserve this loyalty, and as I run my gaze over his frowning face, I realise he's not going to listen to me. At least not if I threaten him. He needs to know the true reason I won't let him risk coming with me. Sighing, I lower my voice, dropping my head as if the confession is shameful. "Noah, I can't risk you getting hurt."

His face softens at my words, and when he opens his mouth to speak, I know he's about to try to appeal to my better nature. He should know better—I don't have one.

Placing a hand on his shoulder, I squeeze slightly in a gesture of friendship. "I need you here. I need to make sure that I have an escape route. If you're here, I won't have to worry about that because I know you'll be keeping me safe in that respect."

He curses, and I know he sees the rationale in my argument. "You've got an hour. If you're gone any longer than that, I'm coming after you."

Emotion clogs my throat and I simply nod, not trusting my voice. The only reason he's allowing me to go is because I showed him some of my vulnerability. Had I forced him into following my rules, I'm sure he would have tried to track me down once he escaped my bindings. Tentatively, I squeeze his shoulder once more and turn in a whirl of fabric.

Shutting down my emotions, I focus on my surroundings, allowing my gorgon's senses to help guide me. The stench of fish and human waste is almost enough to make me gag, the air tainted with rot. Slipping from the warehouse, I blend in with the shadows cast by the other large buildings around us. This part of the docks is empty at this time of night, since it's too dangerous to transport goods in the dark. This works in my favour, but I know I can't let my guard down. I won't be the only person out here with nefarious purposes in mind. My chest is bound, and I'm wearing a dark tunic and trousers, so no one can tell that I'm female—although if my last interaction in the stables is anything to go by, I'm gaining a reputation despite my lack of features.

This section of the docks is busier, and I can see lit torches ahead, so I make the decision to scale the drainpipe for the closest warehouse and cross the docks via the roofs. If we were closer to the city where the main boats dock, I would find this harder, because the buildings are spread apart and the roads are properly lit thanks to the money those large boats bring in. However, this is the poorer end of the docks, so the buildings are less looked after and crammed together, using every scrap of space available. This makes it perfect for travelling unseen above the roads.

It's not long before I find them, although I sense them before I see them. The strange feeling in my chest I experience when they are nearby seems to tug behind my sternum, almost directing me right to them. They said they'd be waiting for me outside one of the large salting warehouses, but thanks to this newfound sense of mine, I follow my gut and take a different route, which brings me closer to the city. What are they doing out here?

That's when I see the three of them skulking through the shadows.

Frowning, I watch them. Why aren't they at the warehouse yet? Their plan had been simple, and they should have been here long before I arrived. Did something hold them up? That's when I see Theo limping. He's hiding it well, and most wouldn't notice it unless they were watching him closely, but the monster in me sees it immediately, picking up on any weakness we can exploit. However, instead of those thoughts, I'm only left with a nagging sensation of...concern? It's not something I'm used to feeling, and I'm left with a sense of frustration. Seeing him also awakens the memories from the library that, until now, I've been so good at hiding. Theo touching my face. The kiss. My lips tingle at the memory, and my heart flutters in my chest. Scowling, I snarl at myself and shake my head as if it would dislodge the thoughts from my mind. I need to focus. I should go to the salting warehouse and wait for them there, but I find myself hesitating. Hissing between my teeth, I make a decision.

Using my gorgon's speed, I jump between the shadowed roofs in near silence, the soft hiss of the breeze against my cloak the only sound of my approach. They don't hear me. In fact, they don't even know I'm there until I drop to the ground right behind them. They whirl around to face me, the moonlight glinting off their drawn weapons. They all seem tense, and as I scan them, I can't help but notice the dark bruise beginning to form on Mason's jaw. Hissing, I step forward and grab his jaw, turning his head into the light so I can see the damage more clearly. No one moves, and even their breaths have stilled.

Mason silently allows me to move his head from side to side as my fingers brush over the bruise. I was so focused on Mason's injury that I hadn't noticed their heavy gazes on me. Jerking my hand away like I've burnt it, I step back and glare at Elias, ignoring the heated look on Mason's face. Elias seems to have managed to arrive unscathed, but that doesn't stop the uncomfortable twisting in my gut.

"What happened?" I demand, looking between Elias and Theo, pointedly keeping my gaze off Mason. I'm not sure what's gotten into him, but that look he's pinning me with makes me uncomfortable.

Elias sighs, wearing a weary, frustrated expression. "We were asking questions, trying to get more information."

"It seems your people don't particularly like us," Mason chimes in, and I have to acknowledge him once more. Thankfully, he just looks pissed off now, his hand rubbing over his jaw.

I want to laugh. Are they serious? Of course it's going to attract attention when strangers turn up in the city and start asking questions about child slaves. They are lucky the guards didn't get involved and they got away. If it gets back to the castle that three foreign males were asking questions that they shouldn't, it's not going to take the king long to realise it's them.

"You're from Saren! They already think you're their enemy, and then you go around asking nosy questions." I stare at them incredulously through my veil, despite knowing they can't see me. "Of course this was going to happen!" I hiss, not quite believing that they'd risk something like this.

"You don't seem to mind us," Theo comments, the usual cheeky lilt of his voice tight with pain. Turning my head to look at him, I just hiss and shake my head.

"I don't like anyone," I reply offhandedly, my attention on the tension around his eyes and the way he's favouring his injured leg. "Should you be here? Is your injury—"

He bares his teeth in a snarl, reminding me of his heritage. "I'm fine."

I stare at him, waiting for him to back down, but he doesn't. Instead, he simply stares back at me as if challenging me to say something else. His frustration is evident, but while I usually would have assumed that was because someone got the drop on him, I get the feeling that it's because I questioned him.

"You know this isn't the first time we've done this, right? We were wearing disguises so they wouldn't know we were from Saren. We don't just blunder in and ask things that will get us into trouble."

This is the most I've ever heard Theo speak, and while the musical note of his siren voice is still there, it's overshadowed by his irritation. For a moment, I get the absurd notion to apologise, but I hold myself back.

Elias steps closer and places a hand on Theo's arm in support. Turning his gaze to me, he releases a long sigh. "The fight started because some drunk took offence that we were talking to his wife. He had no idea what we were talking about, so it won't be led back to us or you. You're safe."

It's not me I'm worried about, but I can't quite bring myself to tell him that. Instead, I listen to his explanation. I shouldn't have assumed they would blunder into this without thought. They had managed to enter the city early without alerting anyone to their presence, after all.

"It wasn't our finest work, but we did find out something useful," he continues, and from the change in the atmosphere around us, I know whatever he's about to say is important.

"We know where they are keeping the children."

Perhaps their trip into the city wasn't wasted after all. This is the one piece of information we didn't have. We had no idea where the children were being kept, only that they were being shipped out at the docks tonight. Knowing this means we can rescue them before they are moved. It would be so much easier than trying to rescue an unknown quantity of children whilst they are being transported.

My gorgon shifts in anticipation, and I allow a smile to pull up at my lips. "Lead the way."

THE WAREHOUSE LOOKS like any other. We're in the wealthier part of the docks now, so it's secure and water-tight, with locks on the large sliding doors. The only difference between this one and the others around it are the guards. They are not standing in front, that would be too obvious. Whoever is in charge wants to stay under the radar. Instead, they stand in the shadowed corners of the other building where the light from the streetlamps can't reach them. If you know where to look, it's easy enough to see them, and from up here, I count four of them. Why so little? Either there are more guards inside keeping the children quiet and under control, or there are less child slaves than we thought. While I hope other-wise, I'm sure it's the former.

Crouching on the corner of the warehouse roof oppo-site the building in question, I run my eyes over it once more. It won't be hard to dispose of the men and break the lock to get inside, but something doesn't feel right. It's all too easy. Scaling down the building, I return to the others.

"I can only see four guards, one at each road entry point." I gesture to each area before continuing. "The warehouse is secure. We can't go through the roof unless we break in, and that will attract too much attention. We're better off going through the main doors." Crossing my arms over my chest, I look at them. "Getting in should be easy enough. We take one guard each and then meet at the entrance. It's likely there are more guards inside, so we should be cautious."

Mason and Theo nod along, but they glance at Elias

for confirmation. The lord purses his lips and hums low in his throat. "This seems too easy."

"I know," I agree. My instincts scream that something is horribly wrong here. "We get in and out as soon as possible."

Elias nods and starts to speak to his companions in a low voice, instructing them on which guard they will each take. Not wanting to interrupt, nor having the patience to wait, I salute them with a flick of my hand and disappear into the darkness, making my way to my target.

The guard is hiding in a protruding doorway, the structure concealing him better than his companions, who are guarding the other roads that lead to the warehouse. I keep my senses open in case I missed anyone when I was scouting the area—I know I didn't, but something is off here, so I'm hyper-aware of my surroundings. Pausing in a shadow, I take a moment to decide how I'm going to do this. Unless I loop all the way around the back of the dock, which will take too much time, I'm going to be approaching him head-on. Even with my speed, he'll probably see me before I attack him, which means he might shout a warning, something I want to avoid. I glance up, choosing my route.

Blowing out a breath, I climb the side of the warehouse as quickly and quietly as I can. This wouldn't work if there were more than four guards, as someone would be bound to see me no matter how fast I climb. Now at the top, I keep low and run to the other end of the roof. This is where things get tricky. In this area of the docks, the buildings are more spaced out, and while I know I can make the jump, I have to do it silently to make sure he doesn't hear me and look up. Heart pounding in my chest, I take a few steps back and focus on where I plan to land on the opposite roof.

In a burst of energy, I sprint to the edge of the roof before leaping across the space. For a split second, it feels like I'm flying, but all too soon gravity catches up with me and I land on the other side. I didn't quite judge the distance properly, however, so I jumped too far, slamming my foot against the corrugated metal roof. Shrinking down and blending into the shadows, I curse internally as I hear footsteps below. Biting my lip, I peer over the edge and see the guard frowning and glancing around for the cause of the sound. Stepping out onto the road, he looks around, shrugs, and slowly returns to his spot. He doesn't even look up. Releasing a sigh of relief and shaking my head, I wait for the perfect moment to pounce.

I'm not left waiting long.

He turns to face the warehouse. Without another thought, I drop down from the building and land on near silent feet. Sensing me, he spins, his eyes wide as he takes me in. Before he has the chance to call out, my hands are already around his neck, twisting sharply to one side. His face goes slack and I let go, dropping his body to the ground. Could I have incapacitated him without killing him? Probably, but I don't take mercy on those who kidnap children and sell them into slavery. I was tempted to rip my veil off and let him see who he was messing with, but if it were reported that a man was turned to stone in the docks, then it would be pretty obvious that the one and only gorgon in the city was behind it. Instead, I step over his lifeless body and ponder what to do next.

My decision is made for me when I see Elias striding

towards the warehouse, clapping his hands together as if
to rid them of dirt. Another flash of movement from the
other side of the warehouse has me turning to find
Mason scowling over his shoulder as he also makes his
way forward. Shrugging, I march forward, arriving at the
large doors at the same time as the three of them. No one
says anything, but I can tell from their alert expressions
that they have dealt with the guards and are ready to kick
butt and get some answers. They are not the only ones.

Theo steps forward and pulls out a lock pick, reaching
for the heavy lock on the sliding doors. Of course he
knows how to do this. Out of the three of them, I'm the
least surprised that it's him. However, it's not needed,
not while I'm here. Besides, just standing out here in the
open while we wait is making me nervous. I hold up my
hand to stop him, waving him away when he opens his
mouth. Grabbing the metal lock, I channel my gorgon
and twist with all my might. It snaps in my hand, and
without giving the guys a chance to argue, I slide the
doors open.

Pouring inside with our weapons drawn, we prepare
to attack, only to be met with...children. There must be
about thirty of them, but they are all sitting quietly and
staring at the floor with blank eyes. Nausea twists my
stomach. Something is horribly wrong here.

"Where are the guards?" Elias asks quietly, confusion
and anger lacing his voice. He turns to the other two.
"Scout the warehouse and look for guards."

They nod and immediately begin to search the area,
but I can already tell no other adults are here. The warehouse is just one open room, and other than the children,
it's completely empty. There are no beds, no sign of any
food, and no bathroom. The smell of human waste and

vomit is so strong, I have to breathe through my mouth to stop myself from gagging. Elias is just staring at the children on the floor, seemingly frozen in place. This is not what we were expecting, and it's obvious that it's thrown him. Shutting the warehouse doors behind us to make sure no one stumbles upon us, I turn back around and try to make sense of what we're seeing.

What I don't understand is why they are so quiet. Children make noise, even frightened children, but there's nothing, not even a whimper. Four strangers have just burst in on them and they didn't even flinch. My instincts are warning me that something is very wrong here. The children are thin and emaciated, obviously having been starved for a long time, but that's not the strangest thing.

Seeming to snap out of his daze, Elias steps forward and kneels beside a boy who looks to be around ten years old. The child doesn't move, even when Elias touches his shoulder.

"We're here to help you. Can you tell me what happened?"

I've never heard his voice so soft before, but it doesn't seem to have an effect, as the boy continues to stare at the ground. My throat goes dry. What the hell has been done to these poor children?

"Let me try," Theo suggests gently as he returns from his search. Kneeling beside his friend and the child, he reaches out and gently brushes the boy's face, guiding it around until he's looking at us. When we see his eyes, grey and unseeing, I can't hold back my gasp. He is looking at us, but I know he's not *seeing* us.

"Tell me what happened, sweet child. Why are you here?" Theo coos, using his gift.

The hair on my arms stands on end at the strength of the power behind the question, and I watch as the child blinks slowly, as if awakening from a deep slumber. "The experiment didn't work on us. We're being sent away." His voice is hoarse, like he's been screaming for a long, long time. He's also still not seeing us, his voice dreamy.

I glance at Elias, noting the horror and anger that he's trying to hold back as he stares down at the child.

"What experiment? Can you tell me?" Theo coaxes softly.

I glance at the other children to see how they are taking this interaction, but they haven't moved. Across the room, Mason kneels beside another child, and I can just make out the low murmurs of his voice, but not exactly what he's saying.

"They made us drink it. It burnt."

Alarmed, I look down and find the child clutching his throat as if just talking about it brings on the pain, but his voice doesn't alter, not even a tremble as he tells us of his suffering. "We were told it would make us strong, that we would serve the king. It was an honour."

I go cold. This is the first mention of Marcus since we arrived. Is he really behind all of this?

"The king did this to you?" I ask, my question sharper than I meant it to be. My voice seems to have an effect on him, and his eyes widen as his head jerks up to stare at me as if he's only just seeing me for the first time.

"It's you," he whispers, real emotion finally crossing his face—a mixture of hope, reverence, and pain. "The guardian. He was trying to make us strong like you. For the king." The boy's eyes glaze over and his head slumps forward as his body gives up. Theo leaps forward and catches him just in time before his body hits the floor.

With my heart in my throat, I feel like my entire body has frozen as I watch Theo and Elias lay the child on the ground, making small noises of distress as the boy's nose begins to bleed. I'm overwhelmed, and I don't know what to do. I came here to help rescue children and return them to their homes whilst trying to find proof of who was behind the slavery. But this is... this is something else altogether. Someone is experimenting on children, that much was clear. Why? How? What did the child mean when he said they were trying to make them like me? He also mentioned a "he" and that they were trying to make them strong for the king. Does that mean Marcus has nothing to do with this and someone else is behind it all? I know it's wishful thinking, and my head is telling me that I already know the answer, but I'm not ready to face the consequences of that answer.

"Maya."

I turn numbly at Mason's voice to find him making his way over with a little girl in his arms. He cradles her limp body closely. Stepping forward to meet him, I look down at the child and see she also has the same dazed expression as the boy, but that's not what has my gut churning and bile climbing up my throat.

I force myself to take one more step closer, needing to confirm what I think I'm seeing. Dozens of small, deformed stumps protrude from her head where her hair should be, and instead of human skin, she has iridescent scales that seem to cover her whole body. She's part gorgon, but something is very wrong with her. Those stumps... They should be her snakes. Were they removed, or did she end up like this thanks to these experiments? Thinking over what the boy said, I realise these children are here because they are failed experiments and are now being shipped away to be used as slaves.

This is so much worse than I feared. I think I'm going to be sick.

"What the fuck is this?" Elias asks as he takes in the deformed child with horror. Slowly, he looks at the other children and realisation sets in.

I almost don't want to say the words aloud, as if doing so will make them true. "Someone is trying to create an army of monsters."

CHAPTER

Stumbling on the rocky ground, I just barely manage to catch myself against the side of the tunnel. To be honest, I'm not really sure how I made it back to the warehouse where Noah was waiting for me. He'd taken one look at me and my dishevelled state and quickly smuggled me into the tunnel. Despite the fact he couldn't see my face, he knows me well enough that he'd recognised something was wrong.

I'm reeling from what we saw in the warehouse, and I can't even begin to put into words what I'd just witnessed. The journey through the tunnels passes in a blur, my mind on the children we left behind. I feel Noah's concerned eyes on me, but he doesn't try to talk to me, knowing I'm lost within my thoughts.

Light comes into view ahead of us, signalling that we're nearly back at the castle, but I just keep putting one foot in front of the other.

I'm yanked backwards, and my steps are abruptly halted as my mind is jerked back into the present. Spinning around to snap at Noah, I'm surprised to see anger on his face that's aimed at me.

"You almost just walked straight out into the corridor. The queen was walking by, but you didn't see her at all!" he snaps, his voice distorted by the rocky walls surrounding us. "You know what would happen if they found you dressed like this. Can you hold yourself together until I get you back to your room?"

I'm a fucking mess. I don't even have the energy to hiss at him, so I simply nod. His expression shifts, and I know he's even more concerned now. This isn't like me at all. He's right—I was on autopilot, and I nearly just screwed everything up, not just for me, but for him too.

He takes control, stepping past me so he's in the lead. As he brushes past, I can almost feel him vibrating with anger. When he reaches the end of the tunnel, he pauses to ensure the coast is clear. Slipping out, he's gone for a second before he reappears and gestures for me to follow. I pull my hood back and step out into the castle, following him as he takes me to my rooms. He's silent as he waits for me to step into the room, closing the door behind us.

There's a beat of silence, and then he spins around to glare at me. "What the fuck was—"

I shove past him, running to the bathroom where I promptly fall to my knees before the toilet and vomit my guts up. Wave after wave hits me, and I retch until my stomach is empty. The acidic taste of bile stings my mouth. I should get up and rinse my mouth out, but a tsunami of exhaustion smashes into me, leaving me drained and draped over the toilet. Eventually, I manage to summon the energy to shuffle to the side, leaning back against the wall as I try to catch my breath. I've never felt so weak, so vulnerable, and I hate it, but what I hate more are the next words that slip from my mouth.

"We had to leave them behind."

Silence greets me, and although I dread it, I lift my head to take in Noah's expression. His brows are furrowed, but he seems more concerned with my slumped physical state right now.

"Who?" he eventually asks, scanning me for injury or an obvious cause of distress.

"The children." The words are like acid on my tongue, and my shame makes my chest tight.

This catches his attention. His gaze flicks up to my veil, and his frown deepens. I can see his confusion, and I don't blame him. After all, the whole reason we'd snuck out of the castle this evening was to rescue the children and free them from slavery. He doesn't push me for an answer, and while I appreciate that, I know I owe him an explanation. He risked his life to help me.

"Someone has been experimenting on children." Leaning my head back, I stare up at the ceiling, unable to watch his face any longer. "They were all..." I trail off, not sure how to explain the dazed, vacant expressions on their faces. Clearing my throat, I try again. "We were able to get one of them to talk, and he said they were the failed experiments. They have all been broken, their bodies twisted with mutations."

Images of that tiny girl's body flash through my mind, and I have to stop for a moment. Who the fuck is trying to create gorgons? It's sick. No one should have to live like this, especially not children.

Taking a deep breath, I tell him, "They all need far more care than we expected. There was no way we could take them. No orphanage would accept them, they would just hand them over to the guards."

We both know what would happen to the children if that occurred—their lives would be cut short. Once the guards were involved, things would go public and people would see what was happening. Whispers would start to circulate about mutated children and monsters in the streets, and it would become impossible to hide any future children.

"Until we can find somewhere safe for them, somewhere that has people who will look after them, we can't move them." I attempt to justify our actions, my throat tightening. Our decision means those children will be lost to us. They'll be shipped off, far out of our reach, and used as slaves until they can't work any longer. "If we took them, they would have only been taken back. We weren't prepared." My eyes sting with unshed tears that I refuse to let fall. "Now that we know, we can sort something out so we can help the next lot of children."

It sounds like excuses, even to me. I hate that we had to make this decision, and guilt eats away at me. I hadn't wanted to leave them. In fact, I argued until I was blue in the face, but the others explained their reasoning to me, so with a padlock Theo happened to be carrying around with him, we locked up the warehouse once more and left the children behind. Elias and the others went back into the city, and I slunk back to Noah. Images of that little girl's limp, mutated body will haunt my dreams forever.

Closing my eyes, I wait for judgement and accusations because I didn't try hard enough to save them. Only they never come. Opening my eyes, I lift my head and reluctantly look at Noah. His expression is torn. His disgust and anger are clear, but understanding shines through. My breath catches in my throat.

"Do you know who's behind it?"

I know what he's asking—was Marcus involved? I shake my head, wishing the answer was otherwise. "The child just mentioned a 'he' and said that they were being created for the king." Nausea rises again at those last three words, but I push through it. "I have no idea if that means he knows about it or not."

He stares at me for a moment, and I know he's thinking the same thing I am. The king *has* to know, at least on some level, even if he doesn't know about the experiments. I need more information. I need to keep looking.

Sighing, Noah rubs a hand across his face. He appears weary, as if the whole evening has drained his spirit. I know how he feels. Stepping towards me, he kneels so we're eye to eye. I really don't want to be touched right now, and he seems to recognise that, lowering the hand he instinctively raised to touch my arm. Instead, his expression softens. "You did what you could, Maya."

I hate those words. It just means that I wasn't good enough, that I failed. If it were just me on the line, then it wouldn't be so bad, but this is so much worse. Shaking my head, I stare down at my hands in my lap. "It wasn't enough."

Part of me wants to go back into the city, wait until they start transporting the children onto a ship, and then slaughter every last person I find. My gorgon hisses in agreement, and my hands ball into fists. It would be so easy. But then I'd be left with the same dilemma—what to do with the children. I can't leave them without anyone to care for them.

A knock at the door startles us both, and for a moment, neither of us moves. The knock sounds again, and Noah pushes to his feet and leaves the room. While he's gone, I try to pull myself together, rolling onto my knees and slowly standing. I suddenly feel my age as everything in my body aches and groans. Moving to the basin, I splash cold water on my face and wash out my mouth, half-heartedly listening to Noah as he opens the door.

"The king requests Lady Maya's presence in his chambers."

My gut sinks, and those words seem to echo around the room so much louder than they should. I don't hear anything else that's said, my ears ringing. How am I going to face the king after what I've just witnessed? I've been dreading this. I knew it was going to come sooner or later.

Gripping the sides of the sink hard enough that my knuckles go white, I stare at myself in the mirror on the wall above. I dare not take my veil off in case Noah comes back in, so I stare at myself and imagine my face is staring back at me. I see him return in the reflection, his expression neutral, and I know that he's going to try and make this better, but nothing is going to make this easier, so I beat him to it.

"I suppose I better get ready then." Pushing away from the sink, I walk straight past him to the wardrobe, pulling open the doors as I decide what to wear.

Time to go and confront the king.

Knocking on the door, I brace myself as I push it open without waiting for his reply. I stride across the threshold with false confidence, pulling the door shut behind me and swaying my hips as I move through the room. Marcus is sitting in a chair by his bookshelves on the other side of the room, a stack of papers at his side on the wooden table.

"Maya," he purrs appreciatively as he looks up from the document. He relaxes back in his seat with a male arrogance that I would usually find amusing, but tonight, it just makes me grit my teeth.

Making my way over to the table, I lean against it as casually as I can, just out of touching distance as he runs his eyes possessively over my body. I couldn't bring myself to dress in the flimsy, provocative outfits he usually prefers, so instead, I picked out this dress. It's form-fitting, showing off my hourglass figure, but it covers every inch of skin. Just the thought of being touched right now makes my skin crawl, so I donned this dress like armour. Thankfully, Marcus doesn't seem offended by my lack of exposed skin.

Throwing the papers he'd just been reading onto the table, he rests his elbow on the armrest of the chair and props his chin in his hand, watching me with a lazy, satisfied smile. "Tell me, Maya, what have you been up to? Have you learned anything about the bastards from Saren?" Although his voice is light, his eyes harden when he mentions the dignitaries, giving away his dislike.

I thought he might ask me this, and I have been mulling over what to say to him for the last day, so I'm prepared with an answer. "They are here for trade," I begin, drawing patterns on the table with my fingertip.

"But they also think you're up to something, and they want me to help them discover what it is."

All true, and by feeding him a small amount of the truth, it will keep him believing that I'm one hundred percent his. I'm sure he already knows Elias and the others have been snooping around. He has spies everywhere, so there is no point in denying anything. I'm also sure that the magic binding me to him would protest if I hadn't said anything at all.

Marcus drops all pretence of being calm and frowns as he leans forward, his hands braced on his knees. "They have been asking questions and sticking their noses where they shouldn't." Baring his teeth, he stares at a point on the table, not really seeing it as he organises his thoughts. Snapping his gaze up to me, he leans back and narrows his eyes as he takes me in. "I need you to keep them busy and distracted. There's something I'm working on that I can't have them discovering."

My heart hammers in my chest. Could this be it? Is he about to admit that he knows about the children? Trying to play it cool, I tilt my head to one side, sliding my hand towards him along the table. "And just what are you working on?" I ask seductively, pushing from the table and taking two steps so I'm close enough to sit in his lap. As I expected, he grins up at me and pulls me down, holding me close with one arm as I run my hand down his chest.

He chuckles, his spare hand sliding up my leg until it comes to rest at my hip. "Nothing you need to worry about," he whispers in my ear.

He's not going to tell me. I should have known. He's always been secretive and kept things from people, just not usually from me. I can scent his desire, and I know where this is about to go, which is where it always goes when he calls me to his room. No, there's no way I can fuck him tonight, not when he potentially knows about the children. Not when the last time he touched me he beat me—not that he remembers that fact.

Trying to make it look casual, I sigh and stretch my arms above my head and climb from his lap. "I should go, it sounds like I'm going to have a busy few days ahead of me."

Walking a few steps away, I glance over my shoulder at him and notice his frown. With slow, sure movements, he stands, his eyes shrewd as he once again looks over me. "You've been acting differently lately."

I don't know how to respond to that. I have been acting differently, but it's not like I can tell him why. Not without revealing that I've been working with Elias to discover the truth as to what he's been up to.

"Is it them?" he demands, beating me to it and saving me from having to answer. He steps closer, and his face twists. "Have they said something? Or have you been fucking them for information and now you've got a taste of Saren cock and I'm not good enough?"

Before I even realise what I'm doing, I slap him across the cheek. "Who are you?" I accuse, my voice betraying my hurt, disgust, and outrage. "What happened to you? This is not the Marcus I knew and loved."

I'm treading on dangerous ground. He's the king, he could order my execution, and given his recent treatment of me, I really shouldn't be pushing him. However, in this moment, I don't care. My heart is being crushed by his words and actions. I feel so fucking stupid for allowing myself to be hurt and used *again*.

Marcus is completely still, the shock of me raising a

hand to him rendering him speechless. Working his jaw and rubbing his hand against his cheek, he brings his gaze back to me. "I notice your use of past tense there." His eyes are shrewd, and I know he's imagining my face beneath the veil. He's the only person alive to have ever seen it. "People change, Maya. *I've* changed. I'm the king, I have responsibilities you can't even imagine." His teeth are gritted, and I get the impression he's trying to hold back his anger, yet I refuse to say anything or move from my position. If he raises a hand to hurt me, I won't allow it. He'll be pinned to the ground faster than he can blink, king or not, and I think he can sense that, can feel how close I am to losing control.

Releasing a long sigh, he shakes his head and his face relaxes, his lips tilting up into a soft smile. "Oh, Maya, I know things have changed, but I still love you. I always will."

There was once a time when I would have melted at his words, accepting that the stress of his position made him speak to me like that. However, I notice how his eyes go to the amulet around my neck as he speaks, telling me exactly what he values about me.

"No, you don't love me." Stepping back, I shake my head with disgust. "You love the power that having me by your side gives you."

Anger instantly replaces his smile, proving my instincts right. "What's gotten into you? You were never bothered by any of this before."

He's right—I've finally been awoken to the realities of my life, and it's depressing as all hell. Instead of making me angry, all of that drains away, leaving me empty. "That's not enough anymore, Marcus." Turning, I walk over to the door, the sound of my dress brushing over the floor the only sound in the room. I pull the door open, and my heart lifts slightly as I find Noah waiting there for me.

"Maya, wait," Marcus calls out, something akin to panic tinging his voice.

I don't even glance over my shoulder as I shut the door behind me and stride down the corridor.

CHAPTER 11

Walking through the hallways of the castle, I march straight past the main hall and in the opposite direction of my rooms. For a few minutes, Noah and I walk in blessed silence, but as we reach the back of the castle, my protector clears his throat.

"Lady Maya, may I enquire as to where we're going this evening?"

I don't blame him for wondering. Usually when I leave the king's rooms, I head straight back to mine to bathe. Tonight, I was with the king for much less time than usual, and I'm certainly not going to my rooms. My relationship with the king isn't a secret, so everyone knows what happens when the king requests my company in his rooms. It's one of the reasons the queen hates me so much, because Marcus flaunts it so blatantly in front of her.

I feel twisted inside, and my mind is a mess. I'm not sure what's happening to me. For the last decade or so

I've been blind to human emotions, not allowing them to touch or affect me. Love and lust were the only things keeping me here, the only emotions I allowed other than the unending anger my gorgon feels. Somehow, because of those blinders I'd been wearing, I missed the rot that's been growing inside Marcus. With the arrival of Elias and his men, my eyes are beginning to open to everything I missed, and I just can't face going back to my room—the room where he beat me and called me a monster.

I had to be rescued.

Rescued. That very word makes me bristle. I'm a gorgon, I don't need rescuing. Over the years, I've allowed myself to become soft. Love, that's what's behind this. I promised myself that I'd never fall for another man again after my first love cursed me. They only ever want to use me. Against my better judgement, I allowed Marcus into my life and fell in love with him. In the early days, I pushed against it, but he was kind, sweet, and oh so persuasive. We had good times together, but now I'm wondering if that was all a lie, a game to him to keep me under his thumb. I should have known better. Stupid, so stupid.

A fire has been awoken inside me, and I need to find a way to contain it before I end up burning down everything around me. I was numb when I left Marcus' room, but with each step I take away from him, my resentment only grows.

I can feel Noah's discomfort at my lack of response, especially as I push through the back doors of the castle and jog down the steps, the cool fresh air of the evening wrapping around us. The icy breeze actually helps clear my mind enough so that I can answer him without snapping. "I'm going to the barracks. I need to train."

"Maya, is everything okay?" I hear the hesitation in his voice and glance over my shoulder to see a mix of emotions playing across his face. "Did the king hurt you?"

Ah, so that's why he's so hesitant. Noah was the one to find me and get help when the king beat me. He's been more protective ever since, and although he's still professional around the king, I've noticed a definite coolness about him during those times.

I ponder his question. Did the king hurt me? Physically, no, but emotionally... Well, that's a different matter. I can't explain all of that to him though, and really, it's not my place. Marcus is still his king, after all.

"I'm fine, Noah. I just need to train."

Facing forward and rolling my shoulders back, I continue across the gardens. Instead of taking the path to the right, which heads towards the stables, I turn to the left. Ahead, the barracks loom like a dark shadow in the night. Most of the building is made up of rooms where the guards sleep and eat, but right in the middle is a large training hall. Glancing up at the moon, I estimate that it must be the early hours of the morning, so I should have the room to myself, which works just fine for me. I don't feel like being watched.

Walking into the building without any trouble, I head straight to the hall but let out a huff of frustration when I hear the pounding of pads. It sounds like I'm not going to be training alone after all. If I just show a bit of aggression and hiss a few times, it should scare them off and give me the space all to myself. A small, devious smile pulls at my lips at the thought. As I step into the hall, however, I see that it's not a guard training late into the night, but Mason, the largest of the three Saren men.

He glances over his shoulder, obviously pissed off at

the interruption, but freezes as soon as he sees me in the doorway. I ignore him as I move farther into the room, find a space on the mats, and begin to take off my shoes. From the corner of my eye, I watch as he slowly straightens and drops his weights to the ground. Making it a point not to look at him, I continue to get ready to train, reaching behind me to unhook my skirt before pulling it away to reveal the leggings I'm wearing below —another reason why I chose this dress tonight.

Mason's gaze is a heavy weight upon me, but I simply focus on the opposite wall and start to go through my warmup stretches. It's been far too long since I trained, instead relying on my gorgon strength and the weaknesses of others. I've been lazy. As I fall into a rhythm, one stretch melding into another, my moves graceful and strong, I let my mind relax into the movements. Distantly, I hear the sound of weights being lifted from the bars, and I know Mason's gone back to his training, leaving me to my own devices.

Body warm and limber, I stride over to the rack of weapons, reaching for a wooden staff. Tossing it from hand to hand, I check the weight and nod to myself. Yes, this will do nicely. Returning to the mats, I fall into a defensive position, the staff held in both hands before me. I lunge forward and thrust it into my imaginary foe, twisting and spinning in a circle, whirling the staff towards his head. Stepping back into position, I do the drill again, over and over, faster and faster, until I can feel the sweat dripping down my forehead. Moving on to the next drill, I repeat the process.

I'm so focused on my patterns that I don't notice someone approaching until they step onto the mat. I lunge, the staff travelling at a speed that could kill if it hit the right place. I realise too late that it's Mason, and there's nothing I can do to stop the impact of the staff. He jumps back instinctively and thrusts his left arm up, taking the impact from the staff and throwing it off course.

"What the hell do you think you were doing? I could have killed you!" Terrified fury courses through me, and my heart pounds so hard, I'm sure it's about to break from my ribcage.

Mason raises a single brow in surprise at my anger. "You didn't," he answers with a shrug. His eyes travel over my body, pausing for a moment too long on my legging-clad thighs. "You look like you need a sparring partner."

A blow like the one he just received would have broken a lesser man's arm, but Mason doesn't seem bothered by it in the slightest, even though I can see a large red welt from the hit. He has to be in pain, but he's offering to spar with me. This man must be a glutton for punishment.

Scoffing with disbelief, I shake my head. "I can't. The only way I can spar with others is if I'm blindfolded."

His eyebrows rise at this, his mouth twitching in one corner, and I just know he's having all sorts of dirty thoughts. Rolling my eyes despite the fact he can't see it, I ignore him and continue to explain. "There's too much of a chance that my veil will come loose in a sparring match, so I have to be blindfolded to prevent anyone from accidentally being turned to stone."

He seems to think on this for a moment, pursing his lips before he simply nods. "Where's the blindfold?"

I can't hold back my laugh. This guy can't be serious.

"I wasn't saying that's what we should do. I was explaining why I can't."

I expect him to challenge me, to call out my excuse, but he doesn't. Glancing around to make sure no one can overhear us, he steps closer, lowering his voice. "Maya, I can tell something has upset you, but I'm not going to make you talk to me, as that's clearly not what you need right now."

My immediate reaction is to pull away and deny that I've been hurt, and I know if he pushed me, I'd simply turn around on the spot and walk out of the barracks. My reputation as a strong, fierce monster has to be maintained at all times, otherwise I'll appear weak and someone will try to best me. Appearances must be maintained at all costs, which is something Marcus has drilled into me since he became king. But even before then, I knew I always had to appear menacing and ready to attack at a moment's notice, as humans will take anything else as a sign of weakness.

Mason seems to sense all of this despite me not saying anything and hums low in his throat. "You came here to pound out your feelings, so let me help."

I stare at him for a long moment and get the impression that this is how he sorts through his feelings too. He's such a physical guy that it makes sense, and he's right—I need to work these feelings out physically. Without a word, I turn and walk over to the supplies, open a small cupboard, and pull out a length of black silky material. Turning my back to him, I remove my veil, keeping my eyes squeezed shut as I lift the fabric to my face. The world goes dark, and I reach behind my head to tie the blindfold, only for a warm set of hands to take it from me.

"Let me." His voice is deeper than usual, but quiet, as he gently ties the material.

My chest tightens at the touch, and I want to scoff. Am I so desperate for intimate touch that even a brush of his hand over mine is enough to flush my cheeks and warm my body? A small part of my mind whispers that not just anyone would cause this reaction and it's wholly tied to *who* is touching me.

"You know that this is a terrible idea, right?" My voice croaks, but I need something else to focus on rather than how close he's standing right now. With my sight gone, all of my other senses are heightened. The heat that's radiating from him warms my back, and the soft sounds of his breath tickle my ear. Oh yes, this is a bad idea.

"Noted." Mason chuckles, and the sound causes the hair on my arms to stand on end.

Needing some space, I step away, working by memory until I feel the give of the training mats below me, then I use the staff to guide myself into position.

"Maya, are you sure this is wise?" Noah asks from the doorway. I immediately feel bad for forgetting he was out there. I understand why he asked. He knows that if anyone finds out that someone else has seen my face, the king will have him killed. Not to mention if the blindfold slips and I accidently turn Mason into stone, it could bring all-out war between our kingdoms.

"I won't let her get hurt," Mason promises, misunderstanding my protector's hesitation.

Noah doesn't say anything more, but I can feel his gaze on me, ready to jump in if needed. Mason's heavy steps pull my attention back to the matter at hand. Expanding my senses, I listen to all the sounds around me as he takes up his position opposite me.

"Ready?"

I don't bother replying, simply jerking my head in agreement and jumping forward in a flash of movement. He laughs as he blocks, immediately counterattacking. It takes all of my focus to fight like this, and I use every sense to defend and work out his next move—the sound of the wooden staff whistling through the air, the change in his breathing pattern just before he attacks, the feel of the mat beneath my feet as he charges towards me. All thoughts vanish as we spar, our bodies a blur of movement.

Mason is an incredible fighter, but then I'd already guessed that. He's much faster than I would have imagined for a man of his size, and there are a couple of blows that I almost don't catch. We continue like this, locked in a battle of wills, as we exchange blow after blow.

"You're good," he grates out with a quick, sharp jab aimed at my ribs that I just manage to avoid.

Jumping back, I shrug my shoulders. "I'm the king's blade. I have to be."

I hear him sigh, followed by the sound of his staff hitting the ground. Assuming he's taking a break, I straighten up and twist my upper body side to side to ease a nagging ache in my back. From the sounds that reach me, I assume he's looking through the weapons rack.

"Let's change weapons," he finally announces, his voice close as he strokes his hand down my arm before taking my staff. The action shocks me so much that I don't fight him, giving up the staff immediately. He presses a wooden handle into my right hand, and I raise it, testing the weight. It's one of the short practice swords the guards train with. Flipping it between my hands, I do a few rehearsal lunges and settle back into a defensive position.

Although I can't see him, I get the impression that Mason is getting into position opposite me, and as he calls out a command to begin, I raise the sword defensively. We circle each other, waiting for the other person to make their move. When he does, I'm ready for him, parrying his sword easily. The only problem with using short swords is that your opponent is so much closer than with the staff or longsword. Our bodies brush as we duck and weave, our breathing and the blows of the wooden swords creating the only sounds in the space.

"Are you okay?" he asks between blows. "After everything that happened in the docks?"

He really wants to talk about this now? If I had time to raise my brows and shake my head, then I would. Images of the warehouse flash through my mind and my attack falters, giving him the chance to push back, and the effort to stop the blow has me gritting my teeth. "No. I'm not okay," I answer honestly. We break apart and jump back.

There was nothing okay about what we saw or what happened. I'm not sure if I'll ever forgive myself for leaving those children behind, but I've made a promise to myself that I will find out what's going on and stop it from happening to anyone else. Horror, guilt, and unease twist my gut.

"I saw Marcus before I came here." The admission leaves me tense, and I leap forward with my sword as I wait for his reply.

He parries, returning the attack with a grunt of effort. "You saw the king? What did he say?" he asks between strikes, barely sounding out of breath.

"I didn't say anything about the children, I couldn't, but he's working on something he doesn't want you to know about," I warn. I should feel guilty for exposing the king like this, but I don't. The only guilt I feel is that I couldn't do more for the children.

"That has to be the experiments," Mason presses, but I wince. Calling those children experiments is cruel. I know that's not what he means, and he's referring to what's actually being done to them, but I feel sensitive about the subject.

Catching my wince, he pauses in his attack, and I feel his heavy gaze on me. "Did he... Did he hurt you?"

That's the second time tonight I've been asked that. I shake my head, wishing I could see his expression. "No, but...I couldn't let him touch me. Not after everything we saw tonight."

There's another heavy pause, and then a low rumbling growl seems to come from him. "I want to chop his fucking hands off and never let him touch you again. The bastard shouldn't have that privilege."

It's a good thing that we're alone, because that comment would see him hanged. Even so, the walls have ears, and his words are dangerous.

"Privilege?" I laugh bitterly. Then, using his distraction, I leap forward until I'm right up against him, disarming him with a single blow before I press my fake blade against his throat. "I'm a monster, Mason. He's the only person to ever see beyond that."

"Not the only person," he whispers, and in a flash of movement, he disarms me and I'm pressed against his chest. I can hardly breathe, not because he's holding me too tightly, but because of *how* he's holding me. I feel him lean down, and before I know it, he presses his lips against mine.

My entire body stills, as if moving might make him stop. For such a large man, his lips are so soft, the perfect juxtaposition. Cradling me in his arms like I'm a precious being, he kisses me until I finally give in to the temptation and kiss him back. I open my mouth with a quiet gasp, and he quickly deepens the kiss, his groan awakening my desire so fiercely that had he not been holding me up, my legs might have given way. Reaching up, I drape my arms over his shoulders and pull him closer so we're flush. His kisses are so different to Marcus', which are commanding and rough, whereas Mason's are deep and consuming, like I'm the oxygen he needs to survive.

I shouldn't be doing this, but not because of Marcus —I don't belong to him, not anymore. I might be bound to him and he might still be my king, but I will no longer share his bed. That decision has been made ever since he beat me, and I've only just had the confidence to admit it to myself. No, I shouldn't be kissing Mason for several reasons. Firstly, he's from a different kingdom, so once he's done with his duties, he'll be returning home and I'll be stuck here. Secondly, Theo's kiss, and while I don't owe Mason an explanation about whom I kiss, I can't deny that I feel a pull towards his companion—both of his companions.

Mason's hands smooth down my back and come to rest on my waist, his hand spanning half of my ribcage. The atmosphere heats up, and I know if I don't stop this soon that we're going to fuck right here in the middle of the barracks.

"Wait." I gently push against his chest, and he immediately steps back, albeit with a dissatisfied rumble. "I have something to tell you. Theo kissed me."

I can't see him, but I can feel his smile. "I know. He told us." The amusement in his voice confirms my suspicion. I'm about to ask more questions, but he stops me by pressing a finger to my lips. "No more questions," he whispers, pulling me against him once more.

This time when his lips land on mine, I kiss him with a passion I didn't know I possessed. He leans down, and unable to resist, I slip my leg around his and trip him to the ground. He lands on his back with a thud, and before he can move, I'm scrambling on top of him, pinning him to the ground.

"I win," I whisper with a satisfied smile, my competitive nature compelling me to be on top. This, however, puts us in an interesting position. My legs straddle his hips, pressing my core against him. He lets out a low, rumbling male laugh, and I wish I could rip off my blindfold and see his expression.

Releasing his arms, I lower myself, and before I have to worry about blindly finding his lips, he presses his against mine in a rush as he leans up to meet me. We kiss until I'm not sure where one of us starts and the other ends. I lose myself in the taste of him, his masculine scent driving me wild.

Mine, my gorgon hisses in the back of my mind, and the claim behind it is so strong that it almost knocks the air from me. Pressing my hands against his chest, I pull back, my breathing heavy. My gorgon is pushing for more, wanting to get closer and practically purring in my mind as he runs his hand up the length of my arm. She's never acted like this before, and honestly, it frightens me a little. Pushing those thoughts away to dissect at a later date, I focus on the here and now, on the man between my thighs. I'm gratified to hear that he's just as out of breath as I am.

"You'll need this," he murmurs, his fingers locking with mine for a moment before he places something soft in my palm.

Puzzled, I sit back so I have both hands free and run my fingers over it. It's my veil. I'm shaking my head before I've even opened my mouth. There's a reason the king blindfolds me when we have sex—other than enjoying the power he has over me. If we're going to get intimate, which I'm hoping we are, it's unsafe for me not to wear it. "I should stay blindfolded so I don't accidently—"

"No, I want you to be able to see me," he insists, closing my fist around the material. "With you blindfolded, I have all the power, and it shows you're beneath me. I won't have that. We are equal, Maya."

I should say no and back away. I would never forgive myself if something happened to him, but his words strike something within me. Equal. That's what I always thought I was to the king, but he's proven that I was wrong. Now that I look back, I can see all the warning signs, comments, and actions I missed before. Mason, however, has always treated me as an equal, even though I'm supposed to be his enemy. To be honest, all three of the Saren males have treated me with respect since they got here. But having a male such a Mason pinned beneath me, desiring me for who I am and not the power I offer, only makes me want him more. I lift the veil and attach it, carefully removing the blindfold from underneath. Letting out a slow breath, I open my eyes and take in his expression. It was worth the wait. Desire burns in his eyes as he looks at me like I'm the most beautiful female in the world.

My hunger for him grows, so I decide to take matters into my own hands. Reaching for his shirt, I start to undo the buttons, leaning down to press a kiss against his lips in the process. He groans into my mouth, sitting up and gently taking my hands in his. Rejection flashes through me, but before I can say anything or act hastily out of hurt, he smiles ruefully and shakes his head before pressing his forehead against mine.

"I'm not fucking you here, Maya," he mumbles with part amusement and part reluctancy.

Confused, I sit back on my heels. I know he wants me, I can quite clearly feel his desire for me pressed against my hip, so what's the problem? "But—"

Scrubbing a hand over his face as if this is the hardest decision he's ever made, he raises a brow. "I said you deserved to be treated better, and I won't go back on my word." Sensing my continued confusion and frustration, he chuckles. "Do I want to fuck you in the middle of the barracks where anyone could walk in?" He shrugs, his grin playful. "There's some appeal if you like that sort of thing. But I want to treat you right, Maya, and fucking worship you." Those last few words are said slowly and with emphasis, making my needy core clench. A full body shiver rolls over me, and the hair on my arms stands on end. I know he saw it from the satisfied noise he makes at the back of his throat.

I stare up at him, not believing what I'm hearing. Swallowing against the sudden lump in my throat, I nod slowly. "Okay, I guess we should go back to my room then."

A smile spreads across his face. Taking that as a yes, I

climb from him and stalk over to where I left my skirt. With my back to him, I reattach the skirt, covering my leggings. All of my actions are unhurried and measured, completely at odds to the raging need within me. Releasing a long breath, I turn and see Mason brushing himself down before strapping his sword around his hips, but his eyes are on me the whole time. Sharing a secret smile, I walk towards the exit, knowing he'll follow.

Coming across a frowning Noah by the door, I feel like a bucket of cold water has been dumped over me. He didn't see, did he? Noah barely looks at me, nodding his head once before glancing over my shoulder. My heart drops when I see his expression as he takes in Mason. The anger on his face tells me he *did* see us. Embarrassment makes my cheeks flush, but guilt prevails. I have nothing to be ashamed of, I know that, but then why do I feel so guilty?

Noah gestures for me to follow him, and without a word, I do, my mood soured. The journey back to my rooms is quiet and awkward. Thankfully, we don't come across anyone due to the early hour. When we reach my door, I see the tension in his shoulders before he turns around and blocks my entry to the room.

"Maya, is this a good idea?"

He sounds angry, despite his hushed tones, his eyes locked on mine.

I feel Mason step up behind me, and the atmosphere in the hall suddenly turns tense and heavy. "That's not really any of your business," Mason replies, crossing his arms over his chest, the muscles of his arms bulging with the action. I can practically taste the testosterone in the air as they face off against each other.

Baring his teeth in a snarl, Noah steps forward. "Her safety *is* my business."

Snorting, Mason shakes his head. "I'm not going to hurt her, and you know it."

They are silent for a moment, locked in a battle of wills. Tired and horny, I let out a quiet huff of frustration. Placing my hand on Noah's chest, I wait for him to look at me. He reluctantly pulls his gaze from the other male and brings his attention back to me. "I'm safe," I promise quietly.

There's longing in his eyes, and I know he wants to say more, but he holds it back, nods his head once, and steps to the side. I don't say anything more, simply opening the door and stepping inside. Low voices sound behind me as the two of them talk, but I don't try to listen, instead making my way over to the bed. I make no move to undress or climb onto it, I just wait. I'm not left waiting long, however, and soon enough, Mason's hands land on my waist and his chest presses to my back as he kisses along the length of my neck.

With a gasp of pleasure, my head falls to one side, giving him better access. His hands skim over my hips and up to cup my breasts. Needing more, I take a step forward so I can reach behind me to start undoing the buttons of my dress, but his hands quickly take over. With deft movements, the dress is soon hanging off my body, and with a simple shrug of my shoulders, it falls to the ground. Stepping out of it, wearing only my underwear, I turn to face him. I don't have a chest covering, since I didn't need one with that dress, so his eyes quickly travel up my hourglass figure and land on my exposed breasts.

"You're a goddess," he whispers as he steps forward,

looking like he can't quite believe this is real. "So beauti-ful." His hand rests on my hip and pulls me against him, while his other hand travels up my ribcage to my breast. He groans as he palms it. I have to bite my lip to hold back my own sounds of pleasure.

"Too many clothes," I bite out, pulling at his shirt. I want to see every inch of skin, read his tattoos like a map of his body, and most of all, I want to taste him.

Laughing, he takes over unbuttoning his shirt, the muscles in his chest rippling as he pulls it off. His entire chest is covered in tattoos that extend down both arms and the bottom of his neck. He watches me as his hands drop to his trousers, which he slowly unbuttons with a sly smile. When his fingers hook in his waistband, I shake out of my stupor and close the distance between us, batting his hands away.

"What—"

Before he can say anything more, I kneel before him. Grabbing his underwear with both hands, I slowly slide it down his legs, watching as his cock is finally freed. It's large, just like the rest of him, and it's so hard it looks painful. Taking him in my hand, I stroke the length of him, enjoying the low groan I provoke. I flick my tongue across the head of his cock, enjoying the taste of his salty pre-cum. No, it's more than that. As soon as the taste of him is on my lips, it's like a switch has been flipped and I *need* more of him. Bringing him into my mouth, I swallow him down as deeply as I can, moaning around his shaft. I go into a sort of frenzy at the taste, trying to take him deeper. My hand is wrapped around the bottom of his cock, and I squeeze with each bob of my head. He grunts and grips my shoulders, and I can tell he's trying to hold back, but my gorgon won't let him, his seed has awoken her.

Mine, mine, mine. The word spins in my mind, over and over, as I feel him getting closer to the edge. His hips jerk and his cock twitches in my mouth as he comes. His cum coats my tongue and I hum, unable to get enough as I lick him, trying to get every last drop.

Giving head has never been something that I was overly enthusiastic about. I enjoyed Marcus' reaction when I did it more than anything, but there's something about having Mason's seed in me. The primal part of me that I try to push away, that's been dormant for so long, well, it's awake now and it wants more.

Mason pants, staring down at me in wonder and shaking his head. He kneels in front of me, and his eyes flash over my veil as if he's trying to read my face. "I've never been so fucking turned on in all my life." He laughs and shakes his head again, his eyes going distant for a second. "Knowing there's a bit of me inside you... Well, it's my turn now." He gives me a seductive grin, his voice low and growly.

He pulls me close and presses his lips to mine before standing in one smooth movement, taking me with him. I automatically wrap my legs around his waist, feeling breathless as he takes me to the bed and places me on the edge.

He frowns as he takes in the perfectly placed cushions and neat bedding. "We'll talk about the fact that the king hasn't provided you with a nest, and instead gave you this monstrosity, at a later date. For now, it's time for me to feast on you."

He's right—I've always hated this fucking bed. It's too high and uncomfortable and unnatural for a gorgon, but I was told I needed to try and fit in, so I was given a bed like the humans. I really don't want to be thinking about that now, however, and as his fingers loop into the waistband of my underwear, all other thoughts disappear from my mind. After sliding them from my legs, he places his hands on my thighs and gently pushes them apart so I'm completely exposed to him. He doesn't waste any time, quickly burying his face in my core. With the first flick of his tongue against my clit, my head falls back in ecstasy. I can tell from every lick, nip, and kiss that Mason is a man who loves to bring pleasure to a woman, and damn is he good at it. He feasts on me with long, languid movements of his tongue, and I can't help but prop myself up on my elbows and watch him. He slides the first finger into me just as his eyes flick up to look at me. I mutter a curse, writhing on the bed as he adds two more fingers, slowly pumping with each flick of his tongue against my clit.

I'm going to come if he doesn't stop soon, and I want to be wrapped around his cock when that happens.

"I need you now," I order in a breathless voice.

Thankfully, I don't have to say any more, because he pulls back with a smug, satisfied expression etched onto his face. "Your pleasure brings me pleasure, my goddess."

My core clenches at his words, aching at the loss of his touch. However, as he stands, I see his rock-hard erection, which shows me he was telling the truth. My pleasure really did satisfy him, and soon after his previous orgasm too.

Lining up his cock with my entrance, he presses so the very tip of his head enters me, but then he moves forward no more. Leaning down, he brushes his lips against mine.

"Say my name," he whispers against my lips.

"Mason," I murmur, my voice equally as hushed, but his name ends on a pleasured groan as he pushes into me, filling me up entirely.

Pausing to give me the chance to adjust to his size, he kisses every part of my face that's not covered by the veil. I'm soon rocking beneath him though, and he chuckles, thrusting into me once. Leaning down, he wraps his arms around me and rolls, switching our positions. I now straddle his hips, and his cock feels so much deeper.

Rocking my hips, I start to pick up a rhythm. With him lying on his back, I can see his expression clearly as I move, tracing my fingers over the patterns inked on his chest. I'm soon distracted, though, as he cups both breasts and rolls my nipples between his fingers until they are tight pebbles, each tweak sending a bolt of pure pleasure straight to my core.

His hips thrust beneath mine with each movement, and I know it's not going to be long until we both reach our climax. One of his hands slides to my hip, encouraging me to move faster, deeper, and I do, savouring his groan. I grip his shoulders as I ride him.

"Mine." The word slips free before I can stop it, and I pause for a heartbeat, worried that he's going to freak out at the claim.

I needn't have worried. A smile spreads across his face, his hazel eyes twinkling. "Yes, yours," he pants in reply, his hand encouraging me to start moving again.

My heart soars. I know I'll have to deal with the fallout of this later, but for now it's nice to be desired for who I am and not *what* I am. My orgasm hits me so hard it takes my breath away. Back arched, I gasp at the pleasure shooting through me. My core clenches down on his cock, which is all he needs to take him over the edge and into his own orgasm. Moaning, he thrusts up, his cock pulsing as he pumps his seed into me. There's something primal about it, and my gorgon practically purrs in my chest. She wants to roll in the sheets that smell like him and be completely surrounded by Mason. Panting and aching, I climb off him and practically collapse by his side.

We lie like this until our breathing evens out, and when I turn my head to look at him, I find him watching me with a determined expression. Apprehensive, I prepare myself for whatever he's about to say next. Is he regretting what just happened? Scanning his face, I see no signs of regret, only happiness.

"Right, goddess." He rolls over as he addresses me, one corner of his mouth pulled up into a smile. "Now, about that nest..."

CHAPTER

As I walk to my bedroom door, it's an effort to stop smiling. My veil only covers the top half of my face, so most of my lips are unobscured, and since smiling isn't exactly something I'm known for here, it's bound to draw attention.

I had the best sleep of my life last night, but that only partially contributes to my good mood. After we fucked, Mason helped me drag all of my bedding into the bathroom and turned the sunken bathtub into a nest for me, much like he did the first time. Once everything was in place, he kissed me deeply and left for his own rooms. It wouldn't do for one of the Saren males to be seen slipping from my room in the morning. I thought I wouldn't be able to sleep, that I'd be too keyed up, but once I was in the comfort of a nest, one that smelled like him, it helped ease some of the tension that I always seem to carry around in my chest.

A knock sounds on the door again, and I roll my eyes at the impatience of whoever it is. Pulling it open, I find

Noah. My smile quickly drops from my face. He looks terrible.

"I thought you were off shift today," I ask as my eyes skim across his face. During the night, he swapped with one of the other guards, so he was not who I was expecting to see when I opened the door. Marcus works his guards hard, but they are all given time off to sleep and rest. Noah looks like he's not slept in days.

"I was. The king has requested both my presence and yours in his meeting room, immediately." His voice is cool and he looks away as soon as he's finished speaking, scanning the hallway.

My heart hurts at his distant behaviour. I know it's because of what happened last night and what he must have seen in the training hall. I'm a grown adult, and I can sleep with whomever I want. He's never acted this way when I slept with the king. Perhaps that's why he's acting like this, because he thinks I've betrayed the king. Sighing, I shake my head and gesture for him to lead the way. "We better leave now then."

He doesn't say a word, nor does he look at me as he glances left and right, checking for danger, before leading the way with me a step behind him. His whole body is stiff and giving off *don't talk to me* vibes, so I give him the space he obviously needs right now. Instead, I contemplate what the king would want to see me about. It's early for him to be in his meeting room. Maybe he wants to ask me more about what I know of the Saren men— not that I can, or will, tell him much more than he already knows. Anxiety twists in my gut as I remember what happened before I met Mason in the training hall. He wouldn't call me to the meeting room to punish me for storming out of his rooms without permission, would he?

And why request Noah? As a witness? No, if the king truly wanted to punish me, he'd do it in front of everyone in the main hall.

Rolling my shoulders back and summoning the courage of my inner monster, I allow a slight, cruel smile to curl up one side of my lips. It doesn't take long for us to reach the meeting room, and I can hear the low murmur of voices within. Two guards stand outside dressed in full armour, and they knock on the door when they see us. Guards aren't usually posted here, so why are they here today? Frowning, I glance at Noah, but his expression is the same distant one as before. The door is pushed open, and Noah hangs back to allow me to enter first. Releasing a long breath, I step in and immediately scan the room to see who's present. The king sits at the head of the table, as usual, and his two closest advisors are on either side of him, but the rest of the table is empty.

The hair on my arms stands on end as my gorgon shifts in my chest, telling me that there are others in the room. The tug in my chest is so strong that I know before I even turn who else is in the room. *Mine*, my monster hisses in my mind, and I have to force myself to stay still as I glance over and find the three Saren males standing to the side. They all respectfully dip their heads in greeting, a gesture I return. Elias looks every inch the lord in his formal jacket, his hair pulled back into a neat bun at the nape of his neck. Theo grins at me in a way that would be disconcerting to others, but I find it charming, and I have to hold back the urge to smile as he winks at me. He probably just did it to piss off the king, but my heart flips anyway. Then there is Mason. He looks fierce and intimidating, as usual, with his tattoos poking out the top of his formal jacket. He's frowning, and his hands are balled at his sides. I can tell he's uncomfortable here, but his eyes are locked on me.

"Maya, how nice of you to join us," Marcus drawls. I turn to him, and although he's wearing a bored expression, I can see the anger he's trying to hide. I was obviously looking at the other males for too long, inciting his jealousy.

I glance at the three dignitaries again, their expressions giving nothing away, although I swear Mason's face softens for a split second as I look at them. Even Theo has stiffened at the king's words.

Returning my full attention to Marcus to avoid any outbursts, I dip into a curtsy. "Your Highness."

The doors shut loudly behind us, and I have to fight my flinch. Two guards, also in full armour, stand on the inside of the doors. Why so much security? The king doesn't usually require this many guards to be present, especially in the meeting room where sensitive subjects are often discussed. I shift my weight from one foot to the other as subtly as I can, trying to settle the urge to fight or flee. My gorgon doesn't like being closed in, and with the armed guards standing by the door, this feels very much like a trap.

"You're probably all wondering why you're here." Marcus breaks the silence and looks between the five of us, his heavy gaze coming to land on me.

"We were hoping it was to discuss the trade deals, Your Highness," Elias replies smoothly.

A flash of annoyance crosses the king's face, but he quickly waves the comment away. "Yes, yes, the advisors are working on that." He sits back in his throne-like chair, and a contemplative expression crosses his face. "I actually have a task for you, if you would be so willing."

I note the surprise in the lord's expression, but he swiftly smooths it into a mask of neutrality. Mason continues to look angry. In fact, I think the king has only succeeded in annoying him further.

Elias dips his head ever so slightly in acknowledgement of the request but is careful not to blindly agree to whatever the king is asking for. "How may we help you, King Marcus?"

A small smile crosses the king's face. "I have a monster problem. Who better to sort it than the greatest monster hunters in the land?"

My body stiffens. A monster problem? Is it something he made up to get rid of the dignitaries, or an actual issue? There's a challenge in his voice, and I know he's mocking them. From their postures, I can see they have picked up on it too, not that it was a subtle dig in the first place. Theo's easy-going nature has completely disappeared, leaving behind a scowling male I don't recognise. Mason looks like he's about to jump forward and attack the king, which would just be disastrous all around.

"What seems to be the problem?" Elias asks, his voice polite but clipped. Gone is the neutral, amicable tone from before.

The king is crossing a line, and from the glimmer of glee in his eyes, he knows it and is enjoying himself. "There's a dragon causing problems in one of our towns in the mountains. I need you to kill it for me."

A dragon. He wants them to kill a dragon. Now, I've heard tales of these three, of the mysterious monster hunting team, and I don't doubt that they could kill a dragon if they wanted to, but this is a dangerous request. If the Saren males go, then they would risk their lives trying to complete a task for their rival king. If they refuse, then they would offend the king and potentially incite war. Marcus is playing a dangerous game here. This is the first I've heard of a dragon causing problems for one of our towns, but it's becoming abundantly clear that he's been keeping things from me.

"Make sure to bring back the head, I want it stuffed. It will look nice on my wall, don't you think?" he remarks with a smile that makes me queasy.

Theo steps forward, his frown severe. "A trip like that will take weeks, if not months, with an army."

The king appears stunned for a moment before shaking his head slightly. He seems particularly sensitive to the siren in Theo's voice, even when he isn't attempting to use his power.

"Surely you don't need more than a few men. For accomplished hunters like you, this should be an easy job," he crows, using that mocking tone once more. A cruel gleam enters his eyes as he looks at me before his gaze flicks to Noah behind me. "Besides, I'll lend you my blade and her best guard."

So that's why the king requested my and Noah's presence. He's sending us away. Suspicion rises within me. This seems like too much of a coincidence. The five of us discovered the children in the warehouse, and the very next day, we're being sent on a mission, one that will take us far from the city.

Looking over at Elias and his men, I realise they don't have a choice. I can tell from the way the king is watching them that he expects them to say yes, but they pause all the same, thinking carefully. None of them speak, but they seem to be communicating silently anyway. After a few moments, I see the king start to bristle and prepare for an outburst, but Elias clears his throat. "We would be honoured to help you, Your Highness. We'll leave first thing in the morning."

Marcus smiles as all of his previous anger washes away, and then he waves his hand in the air, dismissing the lord's words.

"No need. I have horses waiting for you at the stables. You can leave as soon as you're packed. You may go."

The three dignitaries allow their anger at being dismissed so rudely to show, their brows furrowed and hands clenched, but Elias shakes his head and they turn to leave. Moving to follow them, I'm stopped as one of the guards steps in front of me, blocking my exit.

"Maya, stay here for a moment," Marcus calls. Dread rises within me. I've started to hate being alone with Marcus, especially after what we saw last night, but that's not what I'm worried about right now. The others' reactions command my full attention.

Elias stares at the king for a moment too long before slowly turning and gesturing with a dip of his head for the others to follow him. My attention stays on Mason. He's glancing between the king and me, and his body practically vibrates with emotion. I know it's because he doesn't want to leave me alone with the king. His eyes flick briefly to Noah at my side, and he seems to grudgingly accept that I'm safe. With a look that expresses far more than words ever could, he turns and follows after his companions.

The doors shut behind them, and the king gestures for his two advisors to leave, not saying a word until it's just us, Noah, and the two guards. I should be worried that he's made everyone else leave, but I'm not. If he tries to hurt me, I'll defend myself. I'm no longer worried about hurting his feelings. Anyone who touches me out of

anger or without my permission will face the consequences. I'm not called a monster for nothing.

"Come here," Marcus orders, his voice devoid of
warmth.

I don't want to, but I push those thoughts down. Any
reluctance will be taken as a sign of weakness, so I make
my way over to him, pausing just before the large table.

"A dragon?" I ask with a single raised brow. He can't
see it, but he can hear my disbelief and amusement.
Dragons are no laughing matter, but I can't reveal my
true feelings about this.

"It's been terrorising the village for the last year, and I
need an excuse to get those nosy bastards from my city.
This will keep them out of my hair." He narrows his eyes
on me shrewdly. "I think you also need some time away
to re-evaluate your position here. You live in luxury only
because I allow it. Spending a week on horseback will
make you appreciate me more when you return." There's
an edge to the way he says this, and I can tell he's trying
to keep his temper in check.

He really thinks that sending me away will make me
appreciate him and my life here? I used to live in a cave,
so riding on horseback and camping in the wild isn't
going to be an issue for me. Honestly, I hate living in this
castle. It's too closed in and there are too many people.
This will be a holiday in comparison. I won't constantly
have to hold back my gorgon nature to kill every human
in sight, not to mention he's sending me away with a guy
my gorgon just claimed, a male who kissed me and calls
to my monster, and a lord who I can't stop thinking
about—not that I'm going to let the king know any of
that.

Cocking my hip to one side and putting my hands on

my hips, I hiss out a bitter laugh, surprised at how easy it is to summon. "So you're punishing me?"

"I love you, Maya, but your behaviour is getting out of hand. Remember, things could be so much worse for you."

His eyes flick to the amulet on my neck, and my heart thuds painfully. He just proclaimed to love me at the same time as threatening me. He knows what my life would be like if he had my amulet. I would just be a puppet, and he would be my master, making me do whatever he wishes. The only thing protecting me from that fate is that the amulet cannot be taken from the wearer. Even if he killed me, whoever takes the amulet will be cursed to become the next gorgon. The only way to own it without being cursed is for the gorgon to freely give it away. Of course that has never happened, as we cannot allow ourselves to be controlled, so on and on the curse continues.

He waits to see if I'm going to argue with him, and I have to bite my tongue to keep in my remarks. He needs to believe that I'm contrite and that I'll follow his orders, because I know he's not bluffing about making my life worse. After a few tense moments, he lets a smile flicker across his lips, and I think he's going to praise me or say something to keep me sweet, but that's not what happens. "You can leave now," he says, dismissing me abruptly and turning to my protector, completely ignoring me. "Noah, I expect you to protect Maya with your life, and I want a full report on the dignitaries' actions on your return."

Practically spitting with anger, I spin on my heel and stalk to the doors, hissing at the guards until they hurriedly pull the doors open to allow me to leave.

"Yes, Your Highness," Noah answers behind me, but I don't bother to hang around to see if anything else is said.

A low hiss leaves my lips as I stride through the corridors, and anyone coming my way quickly jumps to the side, their terrified expressions only making my bad mood worse. Following the instinctual pull within me, I turn a bend and find the three of them waiting for me just down the corridor. I don't know how I knew they were there or how I knew they were waiting for me, but I'm too angry to figure it out. They speak in low voices so as not to be overheard, but I manage to pick up their words with my gorgon hearing. They have not seen me yet, so I pause and listen to their conversation.

"He asked for us to bring back the head. He wants to ensure we actually follow through on his request and that we're as good as the stories," Mason grumbles with dissatisfaction. "He sees us as a threat, so this way he can see how strong we are and if he can beat us," he states, ever the protector of the group.

Theo shakes his head, his expression uncharacteristically serious as he leans against the corridor wall with his arms crossed over his chest. "No. Dragon tongue has powerful healing properties, but it's rare. There aren't many dragons left." There's a heavy pause, and he seems to come to a realisation at the same moment I do. "What if he wants it for the experiments?"

The other two curse under their breath, but Elias says nothing else, his eyes focused on the wall as if he's deep in thought.

Mason grumbles, shifting his weight from foot to foot. "He gets us out of the way and gains something he needs for his sick experiments at the same time."

I step out into the corridor, and Mason instantly looks

up as if he senses me immediately. *Mate.* The word hisses through my mind. I want to throw myself into his arms, have his scent surround me once more, and to be filled with his cock and cum, and I can tell from his expression that he wants the same. My feelings are so intense it's all I can do to stop myself from running to him, but I have some self-respect—I don't run, not even for him. However, as my eyes flash to Elias and Theo, who are just looking up and noticing my presence, I find my gorgon is also drawn to them. I don't quite feel the same frenzy as with Mason, but I get the feeling if I were to fuck either of them that I'd be feeling the same way. She's never acted like this before. It took a long time before she would even tolerate being around Marcus, so the fact she wants these three men, that she wants to claim them, mark them, and make them hers...well, it's terrifying.

"He's definitely trying to get rid of you. You're causing too much trouble, he told me himself." Pausing in front of the trio, I glance between the three of them. Mason is watching me intently, so much so it makes my skin tingle even at the thought of him touching me. Pushing those thoughts aside, I focus on Theo and Elias. "It wouldn't surprise me if we got back from the trip and found no trace of the children. It also wouldn't bother him if you got killed while trying to slay the dragon."

Elias shakes his head slowly. "I thought as much. I suppose you have your orders to kill us if we act out too?"

His comment takes me aback. Frowning, I turn my full attention to the lord. I don't think the resentment in his voice is aimed at me, but it stings all the same. "I wouldn't hurt you," I say slowly, confused at the sudden change in his attitude.

Realising he's offended me, he sighs and rubs his face,

a motion I'm starting to recognise as something he does when he's stressed. "I know." There's an unspoken apology there as he gives me a soft, distracted smile. "Do you need help packing?"

Deciding to give him some slack, I shake my head. "No, I'll meet you at the stables in an hour."

Elias nods and motions to the other two to follow him as he turns and walks down the corridor. Smiling at Theo and Mason in farewell, I spin and start to walk back the way I came.

"Maya."

Mason's hand brushes my shoulder, and I have the strangest urge to purr, something I didn't even know was possible. I look up at him and take in his conflicted expression. He wants to talk about last night, and a cowardly part of me doesn't want to hear it, fearing rejection. The look in his eyes convinces me not to be scared though.

"Last night... I can't get you out of my head. Your taste, your smell, how you feel..." A low grumble leaves his chest, and my core clenches as desire floods my body. "My every thought revolves around you."

I don't know how to respond to that. Do I tell him that I feel the same way and admit that my gorgon has well and truly claimed him? When the word slipped from my lips last night, he hadn't seemed offended. In fact, he agreed. He steps closer and slides his hand beneath my veil, cupping my cheek. Against my better judgement, I lean into the touch.

I should have heard the footsteps, or maybe I just knew that it was Noah, but I'm slow to react as he rounds the corner. Really, it's probably because I'm so absorbed with Mason and my desire that I wasn't paying enough attention. Noah stops when he sees us, my head snapping around in time to see his eyes narrowing on where Mason's touching me.

He doesn't bother to greet us or waste time with pleasantries, his face hard as he clears his throat. "Maya, you should return to your room."

He's right—I really should. I've got a trip to pack for, and if I stay here any longer, I might do something I'll regret. Mason, however, takes issue with Noah's sharp tone. Stepping around me, he seems to fill the whole corridor as he bears down on the other man, reminding me just how huge he is. "She's not a child you can order around."

"No, she's not, but I'm her protector, and it's my job to protect her from any threat. Right now, in this corridor, where anyone could see you, *you're* the threat."

The emphasis he puts on that last comment brings everything back into focus. I got so caught up in these strange new feelings that I could have just screwed everything up. Had the king walked around the corner, he would have had us hanged for treason. Letting out a shaky sigh, I place a hand on Mason's back. "He's right. I'll see you with the others at the stables in an hour."

He looks at me then, his gaze so intense it's like he can see straight through the veil and right into my eyes. Without another word, he gives me one last simmering look and spins on his heel, marching after the other two.

Watching him leave, I prepare myself for the disapproving look I'm sure to see on Noah's face, but as I turn, I find he's not even looking at me, instead staring daggers at where Mason had been standing. Sighing, I stalk back to my rooms in silence, Noah following close behind me. Once inside, I walk straight over to my wardrobe, pull it open, and frown at the contents. Large dresses are out if we're going to be slaying a dragon, so trousers it is. I'm just gathering the clothing in my arms when Noah slams the door shut behind him. Surprised, I raise an eyebrow and turn to look at him. He looks livid. I've never seen him like this before.

"What's wrong with you?" I challenge, dumping the clothing on the bed and putting my hands on my hips. "I'm not exactly thrilled about the trip, but I'm not throwing furniture around."

"Why do you think I'm angry? I have to spend a week watching you and Muscles make out."

Tilting my head to one side, I ponder his words, and then a sick feeling hits me as I comprehend what he means. Is this because of my relationship with the king? Does he think I've betrayed Marcus? He was there when the king was beating me, so he must know how dysfunctional that relationship had become. However, he is the king's guard and is loyal to him. He's obviously not said anything to Marcus, otherwise that meeting would have gone very differently.

"Noah, if you're upset because I slept with someone other than the king, Marcus and I—"

Whipping a hand through the air, he cuts me off. "I don't give a fuck about the king. What I care about is that you're fucking one of *them*."

His anger is so fierce that I literally take a step back. It takes a lot to faze me, and if this were anyone other than Noah, I'd have them pinned against the wall and apologising in a second. But this is the only man in this castle that looks at me like I'm more than the monster I am—at least he did before the dignitaries arrived.

What I care about is that you're fucking one of them. The

words play over in my mind. This is all about his preju-dice towards Saren? I always thought Noah was open-minded and kind, so this seems really out of character for him. If he doesn't care about what the king would think, then why is he so worked up about this?

"I don't understand you. You went to them for help when Marcus beat me. You trusted them with my safety then, so why is this such a big deal for you?" I demand in my frustration.

"Because I'm in love with you!" he shouts, throwing his arms wide.

I gape at him in shock, unsure how to reply. I must not have heard him right. He's always been protective of me, but I thought that was because he was my friend. He's never said anything.

Looking him over now, I take in his sad, resigned expression, like he's waiting for rejection. My heart clutches painfully in my chest. I hate seeing him look at me like that, like he's waiting for me to hurt him. I slowly take a step forward, extending my hand towards him, and his face shifts, hope shining in his eyes. No, I can't give him hope, not like this, it's not fair. "I had no idea," I whisper, letting my hand drop to my side.

He visibly deflates, shaking his head. "You don't see people. The gorgon in you only sees humans as food or a threat." He's not accusing me, only explaining, but the hurt in his voice still stings. "It was only once *they* arrived that you started to see humans as people. I'd hoped that..." He trails off, shaking his head sadly, and his shoulders fall. "It doesn't matter now. I need to go pack. One of the others will be here to guard you while I'm gone."

He turns to go, and it feels like he's taking a piece of

my heart with him. Panic tears through me. I can't lose him. Even the thought of it makes me feel physically ill. "Noah, wait." He pauses but doesn't move to face me. "I see you, I always have. You're my friend. I trust you with things even the king doesn't know. Please, don't let this fracture our friendship."

Glancing over his shoulder, he pins me with a look of such sadness that my breath catches in my chest. "What if friendship isn't enough?"

Before I have the chance to reply, he leaves, shutting the door quietly behind him.

CHAPTER

I'm led to the stables by one of the older guards, and while he doesn't speak to me much, he does offer to carry my bags. Recently, I have noticed a change in how my protectors act around me, and I wonder if it has to do with what Noah said—that I've only started to recognise humans as people since Elias and the others arrived. Do I act differently around the guards now? Am I becoming soft? My gorgon hisses at the thought and wants me to bite the guard just to reinstate some fear. While at one point, I might have acted on my impulses, I find that I don't *want* to hurt him, he's just doing his job.

Unbelievable. I *am* going soft.

We step from the back of the castle and walk through the garden, the stable building appearing just ahead. I see everyone has already gathered outside and are strapping their bags to their horses. In addition to the three dignitaries and Noah, three other guards are joining us, all wearing armour with the Saren emblem.

My heart clenches painfully as I see Noah, remembering his last words to me earlier. *What if friendship isn't enough*? I barely slept last night, thanks to the hurricane of different thoughts and emotions plaguing me, and now I have this to contend with too. I'm starting to miss the days when I was oblivious to the humans. This is too hard. Feelings hurt.

All eyes land on me as I arrive, some welcoming and others cool and measured. I try not to take it to heart that Noah's response is the latter. Theo watches me with that playful, disconcerting smile, while Mason views me with an intensity that makes me quiver. Elias is standing with the gruff stable master, speaking in low tones as he, too, watches me closely. Taking a set of reins from the stable master, he walks over leading a beautiful white and grey mare. As they approach, the horse's ears flick towards me, her nostrils flaring as she senses the predator within me. Holding my hands out to show her I mean no harm, I lower my head in a sign of peace. Some of the waiting men begin to whisper, not understanding what I'm doing, but I ignore them. I don't have the time or patience to explain it to them. After a few moments of holding my position, my patience is rewarded, and a soft muzzle is pressed into my palm.

Smiling, I lift my head and coo as I stroke the side of her head, telling her how gorgeous she is. The mare huffs and presses closer, receiving a quiet laugh from me.

Elias is watching me like I just performed magic or did something impossible. "This is Rose, your horse for the journey," he explains, but he seems distracted as he watches me with a confused frown. "How did you do that? She was all jittery and jumpy before you arrived. We thought we'd have to get you a different horse."

Shrugging, I stroke her silver mane. "I like horses."

That was all the answer I was going to give, but there's still a question in his expression, and I'm not quite sure why, but I decide to elaborate. "I was raised on a farm when I was a girl before I was cursed," I admit quietly, my voice low enough for only him to hear.

His eyes widen slightly, and I notice how his gaze is locked on my lips as I speak. This continues for a few seconds, and he seems to realise that he's staring. He shakes himself from his stupor, and his expression returns to his usual serious mien that he takes on when he's around others—one I've started to think of as his lord look. When he's just with Theo, Mason, and me, he seems to be much more relaxed, but right now, he adopted this persona since he's around his men. I suppose that's needed from a leader, but I find it sad that he can't be himself all the time.

Clearing his throat, he glances over at the others before returning his attention to me. "It's going to take several days to get to the village. We're going to be riding hard and fast so we can get back here as quickly as possible." He seems more distant now, and I'm guessing it's because we're surrounded by his men. We have to maintain appearances, I suppose. "Get your bags sorted, and we'll leave when you're ready."

I just nod in response and take my bags from my protector, dropping them on the ground beside Rose. Waving the guard back, I ignore his relieved look at being dismissed and focus on the task at hand. I lift the bottom of the saddle, making sure the girth strap is tight enough, and begin lifting my bags. The heavy weight in my hand disappears at the same moment my gorgon hums happily in my chest. Biting back my sigh, I turn and glare up at

Mason who's currently affixing my travel bags to the saddle.

I place my hands on my hips and narrow my eyes behind my veil. "I am capable of doing that, you know."

"I know," he grumbles, not even bothering to look at me as he finishes my task.

Shaking my head, I wait for him to finish. If anyone else tried to pull this, I would have bitten them. Maybe I will still bite him anyway and remind him who he's dealing with. This excites my gorgon, but to my surprise, it's not because she wants to hurt him. Oh no. Images of exactly what she wants to do to him flash through my mind, and I'm glad for my veil as my cheeks heat. It takes a lot to make me blush.

Once he's finally done, he turns to face me and runs a critical eye over my attire. Grunting wordlessly, he reaches out and pulls my travel cloak closer around me, tightening the ties at my throat.

"What are you doing?" I bark out, stepping back in frustration. Does he think I'm not capable of tying my own cloak? Embarrassment and pride war within me, but he just follows me, adjusting the fabric around my shoulders. I'm about to bat him away when Theo walks over, cutting slices from an apple with his dagger, one of his brows quirked quizzically.

"You've bonded, right?" he asks, feeding my horse a slice of apple, his crystalline eyes flashing up to mine. "He's taking care of you. It doesn't happen often in humans, but I've seen a few bonded couples and this behaviour is normal for the first few weeks after bonding. Although between us, Mason's always been a big softie at heart."

Mason grumbles but doesn't dispute the comments. I

look between them, wide-eyed, as I try to work out if he's joking or not.

"Weeks?" My voice jumps up a few octaves, startling some of the horses. Rose pulls her attention from Theo and his apples to butt me gently with the side of her head. Absent-mindedly, I rub her nose as I think about how I'm going to manage the next few weeks with an overprotective Mason hovering over me. Hopefully, he can get it out of his system before we get back, because someone is bound to notice if he's following me around like an overgrown puppy. Theo's words play over in my mind, and something snags my attention. *Bonded*, my gorgon whispers, practically humming in my chest. Snapping my head around, I focus on the half-siren. "What do you mean, bonded?" My tone is dangerous, and anyone else would back away, afraid of my wrath. Theo, however, just grins and feeds himself a slice of apple, the crunch audible. I want to snarl and hiss, my patience fraying, but I manage to hold back until he finishes his mouthful.

Mason seems to realise that I need some space and steps back, glaring at his friend as he moves reluctantly over to his horse. Theo, on the other hand, laughs at the impatience pouring off me. Sliding his dagger back into its hilt at his waist, he throws the apple core to the ground, seemingly unbothered that he has a wound up gorgon breathing down his neck. "You fucked, right? Your gorgon claimed him?"

I look at him suspiciously. For a guy who kissed me only days ago, he looks remarkably fine with the fact that I just slept with his friend. I don't know how he knows. I assume Mason told him or he's worked it out from his friend's behaviour. Their guards are watching our interaction with wary, confused looks, so I know this isn't usual behaviour. He seems to know a lot about all of this, so perhaps he can help me, but for that I need to be honest. I can feel Noah's gaze on me and my stomach knots with guilt, but I know he can't overhear us, so I try to put him from my mind.

"And if she did?" I finally answer, my eyes automatically flicking over to Mason who's watching us.

"Then you've bonded." He grins, patting me on the shoulder, but something in his eyes shifts, like a spark of jealousy. It's gone in a moment, replaced by a look full of mischief, but I know what I saw. "It's an unbreakable bond and will stay with you for life. He'll be your most loyal protector."

Fuck. "Well, this complicates things," I mutter, talking to myself more than him. Panic makes me shift from one foot to the other, and I have to stop myself from backing away—something I never do for a human. However, my agitation isn't due to the fact that I'm bonded to a human forever, but because I'm *not* bothered by that fact. Or at least, not as much as I should be. What the fuck is happening to me? The more important question right now is, how the fuck am I going to hide this from Marcus, and how is he going to react when he inevitably finds out?

Theo laughs at my understatement and looks like he's about to say more when a whistle splits the air.

"Mount up!" Elias shouts, and everyone suddenly bursts into action. Theo winks at me and moves away. I have so many more questions and I know he's the person to ask, but they'll have to wait until later.

Mason is instantly at my side again, offering me a steadying hand to help me onto my horse. My instinct is to wave him away, but I see the strain in his features and I realise that he's already holding himself back, knowing how uncomfortable all this makes me. Gritting my teeth to restrain my hiss, I accept his hand and mount my horse. Settling into the saddle, I slide my feet in the stirrups and take hold of the reins, finally waving Mason away. He doesn't move immediately, watching me closely with a frown pulling at his brow. Instead of asking the question he so obviously wants to, he sighs and walks over to his steed.

Feeling eyes on me, I scan my new travelling companions. Most of them look away as soon as my head turns in their direction, but one person doesn't move—Noah. He's watching me like he doesn't recognise me anymore, and somehow, that hurts more than anything else that's happened between us so far.

The riders begin to shift their mounts into formation, and Noah finally looks away, allowing me to breathe once more as the tight band of guilt around my chest lessens. I gently tap Rose's side, and she starts to walk, the others falling into place around me. Two guards lead the way for our little procession, followed by Elias on his proud steed. Behind him, I ride in the middle, with Mason and Theo on either side of me, whilst Noah and the other guard bring up the rear.

We ride in silence as we make our way from the stables to the front of the castle. No one is waiting to see us off, and although the guards patrolling the castle watch us closely, none of them call out their farewells or well wishes. In fact, several openly glare at the procession of Saren guards, only flinching away when their gazes fall on me. It's quiet here, peaceful, but I know that will change once we enter the city proper.

Our city is built on a hill, with the castle situated at

the top. Upon immediately leaving the castle walls, it appears like you are still within them. The richest citizens live here in large, gated, mansion-like buildings, their gardens so vast and manicured that they rival the castle's for their beauty. Although there isn't a physical wall stopping any of the lower classes from entering this part of higher society, the guards who stand on street corners, turning anyone away, are enough of a deterrent. However, even without the guards, you can almost feel the boundaries shift as you cross from one part of the city to another. All of the houses here are large and well kept, the streets are clean, and fresh running water is readily available. As we make our way farther through the city, though, winding our way down, it's impossible not to notice the streets become more crowded as the buildings become more ramshackle and closer together.

After what feels like hours of travelling, but could only have been thirty minutes or so, we reach the marketplace. It's full of hustle and bustle, a mixture of people from all walks of life, but it acts as a barrier between the haves and the have-nots. Smells of spices from far-off lands mix with the pungent odour of the fishmongers' wares and stalls selling live animals for slaughter. Fabrics, weaponry, vegetables, you name it, if you need it, the market will find it for you—for a price, of course. We attract a lot of attention, and not necessarily in a good way. Pickpockets do well in stealing from passing travellers, but with one look at me, they baulk, and everyone clears a path for us to pass unbothered.

After leaving the market, we are once more back on the main road, heading towards the main gates. We enter the poorest part of the city. The smell of unwashed people, rotten food, and sewage makes my nose wrinkle.

I've visited here before, but I can never get used to this smell. I'd blame it on the fact that I've got more sensitive senses, thanks to my gorgon, but as I glance at my travelling party, I see them trying to hide their own expressions of disgust. This part of the city isn't even that bad compared to the buildings farther away from the main road. The poorest are moved away by the guards who patrol the street, hiding anything the king doesn't want seen. I've not ridden like this in decades and been able to see the city during daylight hours. The last time I travelled to the docks on the east side of the city, we took a carriage and the curtains were pulled for the entire journey. My little midnight jaunt to the docks the other night didn't show me how run-down this end of the city has become.

The streets fall silent as we make our way through, and even the noises of children and the cries of gulls seem to die down as all attention turns to us. Fearful, wide eyes watch us, but I get the impression their uneasiness isn't due to our presence. How has Marcus let the city become like this? I wondered how it was possible that children were being taken and experimented on without anyone raising an alarm. However, after seeing the conditions here and the number of emaciated, homeless children hiding in the alleys, I understand why no one would notice a few missing orphans.

We eventually reach the gates, ones I've not crossed in the almost two decades I've been here with Marcus. Although I'm annoyed at being sent off on this mission, I can't deny the flutter of building excitement at the thought of passing through those gates. I'm especially looking forward to leaving behind the uncomfortable feeling that seeped into me while passing through the lower half of the city. When I return, Marcus and I will be having a long chat.

When we pass through the city gates, I'm dismayed to see ramshackle buildings erected as far as the eye can see. I must make some noise of distress, as Mason looks over at me and grunts, shaking his head. "The slums. I've travelled most of this continent, and I've never seen anything like this."

Slums. Eyes wide, I stare in disbelief. Most of the buildings are made of wood and sheets precariously held together with rope. I lived in a cave for over twenty years, and even I had a better quality of life than this. How has this been allowed to happen? With every step we take through the slums, the ache in my chest increases. Many of our own citizens are living here, but it's also clear from the myriad of skin colourings that people from other nations are living here as well. When Marcus took over our smaller neighbouring kingdoms, he promised a better world, a better life for all involved. An open door policy for people to move to our city for a greater life with more possibilities. But they have all ended up out here in the slums with nothing to their name save for the clothes on their backs. Some of them don't even have that, wearing only tattered, torn scraps of material strung around their shoulders to keep the worst of the winter chill from their exposed skin.

Hungry stares go straight to the guards' pockets and then to the weapons at their sides, weighing up how much they want to risk to fill their empty bellies. However, no one bothers us once their eyes fall on me. It seems that the rumours of my power have reached all the way out here. I suppose that even starving is better than being turned to stone. Despite the urge to turn a blind eye and focus on the horizon, I refuse to do so. These people are marginalised, those who the king wishes to sweep under the carpet and pretend don't exist. I've lived here for decades and had no idea the slums existed. I've been cloistered and kept ignorant all this time. Before, I might not have been too bothered by this, but I've been awakened to the realities of what's happening, for better or worse, and I won't knowingly ignore it. They deserve more than that. So, as we slowly make our way through the ramshackle shelters, I meet the vacant gazes of the ones society forgot, and I make them a silent promise. I will remember them.

It breaks a piece of what's left of my shrivelled human heart.

Eventually, after what feels like a lifetime, we seem to reach the edge of the slums. The only shelters that still remain are built along the river, which winds off to the west, whilst the main road continues south. No one speaks, but the farther we travel from the city and the more the open countryside surrounds us, the dark tension that settled over us slowly lifts, and I feel like I can breathe once more. However, the quiet gives me plenty of time to think, and my mind mulls over the events of the last couple of days. I ponder my slowly declining relationship with Marcus, which I'm still not sure how I feel about, and my heated interaction with Mason and the fact that my gorgon seems to have claimed him—something he doesn't seem to be bothered about in the slightest. Even with him riding just out of reach at my side, I can feel my gorgon preening, wanting him closer. At the same time, I feel that constant pull towards Theo, and if I'm paying attention, to Elias as well. It's impossible for me to get too wrapped up in these thoughts, though, when I feel Noah's gaze on me from behind. In a move I'm hoping looks casual, I glance over my shoulder. He wears a slight frown, but before I can even begin to try and decipher it, Mason growls low in his throat.

Whipping my head around to scan for whatever threat has him on edge, I find him looking directly at me. Raising a brow he can't see, I take in his tightly clenched fists squeezing the reins of his horse and realise that he's jealous. Is it due to the fact that I looked at another man, or Noah specifically? Stifling a groan, I shake my head and look at the road ahead of us. This is going to be a long trip.

Glancing at Theo on my left, I notice he's trying not to smile, his eyes glittering with mischief. I suppose I might as well get more information from him about what I've gotten myself into, seeing as he seems to be knowledgeable on the subject.

Turning on my horse as much as I can without falling, I face the half-siren. "Can you tell me more about the bonding?" I'm aware that Mason can probably hear me, but I keep my voice low to avoid anyone else from overhearing. "You seem to know a lot about this."

His expression turns more contemplative, and an old sadness seems to settle over him. Slowly, he nods his head. "I knew a bonded set. I learned what I know from them and stories my mother told me."

Ah, his mother. That's where I'm picking up the sadness. My gut tells me that this is old grief, one that's familiar to him but hasn't faded with the passage of time. Now isn't the time for me to ask, but I'd like to know more about her, about the woman that brought Theo into the world. Instead, I focus on what he said, on terms I've never heard before, confusion making me frown. "A bonded set? What do you mean?"

Mason is watching us closely, but he stays silent as Theo takes a moment to put his thoughts together, all humour gone from his eyes.

"I was taught that the gods will occasionally bless someone. That person has a great purpose, but one that is so difficult they can't succeed without the support of others. The gods create the people who will support the blessed, and they are destined to be bonded. These people will help the blessed one with their task."

There's a moment of silence as I wait for him to finish his story, but as the silence extends, I realise he's done. He looks like he's bracing himself for backlash, and as I take in his words, I realise it's for good reason.

"And you think that *I'm* one of those blessed?" I ask incredulously.

He shrugs casually, but I can tell it's a front. He believes every word he just said. "Mason is bonded to you, that much is certain. Besides, you've already admitted that you feel drawn to me."

He can't be serious. He thinks that the gods have created several males to be mine? Not only that, but to help me with my divine purpose? I don't miss the fact that he's suggesting he could be one of those males. It's impossible. I'm one of the cursed, not the blessed. Who would ever consider being a gorgon as a blessing? To never look someone in the eye and have everyone fear me? I would give anything to be human again and for this unending anger and hunger to disappear. I could tell him all of this, I could open my heart up to these men who are supposedly destined to be mine, but do I really believe that? Can I get past the fact that I've been betrayed by love over and over again?

Locking the pain and hurt away, I focus on my disbelief and frustration instead, letting it fuel me. Turning in my saddle, I look at Mason. Is he just a puppet in all this? If the gods have decided that he's destined to be mine, then does he have any choice at all? I won't have relations with anyone who's unwilling, I don't care if the gods have decreed it. I've not cared what they thought since I was cursed and abandoned.

"How do you feel about all this? Do you have any say in it?" I challenge, but he doesn't rise to the bait, simply glancing at his friend before returning his attention to me.

"I think Theo's right."

Well, I wasn't expecting that. Exasperated, I gesture towards Theo. "So if I fucked him right now, you'd be fine with it?"

Mason seems to think on it, and I'm surprised to see no signs of jealousy cross his face. After a few moments, he shrugs. "If I can watch, then I have no problem with it."

His words send a rush of arousal through me, and I have to take a few seconds to clear my mind before I can think rationally again. My gorgon is all for the idea, flooding my mind with images of me tangled between the two men, my head tossed back in the throes of passion as they worship my body. Shaking my head, I clear my throat. "And him?" I ask, pointing at one of the guards at random. "Or if I fucked the king?"

I'm not prepared for how violently my gorgon reacts at the idea of fucking the stranger or her sudden reluctance to sleep with the king. I'm also taken aback as

Mason snarls, his horse shifting nervously beneath him. "No. *Mine*," he bites out, sounding much like my gorgon.

A thrill passes through me at his possessive claim. There is something about him saying it that's so different from when Marcus acts possessively, and it takes me a while to work out why. Marcus treats me like a possession, something he doesn't want to share with others, like a child hoarding their toy. Mason's claim, in contrast, ignites a spark within me. Sure, he doesn't want to share me, but he also doesn't want to own me.

Before I can reply, Elias calls out, and I realise that we're now well and truly into the countryside. With a gesture from him, we move our horses into a trot and then quickly speed up to a canter, leaving the city behind us and cutting off any further conversation.

CHAPTER

14

We ride hard for the rest of the day, so much so it's impossible to talk, so my mind just mulls over everything that was said. The sun is low in the sky, and there's one thing that I can't seem to shake from my mind. If Mason really is bonded to me, then what the hell are we going to do when they have to return to Saren? The king will never let me leave—he's got too tight of a grip on me, and the only way to release the spell that binds me to him is to kill him or for him to let me go—so Mason and the others will depart, and I'll have to stay.

My gorgon thrashes within me so fiercely that for a moment, she breaks through my barriers. I manage to pull her back at the last moment, throwing all of my reserves into keeping her locked within me, but it results in a physical reaction and I'm thrown from my horse by the force of the internal blow. I smash into the rough, rocky ground, and a grunt of pain escapes my lips as I roll from the momentum. Agony tears through me as I finally come to a stop, my right side burning where I first hit the ground, but it's the pain of fighting the shift that hurts the most. Injured like this, I'm going to struggle to control my monstrous side if she's released, and I can't risk her turning on anyone and killing them. Instead, I cry out and thrash on the ground, gritting my teeth as I hold her back. I hear the shouts and calls of alarm from the others, the sound of their running feet getting closer.

"Maya!" Mason skids to a stop in the gravel and kneels in front of me, his hands hovering over my body. He wants to help, but he doesn't know how. The best thing he could do right now is keep the others away from me and give me space, and subconsciously, he seems to know this, because he snarls at anyone who comes too close.

With my face pressed against the hard ground, I breathe through clenched teeth, trying to pull myself together, but my injuries have brought my gorgon closer to the surface. Being surrounded by all these humans isn't helping. Steeling myself, I take a deep breath and move so I'm on my side, facing them. I don't have the strength to sit just yet, all of my concentration on holding back the shift.

"What happened?" Elias barks, the command in his voice making me open my eyes. He's moving through the guards surrounding me, his frustration at the hold-up evident. When he sees me curled up on the ground, however, concern flashes across his face. He glances at Mason for permission to come closer, which the big man gives with a nod, and then he slowly approaches before kneeling by my side. Reaching out as if to touch my shoulder, he quickly stops as I flinch away. Frowning, he drops his hand to his lap. "You're injured, let me help you."

I want to tell him that I can't, that if he touches me, it will shatter my control. Only I can't, my jaw locked as my body spasms with pain. Thankfully, someone answers for me.

"She's fighting her gorgon, give her space," Noah calls out, and the guards step back to allow him through. As he stares down at me, I can see my own pain reflected in his eyes, and I don't know how I didn't see his true feelings for me before.

Elias looks up at the guard and seems to assess him for a moment, and after a tense silence, he nods and stands, stepping back. Moving over to his men, he speaks in a low voice and ushers them away from me, giving me the space I need.

Theo, Mason, and Noah stay with me, all several paces back to give me space. There's something about having Mason and Theo close that makes me feel stronger and helps settle my gorgon. After what seems like an age, I manage to push her back enough so I can sit upright. Blinding agony in my right shoulder has my vision flashing white. Hissing through clenched teeth, I grab my arm, noting the pain is a familiar one—dislocation. With one sharp movement, I snap it back into place, ignoring the mutterings of those watching. My left hand comes away bloody, so I look down and see my arm is torn up. I can feel throbbing in my hip and right leg too. I need to shift, but I can't, not while we're out in the open and as the sun is about to set. I'd be too vulnerable right after the shift, so we need to get to safety first.

"What can I do?" Mason's voice is tight, and I can see the strain he's experiencing from holding himself back.

My heart stutters inside my chest, and I know I have to give him something.

Releasing a long breath, I tilt my head up. "I'm fine, just help me back onto my horse." I could probably manage myself, and usually I would, whether I was able to or not. However, his relief at being able to do *something* to help tells me I've made the right decision.

Before he can move, though, Noah is stepping forward, frowning. "She needs to shift to heal these injuries." Admitting that I need help usually indicates it's bad, and Noah knows this.

I feel the shuffling of the other guards who anxiously turn their attention back to me at the mention of me shifting, but I quickly shake my head. "Not here, it's not safe." Noah and Mason are already shaking their heads, for once in agreement on something. Glancing around, I look for Elias, knowing he won't let his feelings get in the way of the group's safety. He's standing just beyond the others, watching on silently, and from his expression, I see he seems to understand.

Re-joining us, but being careful not to come too close, he runs an assessing gaze over me. "There's a place I was planning on stopping not far from here," he starts, crossing his arms over his chest. "It's about an hour by horse. Do you think you can make it?"

I don't answer him, simply standing and hobbling towards my horse. I can manage an hour. Gritting my teeth, I take a few painful steps towards my horse. Someone has taken care of her, and I see one of the guards feeding her a handful of oats as she watches me with solemn eyes.

"Maya—" Noah begins, but he stops when Mason instantly steps to my side. I should feel guilty at the expression on his face, but right now, I'm having to use all my energy just to stay upright and keep my monster at bay.

Wrapping his arm around my waist, Mason leads me over to my horse, letting me lean against him, even though I would usually brush off his attempts. Honestly, it takes the edge off the pain and having physical contact with him helps keep my gorgon at bay, not that I would ever admit this out loud.

"I want you to ride with me," Mason grumbles, and it's obvious that he's expecting me to put up a fight. He's right.

"I'm not riding with you."

"Will you shift then?" When I don't immediately answer him, he starts to growl low in his throat. I pin him with a glare. I know he can't see it, but he seems to be able to feel it and the sound slowly stops. His concern and frustration, however, don't. "Then I'm not leaving your fucking side."

I don't bother to fight him on this, knowing it would be pointless. Instead, I sigh and gesture for him to help me up onto Rose's back. As I put my foot in the stirrup and swing onto the horse, I'm glad for the veil as it hides my pained expression. Once I'm up, I wave him away. He grumbles something under his breath I don't catch before mounting his own horse. Everyone seems to release a breath at seeing me upright and still in human form, quickly getting on their horses and moving back into formation. Elias glances questioningly at me once, and I nod, grateful that he doesn't question me further and takes me at my word, calling out for us to continue once more.

THE JOURNEY IS AGONISING. Mason is true to his word, riding so close that our legs are almost brushing together. Even Theo has been riding nearer, his gaze often landing on me. The horses weren't particularly happy about being so close, but I think they could sense the need to keep moving. Cantering is almost too much for me, but I manage to cling on, using all of my energy to stay in the saddle.

When we finally arrive after what feels like an eternity, I practically fall from my horse. The only reason I don't end up sprawled across the dirt yet again is because Mason is at my side and catches me. One of the guards approaches and takes Rose and Mason's horse away, promising he'll take care of them. It's only then that I take in our surroundings.

We left the main road to pass through a split between the mountains. Had I been fully aware, I might have questioned Elias' decision. Leading ten horses through a narrow, rocky crevice is not what I'd call a smart idea. However, looking around us now, I can see why he did. We're in a small valley, one that's completely surrounded by rocky, mountainous walls. Within the bottom of the bowl-shaped valley is a grassy haven, complete with a small lake. Glancing up at the rapidly darkening sky, I can just about see the stars starting to shine down on us. A light breeze caresses my exposed skin, but the temperature here is far warmer than it had been on the main road, the valley protected from the worst of the elements.

The guards are busy setting up camp, and as I glance around, I see Theo and Elias talking in low voices to one side. Before I can even begin to wonder where Mason is, I feel his warmth at my back, my gorgon humming in my chest at his proximity as he places his hand on the small of my back.

"I need to make sure everyone knows who's doing guard duty tonight. Will you be okay?"

I turn and look up at him. Even with my veil covering my face, I'm sure he can sense my ire at the question. Is he serious? Will I be okay? I want to snort and bare my teeth at the insult, but surprisingly, my gorgon is preening. She *likes* that he's fussing. Had it been anyone else, she would want to bite their head off for implying that we're not capable of looking after ourselves.

"I'm sure I can survive without you for an hour or so," I drawl, my words dripping with sarcasm.

This doesn't seem to bother Mason. His lips quirk up into a smile as he leans down and places a kiss on my exposed lips. "You're going to bruise my ego," he whispers, and I have to fight my shudder of pleasure his kiss brings.

I shouldn't be so shaken by a kiss. It's not like I've never had one before, but he just publicly claimed me in front of everyone. Sure, he didn't announce it loudly, but we're being watched constantly. Not just by Noah, but the other guards as well. Not to mention that I don't know how Elias is going to react. He and Mason might be friends, but he's still the leader of this group.

With my lips still tingling, I step back, momentarily forgetting about my pain as my cheeks flare red. As if he knows the reaction he just caused, a smug smile pulls at his lips. Giving me one last lingering look, he turns and walks over to the guards who are unpacking supplies, clapping one of them on the back in greeting.

We're safe now. I should shift so I can begin to heal,

but I find myself reluctant to do so. Is it because I'm worried about what my gorgon will do once she's released? A little nagging voice in the back of my mind whispers that the true reason is because I don't want to show my monstrous side to Elias and the guys. Sure, they saw it before, during that awful night when Marcus attacked me, but things have changed since then. Mason, for one, but there's that constant pull to Theo and something I can't deny about Elias that makes me feel hopeful for the first time in decades. Noah's seen me as my gorgon many times over the years, but now that I know his true feelings for me, it feels strange to shift in front of him. I'm at my most vulnerable during the shift, consumed by pain, so it takes a lot of trust for me to do it in front of others. Either that or I'm forced to by the magic connecting me to Marcus.

My wounds throb, and I know I need to do something. Letting out a huff of frustration, I slowly limp over to Elias, who is perched on a large rock scanning a map.

"How did you know about this place?"

"We've travelled the continent far and wide on our hunts. There isn't much of it that we haven't seen." He stares at the map, only glancing at me as he finishes speaking.

Somehow, his answer wasn't what I was hoping for, but I'm not sure why I'm feeling disappointed. Am I fishing for conversation? How pathetic. I start to turn away, but he must sense my disappointment because he watches me closely and sighs, a rueful smile pulling at his lips.

"It was on one of my first hunts. It was when I was with a different team," he begins, his voice hypnotic as he tells his story. "I was hunting a dragon, thought that I knew better than the others and got separated from the rest of my group. Unfortunately, the dragon took a particular interest in me and chased me for miles. I was desperate and thought I was going to die when I found the entrance to this place. I slipped between the rocks and waited until the dragon lost interest. However, that took several days, so I went exploring for food and water and stumbled across this."

"Little Lord Elias made a mistake?" I mock, a smile pulling at my lips despite the pain and exhaustion pulling at my body.

"Oh, I've made plenty of mistakes in my past." Despite his smile, he looks haunted for a moment, and grief shines in his eyes. Seeming to realise that he's given too much away, he coughs and grins. All signs of his grief are gone so fast, I almost think I imagined it. "If you tell Mason or Theo I told you that, I'll deny it."

Shaking my head, I clutch my right arm with my left to ease the pain. An orange flash catches my attention, and I see that Theo has just gotten a fire started. Without even realising what I'm doing, I start moving towards the fire, craving its warmth. The soft sound of Elias chuckling follows me, but I don't bother to respond, simply crouching before the flickering flames. Theo glances over just in time to catch my grimace of pain, but he doesn't say anything, instead continuing to build the fire.

We stay like this for some time, and the warmth makes me drowsy, my eyes locked on the dancing flames.

"What set your gorgon off earlier?" Theo's question pulls me out of my stupor. Dragging my gaze from the fire, I look over at him. When I don't immediately answer, he tilts his head to one side, appraising me. "That was why you fell off your horse, right? She was trying to break free?"

He sees entirely too much and asks questions that are hard to answer. Perhaps others wouldn't find them so hard, but the answers he wants are personal, things that I've not even fully admitted to myself.

"Come on." He smiles softly, his musical voice lowering as he realises this is hard for me. "I won't tell anyone."

I think on it for a moment. I could make something up and tell him that she just pushes for dominance occasionally, which she does, but never so violently as today. Theo's part siren, so if anyone is going to understand the warring of my two natures, it would be him, but I'm sure he'd see straight through any attempt I made at lying.

Meeting his gaze through the veil, I see the sincerity in his eyes. Swallowing against the sudden lump in my throat, I look away and stare into the fire once more, not wanting to see his reaction as I admit the real reason for my fall. "It was due to the thought of you guys returning to Saren and leaving me behind."

There's a beat of silence, one that seems to stretch on for eternity. When he does finally speak, I wish I'd never said anything.

"Oh, Maya..."

My heart twists painfully. Not willing to listen to his pity, I force myself to stand, ignoring my discomfort, and make my way around the fire. His response tells me everything I need to know—he pities me. Rejected and insulted, I start to walk away, my heart hurting more than my physical wounds. I'm not sure what I was expecting. Declarations of undying love? Promises that they wouldn't leave me with Marcus? Just because Mason has bonded with me, it doesn't mean any of them owe me anything.

"I'm going for a wash. I need to get this grime off me," I call over my shoulder.

"Maya, can we speak about this—"

"No." Spinning around, I pointlessly glare at him through my veil. "Speaking isn't going to change the fact that I can never leave the king, whether you wanted me to or not." Bitterness makes my words harsh as I hug my injured arm closer to my body.

"Of course I—" He cuts himself off with a shake of his head. Releasing a long breath, he steps around the fire and walks to my side. "I'll come with you to the lake. I have something to show you."

I don't bother to tell him not to, as I know he'll follow me anyway. Our walk down is silent, my thoughts turning over and over in my mind. Reaching the lake, I see there are several large boulders that I can get undressed behind. Sinking down onto one of them, I hold back my sigh as my injuries throb. If I don't voluntarily change soon, it will be forced upon me once all of my energy is drained, and at the rate I'm going, that will be sooner rather than later.

Reaching up, I unfasten my cloak and shrug it off, hissing with pain as I work on undoing my riding jacket. I'm not shy about my body, and I don't really care that Theo's going to see me naked, nor that someone else could come by at any moment. In fact, Theo is watching me undress now, and he's making no effort to hide that he's watching me. Mostly, I believe it's out of concern and he's waiting to see if I need his help, but there's lust in his eyes that he's not trying to hide. He smiles when he catches me watching him, and he begins to undress, removing his jacket and shirt with swift movements. My breath catches in my throat at the smooth expanse of skin on the taut muscles of his chest. As his hand goes to the waistband of his trousers, I look away, busying myself with standing so I can undo my own riding trousers.

Should I feel guilty for looking at him like that and lusting after him when I'm bonded to Mason? I know most human relationships are monogamous, and Marcus would never share me with anyone, yet Theo was the one to tell me about the bonding and point out the pull between us. Mason had even given us permission, in a way, to fuck each other. Urgh, this is all so complicated.

Shaking my head, I focus on peeling away my clothing, hissing as I see the huge purple bruise that's appearing over my hip and down my right leg. After many curse words, I'm finally naked, save for my veil. Crossing the distance to the lake, I sit on the rocky edge and slide into the water, bracing myself for the chill. However, I'm pleasantly surprised by how mild it is. Submerged up to my waist, I move around slowly, finding that some parts of the water are much cooler than others. Frowning, I look around and find Theo already in the water, leaning back against the shore where he's watching me with a knowing smile.

"Is this you?" I ask, gesturing to the water.

His smile turns into a grin, and he shrugs like it's no big deal. I had no idea that Theo had any gifts other than his voice, but I find that I like this one very much. He watches me for a few moments more, his eyes flicking to my injured shoulder. His expression dims, becoming contemplative. "Maya, come here, I want to show you something."

I consider him for a moment. I'm alone and naked

with him in the water, so what could he possibly have to show me? Curious, I slowly move forward, thankful that the water takes some of the weight from my injured leg.

"Did you know that sirens have the ability to heal with water?"

I shake my head as I continue to move closer, stopping only several feet away from him. I know very little about sirens despite having known of one many years ago. Monsters tend to keep to themselves, it's safer that way. Being able to heal with water is not an ability I would have guessed though, not when they have such a bad reputation for luring people to their watery grave.

"Being only part siren, I'm not able to fully heal injuries because it takes too much of my energy," he continues, his eyes flicking up to my face. "But I can take away the pain and get the healing started." Cupping his hands together, he closes his eyes. For a moment, nothing happens, but then a faint vibration travels through the water, and my eyes widen as the water in his hands begins to glow. The water gives off an eerie blue light, bouncing off the water around us and lighting his face in the rapidly darkening valley.

"Give me your arm." His musical voice is strained, but I do as he asks, stretching it out, despite the discomfort the movement causes. Raising his cupped palms, he trickles some of the glowing water down my shoulder. Everywhere the water touches begins to tingle, and to my amazement, the pain starts to fade. Glancing at the wounds, I see they are half the size they were and look like they are days old rather than only having occurred several hours before.

I'm not sure what he can see with only half of my face visible, but it makes him chuckle. I twist my arm, experimenting, and I'm amazed to find only a twinge of pain. Laughing in disbelief, I shake my head. "Thank you." I hope he can hear how genuine I am. He took the worst of the injury away, which means that while I'll still need to shift later, I'll be able to control her much better. He's made my whole evening less fraught.

"I'm not done yet."

Reaching out, he takes my hand in his and pulls me closer until I'm pressed against him. This wouldn't necessarily be a problem, but with us both naked as the day we were born, I can feel every inch of his body, including his rapidly hardening cock. My chest becomes tight, and breathing becomes difficult as lust surges through me, my gorgon awakening once more. "Theo..." My voice trails off as I realise I have no idea what I want to say. Tell him to stop? No, I don't want that. Tell him to keep going? My mind is a muddled mess of hormones, and my body's reaction is so much stronger than anything I ever felt for the king.

I don't need to say anything, however, as he reaches out and presses a hand against my right hip. When he closes his eyes and the water heats around me, I realise what he's doing. Relief and disappointment war within me—relief that I don't have to make a decision whether or not to make him stop, and disappointment because the way my body is reacting to him is going to make for an uncomfortable night.

I watch his face as he continues to will the water to heal me. He looks peaceful like this, but there's definitely something about him that screams other. If I hadn't known he was part siren, I might have guessed he had some connection to the fae, perhaps the pixies. They haven't been seen in decades, but he's got the pointed chin, pale skin, and mischievous glint in his eyes that the fae possess. Opening his eyes, he smiles as he finds me watching him, but it quickly fades before a slight frown pulls at his brow. Before I can ask what's on his mind, he reaches up with his other hand and cups my face.

"Even before Mason bonded with you, we knew we had to get you away from the king. We knew there was so much more for you. Then, as we got to know you, we thought you could help us, and that's when we felt the connection." He's uncharacteristically solemn as he speaks, his eyes begging me to believe him. Everything he's saying is exactly what I want to hear, yet it's also terrifying.

"We would never leave you behind, Maya," he continues. "Not now, not ever."

My heart thuds so loudly, I'm sure he can hear it, and my throat tightens with emotion. Pushing my feelings aside before I can get carried away, I try to focus on the one thing that's going to put a stop to his plan. "But the king—"

Placing a finger on my lips, he cuts off my words as something hardens in his gaze. "Don't worry about him now, we'll find a way to free you."

Frowning, I push against his chest and pull back from his hold. "I don't need knights in shining armour to save me. I'm not a damsel in distress." The implication that I need saving rankles me, and despite my gorgon's relaxed state around Theo, even she hisses angrily in my mind.

"We know you can rescue yourself. You're powerful, strong, and clever, so you'll figure out a way."

The absolute surety in his words takes me aback for a moment. He fully believes what he's saying, he believes in *me*, perhaps more so than I ever have. While I don't need them to save me from my situation, I don't think I've ever believed that I would break away from Marcus. Until recently, I hadn't wanted to. However, hearing how much Theo believes in me makes me think that perhaps there *is* a way around the magic binding me to the king.

Theo reaches out once more, pulling me close until my chest is pressed against his. "What I'm trying to say," he begins, his voice sultry and musical, "is that you don't have to do it alone any longer."

I desperately want to believe him. In the short time that I've known the three Saren males, I've changed in ways I didn't know were possible, but trusting my heart again when it's let me down so thoroughly in the past is absolutely terrifying. My track record with men isn't exactly great.

Taking a deep breath, I scan his face for any signs of uncertainty. Before, I would have shut down to protect myself, but Theo makes me want to be honest, even if it makes me vulnerable. "Every man I've ever trusted has betrayed me." My admission is quiet, but I'm proud to say it's not weak, my voice staying strong.

Theo's quiet for a moment, acknowledging my past pain with a slow nod of his head. Reaching up, he runs his fingers through my hair. "You trust me, right?"

My chest feels tight as I swallow against the sudden lump in my throat. "I want to."

His eyes soften, and his hand moves to caress my cheek. "That's enough for now. I know we have to prove ourselves."

Leaning forward, he brushes his lips against mine in a kiss so gentle that I could almost convince myself it hadn't happened. Moving against me, he kisses me again, and a sense of rightness settles over me, like this was supposed to happen and I'm following a path previously laid out for me. That thought terrifies me, so I push it deep, deep down and focus on the here and now. I return his kiss, nipping his lower lip with my teeth. I smile into the kiss at the surprised noise he makes, one that quickly turns into a groan as I press myself harder against him. His slick, naked body ignites a fire within me, and my skin tingles wherever we touch. His hands slip down to my ass, holding me tight and kneading the muscle as I writhe against him.

I'm on fire, and I feel like I'm about to be consumed by my desire and only he can sate it. More, I need more. Moving my hand to his chest, I slide it down between our bodies until I find his cock, grasping it tightly. He throws back his head and groans. I begin to move my hand, experimenting with the tightness of my grip and enjoying the sounds of pleasure I'm wringing out of him. When he lifts his head, naked desire and pure need shine back at me, his siren side rising to the surface with his arousal. His pupils look different, almost slitted, his cheekbones seem more pronounced, and his blond, almost white hair glistens in the moonlight. He looks ethereal, magical, and oh so beautiful. Some might be put off by the changes in his appearance, but if anything, it just draws me to him all the more. He knows what it's like to be different, to be something others fear and don't understand.

He grins at me in a way I recognise—he's about to cause trouble. Before I can warn him not to try anything, I realise something is happening with the water. Frowning, I glance down, and my eyes widen as the water starts to pulse around me, focusing on my core. It pulses again and again, the rhythm pressing against my clit.

Now this is a use for water magic I've never thought of before. I can see that using his limited power is causing a strain on him, his eyes tight with concentration. Well, two can play at that game. Squeezing his cock once more, I begin to move my hand again, pumping his length in time to the vibrations of the water. Realising what I'm doing, he flashes me a grin and reaches up to palm my breast, rolling my nipple between his thumb and forefinger. My head falls back for a moment, each tweak of the sensitive bud sending a flash of white-hot desire straight to my core.

My gorgon pushes against my boundaries, humming at the pleasure coursing through me. She's not trying to take control, instead encouraging me to take what's mine. Theo. *Mine*, she hisses as my other hand caresses his shoulder. I should probably be more concerned about this, that I could bind another male to me and make an already impossible situation even worse. Although, in this moment, I don't care. All that matters is that I'm safe here with Theo and...

"Mason," I stammer out, guilt slamming into me. Out of breath, I try to push back to put some space between us. "We need to get Mason. I know he said before he would be okay with us—"

A low, familiar chuckle echoes around us, and I spin in the water, finding Mason leaning against one of the rocks with his arms crossed over his chest and a smile on his face. "As you can see, Maya, I'm already here, and I meant what I said." He glances briefly at Theo, nods at the male, and then returns his intense gaze to me. His eyes drop to my chest, where my breasts are just above the water, and a hungry expression crosses his face. "I believe Theo is right—he's destined to be bonded to you just like I am," he continues. "You should complete the bond."

I remember another part of what he said previously, that he didn't mind as long as he could watch, and from the expression on his face and the bulge in his pants, I'm guessing he meant that too. Something about knowing that he's going to watch and find his own pleasure in that only turns me on more.

The water ripples around me, telling me that Theo is moving closer, so I'm not surprised when his hand trails over my back and around to my front, pulling me back against him. My veil shifts, and for a moment, I panic that it's going to come loose, but I secure it in place. Theo slides his other hand around my body and cups my breast. With my back pressed against his chest like this, I can feel his erection against me, but he doesn't let me reach back, holding me in a way so I can't move. Sure, I know if I really needed to get away that I could, but being pinned against him like this, with my chest exposed to Mason, who's watching intently, is a major turn-on. The hand pinning my hip against him moves between my legs, finds my clit, and presses against it. All I can do is hold on. On the shore, Mason slides his hand past his waistband and grasps his own cock, stroking it to the same rhythm of Theo's hand between my legs. Although this is all below water level, what's happening is still pretty clear from our positions and my breathless gasps.

I can feel the pleasure building, and I know he wants me to come, but I just want his cock inside me. In a move too fast for human eyes, I break from Theo's hold and spin around, pushing him up against the bank. As soon as my eyes lock onto his startled smile, something takes over me.

"Mine," I hiss, sounding more like my gorgon.

This doesn't seem to put him off, however, as he reaches up to cup my face with both hands and rests his forehead against my veil-covered one. "Yes, yours."

That's all the confirmation I need. Gripping his shoulder with one hand, I wrap my legs around his waist and use my other hand to guide him to my entrance. With one slow movement, I impale myself on his cock. We groan in unison at the tightness, and the feeling of being filled completely satisfies my gorgon. Once he's fully inside me, I wait for a few seconds, allowing my body to become used to the feel of him. Our lips meet in a kiss, deep and passionate, but it soon turns frantic as I begin to move my hips. Tongue, teeth, lips, and hands are everywhere as we fuck in the lake, the sounds of our panting breaths and the occasional groan from Mason filling the air. I should probably worry that the others will overhear us, but I'm too far gone to care.

My pleasure continues to build, and it's not long before my orgasm hits me. Back bowed, I call out his name, my core squeezing down on his cock. With a strangled noise, he quickly follows after me, and I feel his dick pulsing as his cum fills me. Something snaps into place between the two of us—the bond. It shines within me, and the previous pull I felt towards Theo is intensified as a cosmic sense of rightness settles over us. Humming with pleasure, I continue to move against him, drawing out the last of our orgasms. Exhausted and happy, I cling to him, not quite ready for this to be over just yet. A noise from behind me catches my attention, and I glance over my shoulder to find a satisfied-looking Mason watching us. Seeing my attention on him, he begins to strip off his clothes before he climbs into the water. My mouth goes dry as I take him in, and my core clenches at the thought of fucking him too.

Wading over to us, Mason leans forward and presses a kiss against my lips. I try to deepen it, but he pulls back with a rueful expression. "While I'd like nothing more than to fuck you right now, you need to shift and then rest."

I open my mouth to argue, and he arches a brow at me. Closing my mouth with a small smile, I dip my head once in acknowledgement. I could easily disregard his order, and I'm sure with a few sultry moves, I could convince him to change his mind. However, he's right— I'm exhausted and need to shift. While Theo's water magic started the healing process and gave me more energy, and the newly formed connection with him has strengthened me, it's not enough.

Nodding his head as if he can sense my thoughts, he gestures towards the shore. "Go back to the camp with Theo, and I'll be along shortly."

With Theo's help, I untangle myself from him and leave the lake. Using my cloak to dry myself, I quickly shrug on the rest of my clothing, aware of their gazes on me. Straightening and brushing the dirt from my clothes, I glance at Theo and gesture for him to lead the way. He pulls me against him and kisses me deeply. It's only as he pulls away, as I see the reluctance on his face, when I realise that I've now got two overprotective, fussy men bonded to me.

I just have to hope that I have a chance to explain this to Noah before he figures it out for himself.

Chapter

I didn't. As soon as I returned to the camp, Noah
took one look at me with Theo hovering close
behind and instantly worked out what happened.
He stared at me like he didn't know who I was and left
the camp without a backward glance.

The rest of the night was awkward. It was obvious
that everyone had heard us from the sly glances thrown
our way. Thankfully for me, Elias had found a small cave
for me to make a nest in. It was tight, and I could barely
stretch out my arms without touching the sides, but I was
glad I had a place I could escape to. I'll shift in front of
everyone if I have to, but I don't want them looking at me
differently. It will only remind them of what and who I
am. I don't know when I started to care about what
strangers thought of me, but as soon as I made it back to
camp and Elias had offered to show me the cave, I
jumped at the chance.

Theo had followed me, but I shooed both men away
once I inspected the cave and then began making my nest

with the blankets someone had left by the door. When I did finally allow the shift to happen, it was far more painful than usual. I guess that was my punishment for holding it back for so long.

I spent most of the night jolting awake at every sound my sensitive gorgon hearing picked up. Despite not allowing them in the cave, I could sense that Theo and Mason were close by, that strange connection between us pulling at my chest. My gorgon wanted to go to them, but I still had enough control over her to hold her back.

I've been awake for a couple of hours now, the light of the morning sun shining through the entrance of the cave, but I'm content enough to stay curled up in my makeshift nest. I know I don't spend long enough in this form and that I only make it harder on myself. This journey is going to be long and hard, so I'm making the most of being in my gorgon form now.

"Do you think she's awake?" Elias' voice reaches me. He's speaking quietly, so as not to disturb me, but my supernatural ears pick it up anyway.

"I know she's awake," Mason replies. "I can feel her."

He can *feel* that I'm awake? That's...disturbing. Then again, if he's able to sense that, then that means I should be able to do the same. Closing my eyes, I reach out to the connections, surprised that I can actually *see* them within me. Not in the literal sense, but almost like golden strings, and I know if I followed them, they would lead me to my bonded. I caress the bonds, and my lips tug up at Mason's rumble that echoes through the cave.

"Maya, I can feel you. I'm coming in."

Suddenly nervous about him seeing me like this, I open my eyes and curl my long, muscular tail around myself. Why the hell I feel like that, I don't know. He's seen me like this before and he's bonded to me, so he'll need to get used to it if he's sticking around, yet everything is different than the last time he saw me as a gorgon. Brushing those thoughts aside, I roll my shoulders back and channel my monster's confidence. Reaching up to check that my veil is secure, I run my fingers along my snakes, smiling as they curl affectionately around my fingers.

Mason appears and slows to a stop, his eyes running over me. I get ready for his fear or disgust, but instead, I'm only met with warmth. Letting out a long breath, he shakes his head. "I forgot how beautiful you are in this form. So strong, so powerful." A seductive smile creeps across his lips, and he slowly moves towards me. "And all mine."

A cough comes from the entrance of the cave, and I know before he enters that it's Theo. "Ours," he calls cheekily as he strides past his friend and kneels before me. "All ours." He doesn't move any closer, and for a moment I wonder what he's doing. They don't usually act like this around me. Then I realise he's waiting for permission to touch me, which is very wise when I'm in this form.

"This is a wonderful nest," Mason praises quietly, gaining my attention.

Usually, being crowded like this would make me edgy and defensive, especially with anyone who entered my nest without permission. Only with these two, my gorgon *wants* them here and is practically preening at Mason's words.

"When all of this is figured out, we're going to find you somewhere cosy where you can make a huge nest, one that will fit all of us."

I can almost imagine it in my mind, but I'm not sure where his comment came from. How are these two suddenly gorgon experts? I'm not complaining, but Noah had to explain to them how I needed a nest... Noah, he must have told them how to treat me while I'm in this form.

Extending a hand, I caress Theo's cheek, my snakes all reaching forward for attention. I can't help my grin, exposing my elongated fangs. "They are attention whores, and they seem to have taken a liking to you. They won't leave you alone until you pet them."

Theo laughs, his eyes lighting up. Without a single ounce of fear, he holds out his hands, grinning as my snakes weave through his fingers and crawl up his arm. Mason clears his throat, and I move my attention to him. Pushing up on my tail, I climb from my nest and move before him. I can see he wants to do the same, to do more, to say more, but a figure moves at the entrance of the cave, and I know our time has run out.

Sighing, I gesture for the two of them to leave. "I need to shift. I'll join you outside in a moment."

They both pause, obviously not wanting to leave. Hissing with impatience, I remind them that I'm not Maya right now, but a gorgon. Mason pins me with one last intense look, and then he retreats from the cave, not turning his back on me. Finally alone, I close my eyes and attempt to coax my gorgon back so I can shift into my human form. It's harder than it should be, and I know that's because I've been waiting too long between shifts. Eventually, I manage to wrangle back full control and force the change, gritting my teeth against the agony as my tail splits in two and becomes human legs. Panting on the ground, weak from shifting, I run my hands over my legs. Smooth, unblemished skin greets my assessment, and I know my injuries from the fall have been healed.

Breathing a sigh of relief, I slowly climb to my feet, using the rocky wall to keep me steady. I'm still wearing my chest binding from last night, but my lower body is bare, and it takes me a few moments to stumble around and find my missing pieces of clothing. Finally dressed and feeling stronger, I take a deep breath and emerge from the cave. The bonds in my chest are thrumming, and I can sense both males nearby. Glancing around, I see them standing with Elias, who is obviously trying to say something to them, but both men are just staring at me. This strokes my ego a little, knowing that I can distract them so completely just by entering the same space as them. Holding back my smile, I take in the rest of the camp and see it's mostly been packed away and the horses are loaded and ready for us. My eyes catch on a figure who had been walking towards me, my horse's reins in his hands, but has now stopped—Noah. I can tell from his expression that he saw me watching the three dignitaries and that I didn't hide my feelings as well as I hoped I would.

Shoving Rose's reins into the hands of a passing guard, Noah spins on his heel and starts to walk away, each step agitated. Cursing under my breath, I stalk after him. I won't run, I refuse, but I *need* to talk to him and smooth things over between us. I don't feel right knowing that he's upset with me.

"Noah," I call, and I know he hears me when his back stiffens, but he walks on anyway, intent on ignoring me. "Wait, please, I need to talk to you."

He pauses then. It's not often that I ask for something with a please, and he knows that. He turns and looks at me, his face tight. I can feel everyone watching us, the busybodies, but I pay them no heed. Closing the space between us, I lower my voice. "Did you talk to Mason and Theo and explain how to treat me while I'm in my other form?"

If possible, he seems to stiffen even more before looking away for a second, and I get the impression he didn't want me to know that he was involved. "I didn't do it for you," he remarks, not sounding like himself. He's never been chatty or overly friendly, that's just who he is, but hearing this bitterness in him makes me sad, especially because it's my fault.

"They had questions, and I couldn't have it on my conscience if you turned one of them to stone because I didn't tell them what not to do while you're in your other form," he continues, his face hard.

Despite the fact that his words sting, I reach out and pull him in for a hug. We've never touched like this before, and he instantly stiffens against me. Contrary to what he said, although he might not have done it for me, he's shown some sort of acceptance of what's happening, even if he doesn't know it. He could have let his jealousy change him and kept quiet, letting my two bonded learn about my other form the hard way. Yet he didn't, he stayed true to who he is. Maybe I've not damaged him beyond repair after all.

"Thank you," I whisper. It's only then that he lets out a long breath as he relaxes into the hug, his arms coming around me. I'm not the type of person who gives hugs—you have to trust someone to be able to pull them this closely against your body and not worry about them trying to stab you. Maybe one time, long ago before I was cursed, I would have hugged freely before I learned about betrayal the hard way. I'm not quite sure what motivated me to pull Noah against me now. Perhaps it's the pain that he's trying to hide from me, or that despite it all, he still decided to help me.

We stay locked together like this for several heart-beats, and when we finally pull away from each other, he releases a long sigh.

"I lied," he admits, rubbing the back of his neck sheepishly. "I didn't tell them what I did to ease my conscience. I told them because I want you to be happy, even if it's not with me."

My heart gives a painful thud in my chest. "Noah—"

"Mount up!" Elias calls from across the camp. "We need to get out of here if we want to stay on track."

I watch Noah sadly, the moment between us shattered. He opens his mouth to say something, but his eyes flick over my shoulder for a second and he seems to change his mind. The bond in my chest tells me that Mason and Theo are approaching, but I keep my focus on Noah for a few moments more. My lips twitch into the semblance of a smile, and after a pause, he returns it. Nodding his head in farewell, he glances at the two males and repeats the gesture with them before making his way over to his own horse.

As I watch him walk away, my chest aches. I hate that he's hurting because of me. There's nothing I can do about it at this moment, not while we're on the road and surrounded by guards. Feeling the heavy presence of my two bonded, I turn and find them just behind me. They are both watching me with intense, alert expressions. I see my horse behind them, which they must have retrieved for me.

Mason reaches out, brushing his hand gently against my cheek. "Are you ready?"

Nodding, I walk to the side of my horse, which Mason is holding steady for me. Lifting my leg, I slide my foot into the stirrup and am just about to mount when a pair of hands lands on my waist. Usually, I would lash out at being touched without warning, but from the humming of my bond and gorgon, I know who it is. Glancing over my shoulder at Theo, I notice the lines of tension on his usually smiling face and the plea in his eyes to let him do this, to let him help me. Pushing back my pride, I grit my teeth and nod, allowing him to help me up into the saddle. Once I'm settled, I see him give me one last look before he strides over to his own horse, muttering something about a tight leash.

"Take it easy on him for a few days," Mason mutters quietly, stroking Rose's soft, velvety nose as he glances up at me. "I think the bond has awakened his siren's protective side. It will take some getting used to for someone like him."

The last part of his comment makes me frown. Just what does that mean? Theo may act like a cheeky male who isn't bothered by anything, but I'm beginning to realise he's a lot deeper than his exterior behaviour would suggest. He's not said as much, but I know that at least in part he considers himself a monster. He even plays along with it, showing his all too sharp teeth in a wide grin to disconcert others, but does it go deeper than that? I'm starting to think I don't know Theo all that well. Now isn't the time to ask these sorts of questions, though, so I keep them to myself and focus on my other bonded.

"You didn't seem to struggle so much," I point out, watching him as he takes his horse from a passing guard.

He chuckles as he mounts his horse, glancing over his shoulder with a pointed look. "I was already overprotective of you."

He has a point. Pondering everything I've learned this morning, I sit back in my saddle and wait as the rest of the guards mount up. That's when I notice it. Frowning, I look around again, sure that I'm mistaken. Alarm flares within me as I realise that I'm not.

"Elias," I call, leading Rose over to the leader, who is settling on his own horse. He must hear something in my voice as his head shoots up. Keeping my voice low so not to cause alarm around the others, I bring my horse up alongside his. "We're missing a guard."

Relief flashes across his face for a moment, quickly replaced by a small smile. "Yes, I sent him ahead with a message."

Taken aback, I raise a brow beneath my veil. "Who are you sending a message to? Ahead where?"

"I have to keep my king informed of our progress," he explains, glancing away as he reaches down to adjust his perfectly level stirrups. "We're travelling almost all the way to the Saren border, so I needed to let him know we were no longer with your king."

All of this makes sense. He was sent here on a diplomatic mission, after all, so he would have to inform his king of the change in plans, yet something about what he says doesn't sit right with me. He's hiding something.

Leaning back, I assess him with a critical eye. "What aren't you telling me?"

"Maya—" He cuts himself off, knowing that I'll hear through any lie that he tells me. Sighing, he shakes his head. "This is a dangerous road and things aren't going as planned with the king. I've requested more guards to join us on our return journey."

I sense the truth in his words. I'm not sure what they were expecting from Marcus when they came to our kingdom, but my king has not been particularly forthcoming. His secret experiments certainly haven't helped the situation either. Bringing more guards into the kingdom will only put Marcus on alert. However, considering everything that's happening, I can understand why Elias feels like he needs more guards.

Reaching out, I touch Elias' arm, not missing his startled expression at the casual touch. "Marcus will see that as a threat."

He lifts his gaze from my hand, scanning my veil as if searching for an answer. "That's why I'm hoping you'll help me convince him we're not."

No pressure then. Pulling back my arm, I rest my hands on the pommel of my saddle. If he's waiting for me to respond, then he'll be disappointed. There is no way I am promising anything at this point. Marcus is up to something nefarious, and I'm determined to find out what it is, but if Elias and his men are a threat to my people, then... When did I start thinking of them as my people? I've never cared about the citizens in the city, at least not until we rode through it and I saw the poverty they are living in. Not to mention the poor children who were experimented on and sent away to work as mindless slaves.

Sensing that our conversation has come to an end, he gives me one last look before whistling and moving his horse forward. Everyone seems to take this as a signal to fall into formation, and I soon have Theo and Mason on either side of me. Neither of them says anything, but I can tell they are curious about my conversation with Elias.

Nothing else can be said once our horses start cantering across the land. I have no idea what to do, but I can't help but notice the farther we get from my kingdom, the lighter the weight on my chest seems to be.

CHAPTER

16

I never knew how sore one's butt could get after riding a horse all day. We've been riding for hours now, and it turns out that after forty years of not riding a horse, I'm a little out of practice.

Elias whistles ahead, this one sounding different than the one he used this morning, and then he makes a gesture with his hand. Hope flares to life within me as the horses before us start to slow from a gallop to a walk. I would never vocalise that I needed to stop, my gorgon's pride wouldn't allow it, but I've never been so glad to get off a horse in my life.

Elias turns in his saddle and looks back at us. "We'll stop for a quick rest. Get some water and relieve yourselves, then we're back on the road. There's still another couple of hours to go until we can stop for the night."

I don't know how I manage to hold back my groan at the prospect of more hours on horseback. However, as Theo starts chuckling quietly at my side, I assume that

I'm not as good at hiding my dismay as I thought I was. Ignoring him, I glance around and spot the guards dismounting and leading their horses to a stream that's cutting through the rocky land. Today, we've passed through large, open stretches of land and fields with long grasses that came halfway up the horses' legs, but now we seem to be climbing up into a mountainous area again. I find myself glad for this, because although the fields and wildflowers were beautiful, they were also open, and for the first time in a long time, I felt vulnerable, scanning the grasses for any threats that could be hiding there.

"Fancy a dip in the stream?" Theo asks as our horses slow to a stop. His grin and the flare of arousal I feel from him through the bond tells me all I need to know—he's remembering last night.

"I think it's a little shallow," I reply, my lips turning up at the corners as I try to hide my amusement.

"Oh, you'd be amazed at what I can do with a little water."

I don't doubt it. Shaking my head, I can't hold back my quiet laugh. Mason dismounts and walks over to help me down from Rose's back, sending Theo a pointed look. No longer able to stifle my pride, I wave the man away with a shooing motion.

"I can dismount my horse by myself," I insist, trying to hold back some of the bite in my words.

Mason just raises his brows and holds up his hands in a *don't shoot* gesture, but he doesn't make any move to step back. Theo watches on, his expression tight as he tries to hold himself back. Rolling my eyes and muttering under my breath about being surrounded by overprotective males, I swing my leg over the saddle and dismount, only for my knees to buckle, much to my shame and dismay. I don't hit the ground, thanks to the large pair of hands that scoops me under my arms. Embarrassed, I shove out of his hold and hiss at him.

Anger flickers across his face, but it soon morphs into frustration. "It's okay to accept our help," Mason bites out, and I can tell he's trying to figure out how to say this without snapping, as we both know I wouldn't react well to that. "It doesn't make you weak, you know."

Theo steps forward, glancing between us. "He's right —we just want to help. Not because you need it, but because we want to be there for you."

"No, the bond is telling you to," I hiss, suddenly feeling overwhelmed by everything. Have I made a huge mistake? My gorgon is hissing at me in my mind, telling me to listen to my bonded, but my brain is whirling with so many thoughts, I can't think straight. "I need some space."

Striding past them, I ignore their protests and reaching hands and march towards a small cluster of trees just on the other side of the stream that backs up to a rocky hillside. Noah sees me, and he must have been watching us or he can tell by my body language that something is wrong, as he jumps from his horse and starts walking towards me.

"Maya, is everything—"

"Maya." Elias' authoritative voice cuts him off, slicing through the light, casual chatter that was going on around us. All eyes turn to me. "Where are you going? It's not safe to be by yourself here."

"I just need some peace. I won't be long," I grind out through my clenched jaw. "I'm a gorgon, I think I'll be fine."

There are other calls behind me, but I ignore them, leaping across the stream and disappearing past the tree-line. I can still hear them all from here, I've not gone far at all, but just having this space between us eases the tight band across my chest. I have no idea what I'm doing. I've gone from being magically tied to one man to being divinely bonded to another two, who just so happen to be trying to overthrow my king.

I walk for a couple of minutes, knowing I'll need to go back soon. Finding a large tree, I lean against it and slide down until I'm perched on the ground. Sighing, I reach up and undo the clasp that holds my veil in place, removing it and laying the soft, gauzy fabric on my lap. I know there's no risk of seeing anyone here, and I'll hear anyone approach long before they are close enough to be at risk of my stare. Rubbing my temples, I try to ease some of the tension there. I'm not a social being, and this forced proximity I'm having to suffer by being surrounded by so many males...well, it's taking its toll, and we've only been gone two days. I can't say I'm particularly looking forward to returning to the city, though, even if it is my home.

Home. No, the castle hasn't felt like home for a while now.

The snap of a branch behind me has me freezing, cocking my head, and listening intently. I jump to my feet, and my veil falls to the ground, but I don't bother to pick it up, not when my instincts are screaming at me that something is wrong. I slowly spin in a circle, taking in the woodlands around me. I can still hear my riding party on the other side of the stream, however, the woods have gone eerily silent. I see nothing. I'm sure it was probably just an animal stepping on a branch, but that doesn't explain why my body is tense and ready to fight.

My heart is beating like a drum. I can't see anything and I can't hear anything, but I know something is wrong.

"Maya?" Mason's call reaches me, and I can tell from that one word that he's concerned.

I don't want to call back, not yet. It feels like I'm being stalked, hunted, and I don't want to reveal my location, not yet. I also don't want to draw him right into potential danger.

"What's going on?" I can just make out Elias' voice over the noise of the others, but I'm barely paying attention because I'm so focused on trying to pinpoint whatever has my instincts so fired up.

"I don't know, I have this strange feeling that Maya is in danger."

Their voices are getting louder, closer, and I know they are trying to find me. I should warn them and tell them to stay away. Fear tightens my chest at the thought of them getting caught up in whatever is happening here. I need to tell them to turn around, to run. Stepping towards their voices, I'm abruptly stopped by a shattering pain splintering through my skull. My vision turns white with agony. In a split second, I'm in my gorgon form, my monster practically ripping from me in an effort to protect me. The pain of the shift is nothing compared to the pounding in my head or the throbbing *protect, protect, protect* circling around in my mind as my snakes hiss and writhe.

"Maya!" Mason shouts with genuine fear in his voice as he feels my pain through our connection.

I want to shout out and tell him where I am, but a

strange, blurred figure leaps towards me. The moment they move, whatever spell that's been hiding them is broken and I can see them. His face is twisted with disgust as he swings a bat towards me, although it soon turns to horror as he realises whatever protection he had over him has failed. My eyes glow, my snakes flare around me, and within a heartbeat, he's stone.

Cursing fills the air, and I realise he's not alone. Why didn't I hear them getting so close? They could have been following me for hours and I wouldn't have known it, unable to see, hear, or scent them. Now I know they are there and what to look for. Magic is strange, and illusionary magic often relies on the recipient not knowing that it's being used in the first place. Now that I know they blend in with the trees, I can see fuzzy human outlines, and as soon as they move, the illusion is broken.

Several figures jump at me in unison, and my snakes hiss and flare around me in fury that someone would dare attack us. My skull pounds as my gorgon genes try to heal my injury, but I can feel blood dripping down onto my shoulder, so I know this isn't good. I hiss and glare at each male—four of them that I can see—trying to capture them with my eyes. However, they dodge and duck around me, working together to stop me from using my biggest asset. I try to capture one in my gaze, and I'm suddenly attacked from behind. I spin and try to make them fall to my stare, only to be attacked from a different angle once more. My back screams out in pain from each whack of their bats, my ribs breaking beneath the blows.

This stops now. I may not be able to use my hypnotic gaze, but my entire body is a weapon. Raising myself up on my tail, I twist my torso, extend my long, poisoned talons, and slash at anyone close enough. From the cries of pain, I know I've hit my mark. A vicious smile pulls at my lips, and my fangs extend down over my lower lip. My head is still throbbing, and I know I need to end this soon, because my top is soaked with my blood.

"Maya!" Mason's frantic voice, so much closer now, distracts me. Jerking my head in the direction of his voice, I look around for my bonded, only my attackers use my distraction to their advantage. Another blow to the back of my head sends me careening forward, and my vision turns dark as unconsciousness claims me. The last thing I hear is Theo screaming my name.

GROANING, I roll over in my bed, my head pounding. I must have drunk too much mead at dinner last night. It takes a lot to get a gorgon drunk, and I've not felt this awful in years, so it must have been some party. I don't even have any memories of what happened, and why is my bed so hard?

"I think the monster bitch is waking up."

The harsh, accented voice makes me freeze. I've heard it before, but I can't think where... Then it hits me. I'm not in my bed in the castle. I'd been travelling with Elias and the others to hunt down a dragon on behalf of the king. We'd been on the road for a couple of days, and I was attacked. The man whose voice I recognised was one of the men who attacked me.

I peel my eyes open and feel my heart drop to my stomach. I'm in a cage, and a sheet has been thrown over the top of it, blocking my view. I must have shifted back into my human form at some point, as I can see my legs sticking out from under a grubby sheet that's been thrown over me. The bottom and top of the cage is made of thick wood, and metal bars surround me. In human form, I can only just straighten my legs diagonally, and as I sit up, I notice that my head almost brushes the top of the cage. How they managed to fit me in here in my gorgon form, I have no idea.

I feel weak, every part of my body hurts, and as I shift around in the small space, a chinking noise catches my attention. Glancing down at my wrists, I see an intricate pair of cuffs. Why use something so fancy? Unless... I've seen magical cuffs that look like this before, and I feel a little nauseous as I contemplate what that could mean if it's true. Reaching inside for my gorgon, needing her strength, I gasp as I realise I can't feel her or my bonds to Theo or Mason. I was right—the cuffs must nullify my gorgon. I always thought I'd be glad to see my monster gone, but now, in this situation, I need her strength, not just physically but emotionally too. She helps me face situations like this without allowing fear to cloud my judgement.

Taking a deep breath, I close my eyes and make myself focus. I can do this. I can survive this. Pushing away all distracting thoughts, I mull over what I know. Knowledge is power, after all. I know that at least five accented men tracked me with magic and attacked me, and at least one of those men is now dead, turned to stone. I also know that they have managed to capture me and block my connection to my gorgon and bonded. I'm in a cage, which, judging from the way my body rocks from side to side, is moving, so they are taking me somewhere. Now I just need to work out the rest of it.

A loud clanging on the bars has my eyes shooting

open, and I hiss as I look around for the source of the noise.

"Wake the fuck up, freak." Cruelty and amusement lace the man's voice, and I realise he's the same male who spoke before. Peering through the sheet that's covering my cage, I can just make out his form. He's shorter than the men from my kingdom, but broader and more muscular. From the way he leers down at me, I'm guessing that whatever is covering my cage allows them to see in without me being able to see out. The fact that he's also staring me straight in the eye tells me that this fabric protects them from my stare. What is this strange magic they seem to possess? I know of no local kingdoms that possess magic such as this, not even Saren, so they have to be from beyond that on a continent we've yet to explore.

"Don't antagonise her. You saw what she did to Romari," an older, more authoritative voice calls out. Squinting, I follow the first man's narrowed gaze to another man who walks ahead of us. He has the same build and accent as the other man, but his skin is pale, whereas the other male's is dark. Grey peppers his sandy hair and neat beard.

The first man scoffs, staring daggers at the apparent leader's back. "She's locked up and her eyes can't reach me through this. Plus those cuffs will keep her down."

"I said don't antagonise her. Stand down, Mika."

The first man, Mika, grumbles under his breath, muttering some expletives about the other man who is obviously in charge. It seems that Mika isn't happy with his leader. Perhaps that's something I can use to my advantage. I can't see the other men, they must be farther away, but I do know one thing—each and every man here will pay for taking me from my bonded.

We travel for several hours, and the farther we go, the more I ache for Mason and Theo. Not being able to sense them feels like a part of me has been left behind. I have no idea if they are okay, and my chest literally hurts with each mile that's put between us. During our journey, I have nothing else to do but sit under my sheet and think about what I'm leaving behind. It's not just my bonded that I ache for, but Noah too. Since his confession, I've started to imagine the two of us together, playing over every interaction we had in the past and wondering if I led him on. I've only started to feel human emotions again since the Saren dignitaries arrived, and slowly, my feelings for him have been put into question. I certainly don't feel a pull towards him like I did with Mason and Theo, or even Elias, but there's *something* there that I can't ignore. Not that I'll have a chance to now. Nor will I ever get to explore the pull I feel towards Elias, not unless I can get out of this.

The sun is beginning to set when we finally stop for the night. The strangers set up a fire and mill around, getting ready for the evening. I stay silent, watching what I can through the covering over the cage. There are more of them now, nine in total, but I don't know if they just joined us or if they were out of sight the whole journey here. They are not a talkative bunch, so I've not been able to learn much, but what I have discovered is that the male in charge is called Joha. Most of them keep to themselves, ignoring me other than giving me an occasional sneering glance. It's Mika who I need to keep my eye on. I've caught him leering at me several times, reminding me that below the dirty sheet covering me, my lower half is exposed.

One of the men starts cooking whatever he was able to catch in the woods, but it makes my stomach rumble. It serves as a reminder that I've had nothing to eat or drink since this morning. Swallowing against my dry throat, I try to ignore my thirst. My most pressing concern now is that I'm no longer bleeding. I won't ask for water though, my pride won't allow it and I would rather die. It won't come to that, however. If they wanted me dead, they would have already killed me. Capturing and transporting a gorgon isn't easy, so they have taken me alive for a reason.

The crunch of footsteps in the undergrowth has me looking up, and I see Joha, their leader, walking towards me. Realising that he's coming right up to the cage, I back up as far as I can, letting out a hiss of warning. He ignores it, lifts the sheet, and throws something through the bars. I catch it instinctively and realise it's a water skin. Unable to hold myself back, I rip off the top and gorge myself like a gluttonous dragon. If I were smart, I would keep some back, but in this moment, I don't care about the future, only that I need water, and I need it now.

"You'll make yourself sick if you continue like that."

He's right, and I hate him for it. Hissing half-heartedly, I reluctantly put the top back on the skin, but I don't let go of it, afraid he'll try to take it from me. He can try if he wants to lose an arm.

"Are your talons poisoned? Is there a cure?"

Frowning, I turn my full attention to him, finding him sitting on a tree stump not far from me. Mulling over his words, I remember lashing out with my nails when they took me. He looks tired, but he doesn't look like he's suffering from my poison. Sensing my assessment, he gestures with his head, so I follow the movement and see one of the males slumped against a tree trunk, his breathing laboured and a sickly sheen coating his skin. I feel absolutely no regrets about it, and perhaps that makes me the monster that everyone thinks I am, but they hurt me and are taking me away from my bonded, from my friends. I won't feel guilty for defending myself.

Scoffing, I look away from the dying man and back to Joha. "Why would I help you?"

He scoffs and leans back with a calculating gleam in his eyes as he continues to study his companion. "Personally, I don't care if he lives or dies, but he's my boss' relative. It'll be a major pain in my ass if he dies."

His callous reply only confirms what I already know —these guys are bad news and there's no point in trying to call to their better natures. They don't have them.

"I'm *so* sorry, but I can't help you." My words practically ooze sarcasm. It doesn't have the reaction I was expecting, however. Anger, frustration, and insults would be a usual reaction, but instead, he chuckles and shakes his head as if I just told him something amusing. Who the hell are these people?

It's time to get some answers, and he seems to be in a talkative mood. Swallowing back my hatred, I force my voice to be steady. "Why am I here? Where are you taking me?"

He finally looks back at me, shrugging his shoulders casually. "We were hired. It's nothing personal."

My false calm snaps, and I hiss as I crawl forward, almost pressing against the bars as I twist and show him my back through my ripped clothing, now purple and black with bruising thanks to the beating they gave when they captured me—not to mention the blood that's dried to my face and shoulder from my head wound. "It seems pretty personal to me. Let. Me. Go."

"I can't do that."

I didn't expect him to just jump up and free me, but frustration makes me grit my teeth. Time to try a different tactic. "How did you get me away from my group?"

He smiles, looking pleased with himself. "We have some tricks up our sleeves. How do you think we tracked you?"

"Magic." It's more of a curse than an answer, but he nods his head anyway.

He opens his mouth to say something else when a shout goes up. Frowning, Joha jumps to his feet and strides forward, his hand instantly going to a huge dagger I didn't see before. I move back in my cage, prepared to fight my way out if whatever's caused the alarm is a threat to me. Not that I'll be able to, not in human form with my hands bound and with my current injuries. Pushing the negative thoughts aside, I squint and stare through the sheet, desperate to see what's caught their attention.

"What is it?" Joha barks, becoming menacing in a way I'd not seen until now. Seeing how the others react to him, jumping to attention as he strides forward, makes me think I've underestimated him.

"We caught someone following us," an unfamiliar voice calls out. "Seems the monster whore has an admirer."

I stop hearing everything else as two burly men enter the makeshift camp, dragging a beaten and bruised body between them. I know who it is before my eyes even have the chance to fully lock onto him. My heart stops in my chest, and for a moment, I swear I feel my gorgon raging within her prison. The feeling is gone again the moment the beaten male lifts his head, and I can't hold back my choked cry of dismay.

Noah.

CHAPTER

Noah. They have Noah.

Why had I assumed he wouldn't follow me? Of course he would, the stubborn idiot. As soon as he realised I was gone, he was probably tracking me. Does that mean the others are with him too, or did they let him come alone? My stomach twists at the thought that they'd just leave me, but I don't have time to feel sorry for myself or mope. My escape plan has just become so much harder, as there is no way I can leave him here, not after he's come to find me.

"Well, well. What do we have here?" Joha asks with a raised brow, his lips quirking up into a smile as he crosses his arms over his chest.

"Looks like someone fancies himself as a hero who's come to rescue the damsel in distress." Mika flutters his eyes mockingly, pressing his hands to his chest. Sneering, he strides forward and grabs Noah's chin roughly. "You need to get your eyes checked. She's no damsel, she's a fucking monster," he taunts, putting his face right up against Noah's. I know he's trying to intimidate him, but it takes a lot to shake Noah. He's been the close protector of the king's blade for years, a job that even hardened soldiers quake at.

True to form, Noah just sneers at Mika. "If you lay so much as a finger on her, I will tear you limb from limb."

The group of strangers laughs loudly—at least they do until Noah spits in the other male's face. Rearing back in disgust, Mika wipes at his face, looking down at his hand as if he can't quite believe what happened. With a roar of anger, he lashes out, backhanding my friend. If he hadn't been held up by the guards, I know this blow would have sent him stumbling back.

"Mika," Joha calls out in warning, and the brute reluctantly steps back under his leader's unspoken order, his hands clenching and unclenching at his sides. Shaking his head, Joha looks Noah over with an appraising gaze. "It seems we've got a snack to feed our guest." With a jerk of his head, he gestures towards me, and the two males holding Noah drag him over.

I can't quite believe they are letting him inside my cage. Are they not worried that we'll try to escape? The cuffs on my wrists clink, reminding me that I'm about as effective as a human without my gorgon. They must hold a lot of faith in the magic imbued in the cuffs, otherwise they wouldn't risk keeping us together. Either that, or they genuinely think that I'm going to eat him. I'm not about to tell them otherwise.

The cage opens, and I immediately receive a blow to my shoulder as one of the males kicks me, throwing me back against the bars. Hissing in pain, I go to glare at them but realise I can't risk using my gaze, not with Noah being shoved into the cage. Turning my head away, I clutch the bars and press myself as far away from the exit as possible. Shuffling and cursing ensue as another body is shoved into the tight cage. I'm desperate to look, but I hold myself as still as the statues my gaze creates.

The loud clanging of the metal door makes me wince, but I stay still as I listen to the sound of the males walking away and the low conversation Joha is having with his men.

"Maya?" Noah's voice is uncertain, and I feel his hesitation in his touch as his hand lands on my shoulder.

Squeezing my eyes shut against the emotions that suddenly flood me, I take a deep, ragged breath. Feeling for the sheet covering my lower half, I rip a strip off to cover my eyes, which is far more difficult than I thought it would be without my sight and with the cuffs hindering my movements. As soon as my eyes are covered, I let out a sigh of relief, even if I've effectively blinded myself. Turning, I reach for Noah, patting the air until his hand finds mine. Our fingers lock together, and for a moment, I allow myself to feel comforted by his presence. That soon ends, though, as my anger takes over.

"What the hell did you think you were doing coming here by yourself?" I hiss, yanking my hand from his and trying to keep my voice low so we're not overheard, but it's a difficult task. I'm exasperated that he would risk himself like this. I don't know what I'd do if he died, especially if it were because of me.

"I couldn't let them take you." He makes it sound like it was such an easy decision.

"So you followed me and got caught? Congratulations," I rage, choking out a laugh. "Was this all part of your big plan?"

His sudden silence stops me dead. This was all part of his plan. He got caught because he knew he would be brought to me. "You got yourself caught on purpose?" I hiss quietly so no one else can overhear us. Does this mean that the others are coming? That they haven't abandoned me? I don't speak my suspicions in case someone is listening in, but if it's not true, it might hurt worse than all of my physical injuries combined.

"I needed to know you were okay." His hand touches mine, and I wish I could look at him and see the expression on his face.

Heavy footsteps march towards us, and I'm pretty sure I know who it is before they even start speaking.

"This is no fun," Mika drawls, confirming my suspicions that it was him watching us. I turn my head, and even though my eyes are covered, I glare at him with a look that makes grown men shudder. Even Noah shuffles awkwardly beside me. However, Mika is either stupid or he just doesn't give a shit, because he chuckles low in his throat. "Perhaps the monster needs her meal tenderised a little more."

"Don't you dare touch him," I threaten, thrashing around as the cage door is opened and Noah's warm body suddenly disappears. "No!" I shout, surging forward and trying to get through the open cage door, only to be thrown back as the door clangs shut. My heart plummets, and I rip my makeshift blindfold off, finding Noah being dragged across the camp.

Noah grunts and tries to keep his feet under him, but they move too fast, and he ends up being partially dragged along the dirt. Someone throws the sheet back over the cage, and I shuffle to the front, grabbing the bars tightly as if I could rip them apart with my bare hands.

The two grunts who found him stroll over, each grabbing him by a shoulder and hauling him upright. Mika glances over at me, his face twisted into a cruel grin.

I know what's about to happen, but it doesn't prepare me for it. Mika twists around and throws a punch into Noah's gut. Grunting with pain, my friend and protector bows over with the force, only to be dragged upright again as Mika hits him over and over.

"Stop," I demand. "Stop this. Stop it now!" I scream, my voice breaking. I swear the ground feels like it's shaking beneath me, but that's probably just my rage making my limbs quake. Some of the watching males curse and look around with furrowed brows, but I'm too busy staring at Noah to notice.

"Mika..." Joha calls, a note of warning in his voice, but he doesn't do anything to stop him, just watches with a frown.

Noah is now sagging between the males, and they let go of him in disgust, his body falling to the ground like a crumpled piece of paper. He groans, the noise full of pain, but as he raises his head, he looks straight at me and mouths one word.

Sorry.

No. Sorry means he's giving up. Sorry means that he can't hold on any longer. Sorry means he thinks he's dying.

Something seems to snap inside me, and it's only as all of the strangers turn and look at me that I realise I'm screaming. A crack sounds from somewhere deep in the ground beneath us as I realise it's not me who's shaking, but the very earth we stand on, and I have something to do with it. I should stop whatever this is, but I don't. I need to help him. I'm no hero, but if Noah dies, I will tear a path through this land, tracking down and killing every last person who had anything to do with his death.

The amulet around my neck becomes hot, and a green light emits from it. All at once, I feel a rush of power and fury as my gorgon awakens within me. Searing heat flares around my wrists, so I look down and see the cuffs glowing red. The burning metal hurts, and the skin beneath turns red and blisters, but I don't care. Borrowing the strength of my monster, I rip the cuffs off, ignoring the pain the action causes, then I grip the bars of the cage and heave, pulling the metal apart until the gap is big enough for me to step through.

Shouts rise up as they realise what I'm doing, and several of the males rush towards me with their swords drawn. I don't have the energy to shift forms again, but I have my gorgon's strength and speed, not to mention my greatest weapon—my eyes. Spinning, I turn to face my first attacker with a hiss, and despite himself, he meets my gaze, instantly turning to stone. Sensing an attack from behind, I duck in a move too fast for humans to follow, feeling the air move as a sword swings above me where my head had been only moments before.

For the first time in a long time, I listen to my monster, to my instincts, and work my way through my attackers. It's going to be tough fighting this many at once, but I know I have to if I want to save Noah. Cursing goes up from the other side of the camp, and the sound of swords clanging reaches me. I glance over, and my heart soars as I see Elias, Mason, and Theo entering the clearing, fighting the other males who took me.

They came. They came for me. My bonds glow in my chest as Theo and Mason come into view, our connection no longer disrupted now that the cuffs have been removed. The two of them work together in sync, as if they are of one body, their weapons flashing in the firelight. Mason lets out a war cry as he decapitates one of the strangers. His weapons fall to his sides, and his gaze locks on me. I quickly avert my eyes—now would not be a good time for my deadly stare. I watch him walk towards me as if in slow motion. Battle rages around us, but right now, my bond is pulling taut and I know he needs me. Staying completely still, I watch from the corner of my eye as he stops in front of me before he raises a bloody hand and pulls me against his chest.

"Maya," he whispers into my hair, and my heart nearly breaks at the emotion I hear in that one word. "I thought you might need this." He presses something soft into my hand, and although I'm not ready to pull away from his embrace yet, I glance down and see it's my veil. He must have found it. Reluctantly, I back away and lift the veil to my face, fastening it firmly beneath my hair. Finally able to look up at him freely, I run my eyes over his face, looking for any signs of injury.

It's clear that he's doing the same, snarling as he sees the dried blood down my neck. "I'm going to kill those bastards."

"Some help here would be nice," Theo calls out. He's helping my injured friend to his feet. I can sense how much Theo wanted to rush over to me, but he also knew that I would be worried about Noah, so he made that his first priority after he knew I was safe. I appreciate the action more than I could possibly put into words, but I know he'll be able to feel it through the bond. Stepping back from Mason's embrace, I ignore his disgruntled grumble and hurry over to Theo and Noah.

Noah can barely stand. His knees give way, and the

only reason he doesn't slump to the ground is because Theo's holding him up. I brush my fingers across Noah's cheek, lifting his head as gently as I can. I hiss through my teeth as he winces and I see the full effect of the beating he just took. He's bleeding from a cut above his eye, his jaw is bruised, and his lips are swollen and split, and those are only the injuries I can see. Something stirs within my gut, something angry and full of wrath. Fighting continues around us, but that's probably a good thing, as I need to let this rage out of me and I can't risk it being directed at one of my party.

"Look after him," I bark at Theo, and before anyone can stop me, I dart forward, take one of his blades, then spin away and enter the fray. I hear Mason curse, but he doesn't get in my way, instead following behind me and protecting my back as I duck, slash, and bite. I don't use my eyes now that my guys are here, not willing to risk it, but there's something satisfying about doing it this way. I lose all track of time, only knowing the feeling of Mason at my back and my blade in my hand.

When the last of the strangers falls dead at my feet, I look around for the next foe, my breathing ragged and body covered in the blood of my enemies—only there's no one left.

"I told you she didn't need rescuing."

I turn at Elias' voice, raising a brow as he wipes his bloody sword on the tunic of one of the fallen assailants. Sheathing his blade, he finally looks up and pins me with his intense gaze. "Maya can save herself."

"She's one of us now," Mason grumbles, stepping up beside me and crossing his arms over his chest. "We have her back, even when she doesn't need us to." I can't decide if he's saying this for my benefit or if he's making a point, and from the way he's staring at Elias, I'd say it was the latter.

Theo laughs, the musical sound lifting my spirits. "It's been a while since we've been able to fight anyone anyway."

I look between the three of them, and the repressed emotions from the day finally hit me. This time, when my hands quake, it's not because the ground is shaking. "You came."

Those two words hold more emotion than I've expressed in a long time, and it seems to take Elias by surprise, cracking his hard leader exterior. "Of course we did. I merely said we didn't need to rescue you, not that we wouldn't come for you."

Mason slides a hand down the length of my arm, and I slowly turn to look up at him. "I would cross the world to find you, Maya." His words are quiet, not to stop anyone from overhearing, but because of the emotion held there. One of the guards hurries over and passes him a length of fabric, which he wraps around my hips, reminding me I'm naked from the waist down—not that I really care right now, too worried about Noah to be bothered.

Elias chuckles low in his throat as he strides over. "I thought he was going to kill me when I said he couldn't just go running into the woods after you, that we had to plan." The lord grins at his friend who just huffs in resigned amusement.

"I nearly did kill you," he admits casually, his hand warm and comforting on my lower back. Something about his ruthless comment makes me smile. Mason is a good man, but he can be just as bloodthirsty as me if the occasion calls for it. Elias too, from what I've seen today.

"Maya."

I turn at Theo's call, my light-hearted mood suddenly broken at the concern in his voice. He must have moved Noah, who is now slumped against a tree trunk, his eyes closed and his breathing sluggish. Panic suddenly flares within me, an emotion I'm not used to, and frankly, that terrifies me.

Acting out of fear, I spin to face Elias and point a finger at him accusingly. "You allowed this to happen. You let him be the distraction." A small part of me knows that this isn't fair, that Noah is a grown man who makes his own decisions, but I'm not listening to the voice of reason right now.

Elias frowns but makes no move to step away from me. Brave. Most wouldn't stay in the path of a raging gorgon. "Noah insisted," he explains, gesturing to the male in question. "He would have come alone if we didn't agree—"

"Look at him!" I scream, all calm and logic lost to the fear of losing Noah.

A rattling cough tells me that he's awake, and he mumbles something unintelligible. I hurry to his side and kneel beside him. Taking his hand in mine, I rub my thumb over the unblemished skin, the only part of him I risk touching in case I hurt him.

"Maya," Noah mumbles again, but this time I realise he's calling my name. My eyes sting with tears, but I refuse to let them fall. "He's right. I was already tracking you before they even realised I'd gone. I wasn't going to leave you alone—" A rattling cough cuts him off, and I share a worried glance with Theo.

Theo looks around, and with a sigh, he removes a water bottle from his belt. I watch him with a frown, wondering what he's doing as he pours some of the water into his palm. It's only as he closes his eyes that I remember Theo can heal with water. Hope blooms in me like the first buds of spring. The water in his hand glows, and he raises it to Noah's lips. Without questioning it, Noah drinks the water. The process is repeated over and over again until the water bottle is empty.

Noah already looks better than he did, the cut on his forehead scabbed over and the bruising more of a green brown rather than the bright purple and black they had been before. His eyelids look heavy, and after a long breath, they fall closed and his head rests back against the tree trunk.

Theo stands and rubs his forehead, his face strained. "He needs to sleep now and let the water work."

With one more look at Noah to make sure he's okay, I stand and cross the short distance until I'm close enough to take Theo's hand in mine. "Thank you for helping him." Something in my chest flutters, and I swear he looks brighter from just my touch. He opens his mouth to say something, but Elias clears his throat.

"We'll make camp here tonight."

There are noises of agreement as the guards begin to move around, setting up camp in a way that we can use it. I watch as they move the bodies of our fallen attackers, but I feel no remorse, not after what they did to Noah. Mason's angry rumbling catches my attention, and I find him by the cage where I was kept. He roughly kicks it, and to my surprise, it flies back several meters. I knew Mason was strong, but this is a whole new level. It took several men to carry my cage off the cart that dragged it here, yet he easily moved it with one kick.

"Lord Elias!" someone shouts, and we all spin to see

two of our guards dragging a struggling body between them. A sense of déjà vu hits me as I remember Noah being brought in this way, but I shake it off and try to concentrate on what's happening.

"We found this one trying to escape," the second guard says through gritted teeth as their prisoner struggles against their hold. I know exactly who it is before he raises his head, and I bare my teeth—Mika. My gorgon wants to shift and rip his head off, but we're not strong enough for that. She's still groggy from whatever spell the cuffs had on them.

"Tell Marcus we said hello," Mika spits, blood spilling from his twisted lips as he glares at me.

What the hell does that mean? Is it a threat towards Marcus because they took the king's blade? Or do they know him because... because he hired them to take me? No, I can't think like that, he's just trying to shake me. I have no evidence that Marcus hired these men.

Elias starts forward, snarling as he pulls his blade from the sheath at his waist. He points it at the man then stops and glances over his shoulder at me. "His death is yours if you want it."

I can feel everyone watching me, and I get the feeling that no one would judge me if I chose not to. However, I'm not some sheltered princess. I fight my own battles. Flashing a grin at Elias, I step forward and reach for my veil. I think it's fitting that he should die from my gaze when he went out of his way to avoid it thus far.

"Fuck that, you monstrous bitch," Mika spits, and before we can do anything, he cracks his jaw and bites down on something hard. He grins and starts laughing maniacally as he begins to foam at the mouth. He soon stops laughing as his eyes roll to the back of his head and his body moves in spasmodic jerks. After a few seconds, he goes still, and I know he's dead.

Stunned at the quick turn of events, I stare down at his corpse. I wasn't expecting that.

"Poison," Mason sneers, shaking his head as he joins me, his arm brushing against mine. "He would rather die like that than be turned to stone." He pulls back his upper lip in a snarl. "Coward."

"Did you expect anything less from Joha's lot though?"

I jerk at Elias' comment. They knew Joha? What does this mean? Seeing my confused look, Elias sighs and runs his hand through his hair before gesturing to the body on the ground. "We know them," he admits. "They are rival monster hunters from a kingdom far from here. They usually never cross Saren and travel into this part of the continent though."

My instincts are telling me that there's more at play here. Why would someone from a distant kingdom want me? My doubts creep up in my mind again, suggesting that Marcus could have something to do with this. I feel overwhelmed as my thoughts spin. As if sensing it, Theo walks over and stands at my other side, close enough that his body brushes against mine. With the two of them touching me, even casually like this, it settles the waves of uncertainty inside me.

Theo touches my cheek and turns my head, trying to examine the wound on my scalp, but I pull back and wave him away. Raising a brow, he tries again. "Let me take a look at your injuries." There's a question in his request—will I allow him to heal me? The stern look in his eyes tells me I don't have much of a choice in the matter.

Snorting, I cross my arms over my chest, glad for my

veil, as it hides my wince the action causes. "You're exhausted. Don't try and hide it from me."

Rubbing his hands together, he flashes me a little grin, and I see the cheeky Theo I've come to know. "I've still got a little more within me," he promises.

Mason grumbles in agreement. "Let us take care of you, Maya, for our sake if nothing else."

I look between them, sensing the strain that holding themselves back is causing them. I can't even imagine how difficult it must have been for them to find me missing. Even imagining if one of them had been... My gorgon rises within me so fast that it's like a physical jolt, and I have to close my eyes for a moment to settle her. It takes a few moments, and neither of them disturb me as I take slow, easy breaths. I know the answer to my earlier question—I would tear this land apart to get them back.

So, with a sigh, I open my eyes and reluctantly nod, allowing myself to be led to a quiet spot where my bonded care for me.

CHAPTER

18

S troking the soft muzzle of my horse, I lean my
forehead against hers. She lets out a long sigh,
which brings a small smile to my lips.

"I know how you feel," I reply quietly, enjoying the
peace of the moment.

At some point during the night, the guards retrieved
the horses from where they'd left them, along with the
rest of our bags. I'd been given some spare riding clothes
to change into and then spent the rest of the night curled
up against Theo and Mason. I hadn't slept well though,
and the sleep I did manage to get was plagued with
dreams of Noah being beaten. Every time, I would wake
with a jolt and desperately look around until I found him
sleeping on a bedroll on the other side of Mason.

He does seem better this morning, thanks to Theo.
He's been up and about and even brought me hot tea
with breakfast. We've not spoken about what happened,
nor the fact I managed to melt magical cuffs from my
wrists to save him—something that should have been

impossible. He's limping, and I don't miss his occasional wince, but I know he'd hate it if I pointed it out in front of everyone else, so I bite my tongue and talk to my horse instead.

I can feel several people's gazes on me, but I don't bother to acknowledge them. I'm tired and sore, so I don't have it in me to be chatty today. I sense Mason approaching, and I turn before he reaches me, crossing my arms over my chest.

"Are you sure you don't need to shift?"

He'd been trying to convince me to shift all night, knowing it would speed up my healing, and each time I told him the same thing—no. My gorgon needs time to heal too, and those cuffs and whatever I did to break out of them drained her.

"I'm fine, Mason. The wounds are mostly healed now."

He grumbles but doesn't push the matter. Instead, he hovers nearby, scowling at anyone who comes close. I don't think he's trying to warn anyone off, not really. He knows none of his own people would try anything, but I feel his anxiety through our connection. When I was taken, it shook him more than he expected, and now he's not prepared to let me out of his sight. Theo has also kept me within view since they found me, he's just better at hiding it than Mason. This man has no subtlety. Maybe that's part of the reason I love him.

My body goes rigid. Love. Is that really how I feel? *Shit, shit, shit, shit.* No, I can't be in love, I *won't* be. Everyone I've loved has always betrayed me. I'm cursed to endure life like this because I trusted my heart with the wrong person.

"Maya, what's wrong?" Mason's low voice cuts

through my panic, and when he places a hand on my arm, I glance up at him, examining his face. He's a good man, honest, and protective, and he would defend me until his last breath, even if I didn't need him too.

A little part of my mind whispers that just because our relationship has developed and I feel love towards him, it doesn't change who he is fundamentally. He will still be Mason, the kind man I've come to know. Love doesn't make people lie and deceive. Those people who hurt me before always would have betrayed me, whether I loved them or not. Still, I'm definitely not ready to admit that out loud right now.

Releasing the breath I hadn't realised I was holding, I force my lips to tilt up into a smile. "I just had a thought. I'm fine."

He purses his lips, clearly not believing me, but he doesn't push the issue.

Everyone starts to mount their horses, and I reluctantly accept Mason's help up onto my mare, secretly glad as pain lances down my back from the attack. Mason grumbles under his breath but says nothing, waiting until my feet are in the stirrups and I'm settled in the saddle before mounting his own horse. While he does that, I watch Noah. I can't help it. Every time I look away, I find my gaze being drawn back to him, the new tightness in my chest easing when my eyes fall upon him. The thought of losing him, of never seeing him again... My gorgon practically shudders within me, hissing, *Mine*, in the back of my mind. This is something I'm starting to recognise now. She only claims those I'm supposed to bond with, yet this feels different. I don't feel that same pull to him that I do with the others, but she still put a claim on him.

Noah turns in his saddle and looks straight at me with a raised brow and an exasperated expression. Instead of jerking my gaze away now that I've been caught, I meet his stare through my veil and tilt my head to one side. Realising he's not going to win a staring contest with me, he sighs and turns to face forward once more, but I don't miss the ghost of a smile he's trying to hide.

Now all packed up and in position, Elias calls out and we begin moving. I learned that we're not that far from our original path, which makes me wonder just where Joha had been taking me. However, because of this, it shouldn't add much time onto our journey, thank the gods.

We've been travelling through this wooded area for a while now, the uneven ground meaning we have to walk so as not to trip the horses. This just gives me plenty of time to think, which I really don't want to be doing right now. Glancing to my left, I spot Theo looking at me. He flashes me a grin, and I return it with a smile, tilting my head to one side as I consider him.

"Theo," I call, my curiosity getting the better of me. "Tell me more about yourself. How did a half-siren end up as part of one of the most famous monster hunting teams in the land?"

Surprise crosses his features, but his expression soon turns contemplative as he faces forward. For a moment, I wonder if I've offended him, but I don't feel anything through the bond other than a mild sense of sadness.

"You must have realised by now that the monster hunting thing is a front, right?" he asks, turning his attention to me once more. "It allows us to get to places we otherwise wouldn't be able to. Sure, we do kill some monsters, but some of the worst beasts we've come across are the humans who hire us."

I assumed that their real purpose wasn't hunting monsters but something deeper. It seems I was right. However, hearing him say it so easily still takes me aback. He's right though—some of the worst things I've witnessed or experienced in my long life have been committed by humans. I knew they'd come to my city to investigate the king and discover his crimes, but by association, that should make me guilty too, and I really *am* a monster.

"Why didn't you kill me?" I've asked this before, but everything is different now and I want to hear it again.

"We told you before. We'd heard about you and decided to hold judgement until we met you. Then you confirmed our suspicions that day in the stables when you were trying to help the orphans."

I face forward, but I let his words roll over me. Mason watches me from my right, listening to the conversation but not getting involved. I can't help but wonder what might have happened if I hadn't gone to the stables that night. No, I can't think on what-ifs, no good ever comes from it.

Theo obviously senses my twisting emotions, but he simply clears his throat and continues, "I find that being part monster myself actually helps with monster hunting. We can talk to the creatures we've been sent to kill, settling tensions and occasionally faking a death. Most of them are misunderstood or their territory has been encroached on by the humans, so they are trying to protect it." I glance over as he speaks. I don't think I've ever heard him say so much before, and his voice calls to me. "Like I've said, there are those that kill indiscriminately, so we do have to kill occasionally, but we try to avoid it where we can."

I'm just staring at him now. This is all so much bigger than I ever suspected. They are not killing the monsters, they are helping them. Somehow, knowing these men as I do, this doesn't surprise me. What they do though...it's so dangerous. Not just working with the beast they have been sent to kill, but the humans too. If what they really did was discovered... I shudder at the potential consequences.

A thought suddenly occurs to me. Am I just one of their projects? Are they wooing me so I stop helping the king and make their job easier? I look at the group of men surrounding me, my eyes snagging on Theo, Mason, and Elias. Perhaps that's what this started as, but my bond is practically singing in my chest. No, they can't fake this. What they feel for me is real. At some point though, they are going to have to move on and leave me behind. This is not going to be easy for any of us, but it will be particularly difficult for them. The monster hunters tied to a monster.

"You're not a monster, Maya," Theo practically growls, picking up on my thoughts. "You're just not human, and being different is something many of them believe is abhorrent."

Shaking my head in disbelief, I laugh quietly. "I've killed people, Theo. Isn't that monstrous enough for you?"

He's going to argue, I can see it from the way his body stiffens and his face becomes tense, but Mason cuts him off with a look.

"Change the topic," he rumbles.

Several of the guards around us have clearly been

listening to our conversation. It seems they need a distraction just as much as I do. Everyone has been quiet this morning, and the atmosphere is tense. I don't know what to make of it, but I am putting it down to the attack. Elias has been particularly tense, his face hard as he scans the trees around us. I started up the conversation with Theo because I hadn't wanted to ride in silence under this heavy atmosphere. Thankfully, Theo seems to realise I need a distraction and nods his head at Mason's demand.

"My mother was a human, and my father a siren. She died giving birth to me, so I was raised by my aunt. She hated what I was, and I was treated like a slave. It wasn't until I came of age that I joined the king's guard, and that's when Elias found me." He shrugs his shoulders and flashes me a smile. "And that's it, I've been with him since."

"Elias!" Mason suddenly calls out, startling me. Has he seen something? Jerking my head to the side, I scan the area, only to find Mason pulling his horse to a stop before throwing his leg over the side. Elias has also stopped his horse and is looking at us over his shoulder with sharp eyes, searching for any threat.

Mason walks over to his lord and they share an intense look. "I need a moment," is all my bonded says by way of explanation. I'm expecting Elias to bark at him to return to his horse, but both males appear tense. I don't know what I'm missing, but I'm beginning to think it's more than just them being overprotective after my abduction. Elias glances up and looks at me. I can't explain what I see in his expression, but it makes a shiver travel down my spine. Returning his attention to Mason, he jerks his head once in agreement.

Mason doesn't hang around, striding straight up to me. "Come with me for a moment."

Raising my brows in surprise, I glance at Theo who simply shrugs but starts to dismount. Ignoring Mason's proffered hand, I swing my leg over the saddle and climb from my horse. Placing his hand on my lower back, Mason silently guides me with Theo close behind. I turn back once and see Noah watching us with a frown, but he makes no move to follow us.

We weave through the trees, not saying a word until we're far enough away where I can only distantly hear the others.

"What's going o—"

I'm cut off as Mason spins me and presses his lips against mine, his kiss urgent as he backs me against a tree. Lust and need surge within me so fiercely that all I can do is kiss him back, sinking into his embrace.

Pulling back, he rests his forehead against mine, his breathing ragged. "I thought I was going to go crazy when you were taken." The emotion in his voice makes my chest ache, and I can't help but rest my hand on his cheek as he continues. "I knew something was wrong, I could feel it in my chest. When I got to the spot where you'd been taken, and I saw the statue and your veil on the ground..." He trails off with a growl.

Theo steps over and taps Mason's shoulder. The larger man grumbles but steps to the side, allowing Theo to take his place and press up against me, brushing my jaw with the back of his hand.

"When you were taken," Theo starts, his voice croaking, "it was like a piece of me had been ripped from my chest." He shakes his head and takes a deep breath. "I don't let people close to me other than my brothers-in-arms, as I've learned from experience that everyone is only out to hurt you. I learned to stay quiet, to stay out of the way, but you..." He laughs at himself, the sound sad. "You make me want to sing."

My heart breaks for him as he speaks. I want to find those who abused him in the past and tear them to pieces. My gorgon and I are in full agreement on this. Theo is cheeky and a bit of a trickster, but he's also kind and generous. He doesn't have to share his healing gift with anyone, especially after the way he's been treated in the past, yet he does so anyway.

"I didn't ask to be bonded," he continues, "and frankly, it's terrifying. However, I know it's just as scary for you. I will cherish you every day for the rest of my life."

He's right, it is terrifying, but knowing that this is just as hard for him, well, it eases something inside me. The two of them seemed so accepting of this bond that I just assumed it was easy for them. His declaration also settles my growing fear that they'll just leave me with the king and return to their kingdom alone once their mission is complete.

All of a sudden, large hands land on me and I'm moved in the blink of an eye. I'm not sure how, but I find myself pinned against Mason's chest while I'm kissing Theo with deep, passionate kisses. My blood is on fire, pounding through my body and igniting me. I need them, I need them *now*.

Just as I'm deepening our kiss, Theo pulls back and I see a small frown pulling at his brow. "We just needed you to know that whatever happens, you're our bonded and you can trust us."

This instantly puts me on edge. Pulling from their

grip, I step back to put some distance between us as I look between them. I can't focus when they are touching me like that. Is something about to happen that I don't know about, or are they simply worried we might be separated again? "What does that mean?" I ask, suspicion lacing my words.

Mason steps towards me, his hand outstretched. "Maya—"

"Mason, Theo, mount up, we need to go," Elias calls out, his voice distant but final.

Mason's expression shuts down, and it fills me with fear. What the hell is going on?

Theo sighs and takes my hand in his, leading me back to our group. Everyone seems tense, but they are silent as we mount. With a gesture from Elias, we begin to move once more.

The path eventually becomes flat enough that our horses can canter without injuring themselves, and any thought of talking disappears as we focus on riding. Falling off is definitely not what I need right now. The farther we travel, the more I become convinced that something's going on. All of the riders seem to become tenser with each minute that passes.

Light catches my attention, and I realise that we're finally about to exit the woods. Cantering out into a large valley full of wildflowers, I let my head fall back and soak up the sun as it shines down on us. We follow the rocky mountain on our right, riding up the valley until we eventually reach the top and find ourselves on a large, flat plain.

The roar of the dragon is what I hear first. Hissing, I hunch in my saddle and look around for the threat. Above us is a huge grey dragon. The beat of his wings sends gusts of wind down on us, and as the beast throws back its head and roars once more, a stream of fire bursts from its mouth. I can feel the heat from the flames all the way down here. How the hell are we going to take down a beast that size?

Looking to Elias for guidance, I see he's wearing a grim expression but doesn't seem worried. He waves his hand for us to stop, and we all do, but I'm too busy looking up at the dragon to notice everyone dismounting. A hand on my knee jerks me to the present. It's Mason's hand. Blowing out a shaky breath, I take his hand and slide from the horse, frowning as I see everyone has done the same. They are all waiting expectantly, although none of them have drawn their weapons. Glancing towards Elias, I see him staring ahead. Not at the dragon, but at...

Eyes wide, I see what he's looking at—rows upon rows of soldiers, all dressed in the battle armour of Saren. I'd been so distracted by the dragon that I hadn't seen them. They'll be here within minutes. Noah makes his way to my side, eyeing the others around us, his hand on the hilt of his sword. The dragon roars again, causing Noah and me to duck. No one else moves a muscle. I watch with growing dread as the dragon circles the approaching army before landing and tucking his wings in close, and I come to a horrifying realisation.

The dragon belongs to Saren.

Spinning, I bare my teeth and back away from Theo and Mason, remembering their words just a few hours ago. They said I could trust them no matter what happened. I want to laugh and cry and rage. My eyes sting behind my veil. "You betrayed us."

Noah seems to realise this at the same time I do, drawing his sword and pressing his back against mine.

My gorgon howls within me, fighting me for dominance, not believing that our bonded would betray us. This is why everyone's been so tense and cagy today, they knew this was coming—an approaching army and the dragon we were sent to hunt is somehow tied to them.

"Maya, let us explain—"

"How could you? You said I could trust you." I hate that my voice cracks as I scream at them, my heart feeling like it's about to tear itself in two.

"Maya, hear us out," Elias orders, striding towards me in full lord mode. Any sign of the kind man I was beginning to know is gone. Was that all a lie too?

"Why should I?" I hiss, baring my teeth, my body jerking as I fight my gorgon.

Roaring cuts us off, and I turn towards the biggest threat I face right now—the dragon. I don't think Elias or the others are going to hurt me, not when they have gone through great lengths to get me here. The approaching army seems to split into two, creating a pathway for the dragon to walk through. With heavy steps that make the ground rumble from the force, the beast stalks towards us with a gleam in its yellow eyes.

My breathing speeds up, and fear causes my heart to pound in time with the dragon's steps. Noah watches the beast closely, his sword raised.

As one, the Saren males all drop to their knees. The move startles me, making me think they are ducking, but I realise with horror that they are bowing and showing reverence to the dragon. I look up again just in time to see a strange shimmer pass over the dragon, and if I hadn't been looking, I wouldn't have believed it. The creature begins to shrink until only a man is left in its place.

Taller than a normal human, he walks confidently.

Long, silky-looking silver hair trails down his back, and he wears a flawless dark green tunic. He's handsome in a harsh way, his cheekbones sharp beneath yellow eyes that don't miss a single thing. The only feature that would indicate that he was just the huge dragon before us are the large grey wings that seem to jut from his back. Lastly, I notice a simple golden band sitting atop his silver hair.

I feel sick as I realise who I'm looking at. I didn't even know that dragons could shift into human form, but there is no other explanation. This is the King of Saren. Somehow, the king of our rival kingdom is a dragon.

"Your Majesty," Elias greets, slowly standing from his position, his head still bowed in respect as he confirms what I just realised.

"Lord Elias." The king dips his head in acknowledgment before pinning me with his golden yellow eyes. "And you must be Lady Maya, King Marcus' blade and the rescuer of orphans."

I can't tell if he's mocking me or if he just finds this whole situation ridiculous. He's not the only one. I'm so close to ripping off my veil and letting my gorgon loose, but she shies away at the thought. A moment ago, she was fighting for dominance, but now she doesn't want them hurt. The sudden realisation hits me like a physical blow—she was trying to protect her bonded from me. I'm at war with myself. Somehow, after everything, my monster still trusts them, despite the fact they lied to me and brought me out here.

At an impasse with my gorgon and knowing I can't fight my way out of here without getting myself and Noah killed, I let out a long hiss. "King Kai, I assume."

"You assume correctly." His mouth turns up on one

side, his eyes flashing as he takes me in. "I'm sorry for all this. I didn't think you'd come if you knew the truth."

I bark out an unamused laugh, very aware of Theo and Mason behind me, our bonds taut as they reach for me. Shoving the bonds away, I keep my attention on the rival king. "And what is the truth?" I demand.

His expression becomes serious, all previous signs of humour gone. "I need you to help me kill the king."

The End

**Maya's story will be continued in Betrayal and Curses
Coming soon**

Acknowledgments

Going into this story I knew that I was going to enjoy writing it, but I had no idea just how much I would fall in love with these characters. Maya is strong and fierce, and certainly doesn't need rescuing, but begins to learn that just because she can take care of herself, doesn't mean she has to do it alone. This is something that resonated in me and I'm sure it will with many others.

A huge thank you goes out to my team who support me throughout writing this book, as always, I couldn't do this without you. My amazing editing and proofreading team, alpha and beta readers, my formatter, and of course my family who are my cheerleaders.

I hope you love this story as much as I do, and a huge thank you for reading it. If you would consider leaving a review, I would be most grateful.

All my love,

Erin xoxo

About the Author

Erin lives in the UK with her husband and now works full time as an independent author. She started writing in 2018 when she published her first book, *Hunted by Shadows*. She specialises in writing fantasy and reverse harem paranormal romance.

She met K. A Knight in 2018 when they became partners in crime and began writing together. In 2019, she became co-authors with Loxley Savage, writing fantasy reverse harem.

She's Disney obsessed, loves cookies and baking, and is always planning her next story.

Make sure to follow her on her social media pages for updates on what she's currently working on:

Facebook Group:
https://www.facebook.com/groups/ErinOKanesShadowRealm

Facebook Author Page:
https://www.facebook.com/ErinOKaneAuthor

Newsletter:
http://eepurl.com/gJhSd9

Instagram:

https://www.instagram.com/erin.okane.author

Also by Erin O'Kane

The Shadowborn Series:

Hunted by Shadows

Lost in Shadow

Embraced by Shadows

The Shadowborn series- the boxset

Born From Shadows Series:

Demons do it Better

The War and Deceit Series:

Fires of Hatred

Fires of Treason

Fires of Ruin

Fires of War

Fires of the Fae:

A Lady of Embers

A Spark of Promise

A Legacy of Hope and Ash

CURSED WOMEN:

Venom and Stone

Co-writes

Erin O'Kane and K.A Knight

Her Freaks Series:

Circus Save Me

Taming the Ringmaster

Walking the Tightrope

THE WILD BOYS:

The Wild Interview

The Wild Tour

The Wild Finale

The Wild Boys Series- The boxset

Standalones:

Hero Complex

Dark Temptations

ERIN O'KANE AND LOXLEY SAVAGE:

Twisted Tides

Tides that Bind

Printed in Great Britain
by Amazon